FIND
HER
FIRST

EMMA CHRISTIE

WELBECK

To mum and dad, for *that* song.

And to Mari, for listening.

Published in 2022 by Welbeck Fiction Limited, an imprint of
Welbeck Publishing Group
Based in London and Sydney
www.welbeckpublishing.com

A CIP catalogue record for this book is available from the
British Library

Paperback ISBN: 978-1-78739-698-2
Ebook ISBN: 978-1-78739-699-9

Printed and bound by CPI Group (UK) Ltd., Croydon, CR0 4YY

10 9 8 7 6 5 4 3 2

PROLOGUE

Please. Don't.

Even now the words lingered; static, utterly unchanged. The passing months had done nothing to them, like those old mines dredged up from the sea-bed, somehow still capable of blowing up a boat and all humans within.

Please. Don't.

Depending on the day, different details would come to the fore; the slight slur that blurred the edges of those words, the tiny balls of saliva on dry lips, the desperation in those eyes. Clouds of breath swirling in slow motion between them, lashes clogged with tears that were still warm when they were wiped away, afterwards.

Please. Don't.

There were numerous moments when the space between one inhale and the next would stretch on and on, threaten an ending. The sound of that laboured breath threw up images of chain smokers, lungs painted with thick black tar. But that wasn't the case here. Even at the end those lungs were healthy; pink and moist and filled with crisp mountain air that held the scent of the pine needles in that light-dappled forest.

That's the kind of place most people would choose to die, isn't it?

Given the choice.

CHAPTER 1

Present day

The courtroom was lit by tube lights hanging on chains, dead flies crisping inside the plastic cover. *A miserable way to go, that.* Andy Campbell's paramedic pals would have laughed if he'd said that, asked him if there was a good way. *Plenty,* he'd say, then happily roll out his theory about death and dying, tell whoever was listening there were only four ways to die.

Suddenly, unexpectedly, peacefully or after an illness – short or long, delete as applicable. Folk would often suggest 'surrounded by family and friends', but Andy would argue that was the context of the death as opposed to an actual way of dying.

All you had to do was read the obituaries section of the papers and you'd realise he was speaking the truth. The only way anyone in their right mind would chose to go was peacefully, but that was the one that rarely happened.

He'd first learned that lesson at home, age nine. All it took was a warm bath and a back turned. One minute he was a helpful big brother and the next there were blue lights and his baby sister silent in a hospital bed; a machine breathing for her. When death came the blame was unspoken but impossible to ignore. From then on he'd vowed to do all he could to sustain life, and as a paramedic Andy spent his days doing just that; battling against disease, accidents and killings, intended or otherwise.

Within those groups there were thousands of variations but every single death shared the same common denominator: failure of the human body or of the human mind. Andy used to be totally sure on that one, so keen to avoid condemnation. And now?

No comment.

The first time Andy attended court he'd been surprised how familiar it felt, like walking on to a TV set. The petty offenders were huddled near the main door, relaxed, eyeing the pub across the road and nipping across for a sly half-pint if time allowed it. They'd be smoking and spitting and wearing tracksuits and not giving a shit if you excused yourself and said you needed to get past. Grey skin, eyes in pits. They're the regulars, the folk who break into your shed when you're on holiday, the ones who get lifted for throwing abuse and bottles at paramedics.

But he hadn't been prepared for the silence on the inside.

Court, in general, was a muted tragedy.

Whole worlds were changing and not a word could be said, not a voice raised. Andy had witnessed wee grannies mouth off at librarians when their reserved book wasn't available and tourists lose the head with airline staff when their carry-on bag was deemed too big for the overhead locker. Folk regularly shouted at delivery drivers, receptionists, customers who pushed in ahead of them in a queue. And the worst part? Usually the person in a rage would have lost very little, if anything. Maybe some time, maybe a few quid, but nothing that couldn't be fixed, repaired, replaced, earned again, forgotten about by teatime. They were all things that left no scars.

Yet here, now, in the courtroom, everyone managed to maintain and respect a call for silence despite the fact someone who was loved had died – and someone else had made that happen. It was like being underwater, watching a film on mute.

Voices would come but only when their name was called, then ticked off a list, and only when they were answering questions put to them by someone else. It was absurd, insulting.

How could Andy's grief possibly be contained?

Shouting was honest. Hating was honest. But these were things that could not be measured and labelled and put in a file and they were not welcome in this room.

Little by little he'd learned it was a place for silence or for words that were carefully chosen and euphemised, rough stones rubbed by lawyers and journalists until they were transformed into smooth, round pebbles that fitted neatly in your palm and no longer scratched.

He dropped his head and stared again at his own hands, was glad they couldn't talk.

Journalists could, though, and did, too loudly.

As if on cue, he heard swirling whispers from the press bench as the last few reporters squeezed into place, thigh to thigh, elbow to elbow. There must have been a dozen of them, hunched over notepads, clicking pens, flicking pages, knowing today was one of those days they'd give readers what they wanted: a verdict.

The judge strode up to the bench, tugging his black gown on to his shoulder. He glanced at the public gallery then sat down and signalled for the lawyers to do their bit: turn actions into words, blame into a decision, an ordinary human into a killer.

CHAPTER 2

Six months earlier

Betty didn't discriminate. It didn't matter what age they were or where they'd travelled before she encountered them. She enjoyed inventing their histories, creating vivid images in her mind of the many fingers that had touched the lucky pennies before she had. When she wasn't cleaning other people's dirty houses she spent her time among those imagined lives, giving names and shapes and purposes to people she'd never meet but with whom she felt a palpable connection. Here she was, Betty Stevenson in Portobello, linked by the glorious frivolities of life to bearded businessmen in Perth and tubby little boys in Nethy Bridge and an eccentric granny in Kirkcudbright and maybe the ginger woman who worked in the butcher's just down the road and who had a terrible stutter and took twenty seconds to say the word 'mince'. Here she was, holding a moment of all those other lives in the palm of her hand, closing her fingers around history; human tattoos pressed into copper.

But the joy wasn't in the keeping.

Betty bent down next to a street lamp on Portobello Promenade, pretended she was retying the lace of her shoe. Then, quietly, she placed the one-pence piece, Queen side up, on the ground.

She glanced over her shoulder, conjuring up the image of her wee brother hunched down beside her, eyes crusted with sleep from his nap, his fast, hot breath reeking of strawberry sweeties as he watched his big sister at work. Back then he'd take her hand when they walked and her word when she spoke. It was Betty who'd told him coins had heartbeats, made him sit in silence with a penny held tightly between two fingers until he could feel the unmistakable rhythm of a pulse. He'd believed it for years, only stopped when the big boys from the flats heard about it and made him chew so hard on a penny that his teeth broke.

Betty had blamed herself.

But she'd never lost her faith in the coins.

There were few things more gratifying in Betty's life than witnessing the pure delight of a Finder when they took a moment out of their busy lives to pick up a lucky penny from a spot on the ground that she'd chosen, with precision. They'd be lost in the automatic motions of their commute to work or their walk home or their lunchtime jog and a chance glance would lead their eyes to a tiny circle of copper on the ground. The coin itself was familiar but when they encountered one in an unfamiliar place their routine would stutter and stall and for a moment it would stop altogether. Suddenly they'd act like a child again; do something which made no real sense and which had no logic and which offered no financial gain of any significance. All it offered was luck, put in place by Betty.

On average her pennies would be spotted and retrieved within forty minutes. Usually within that time she'd observe a Hesitator, somebody who saw the coin but decided not to touch it, either because they were in a rush or because their mother or son was pulling their hand or because they were ashamed or embarrassed at the thought of taking lost money from the street. Betty used to think that the only people who'd pause and pick up lucky coins were people who believed in magic but after detailed observation she realised it wasn't the only factor. The key element was not belief in magic itself, but the willingness to expose and act upon that belief in a public place. She'd witnessed it countless times, that moment of conflict; someone who actively chose head over heart, logic over luck.

It was agonising to watch.

At least, that's what she'd tell people if she ever openly talked about it. But if you asked Betty why she'd returned to the habit of her youth she'd dismiss its importance, tell you it was just her way of spreading goodness in the world; then reel off a range of clichéd phrases that she'd heard elsewhere and hoped applied to her, like Every Little Helps and It's The Giving That Counts. But if you scratched beneath the surface you'd discover that Betty didn't believe in any of those ideas at all; what you'd see was Betty, collecting and distributing lucky pennies day after day in the hope her hands would start to smell of copper instead of blood.

The coin she'd placed on Portobello Promenade that Monday morning was immaculate despite being minted in 1988. She'd found it in the grounds of a castle, along the coast from Edinburgh. There was a fountain there with a sculpture that was supposed to be a swan but it wasn't nearly graceful enough – more like a goose than its royal cousin. The bird's mouth was wide open but instead of a tongue there was a tube from which water perpetually trickled. Betty had felt nauseous looking at it, imagining the pipe being forced into the bird's throat, filling it, leaving it forever rasping or mute. From time to time a drip had escaped the slimy mouth of the pipe then trickled down the smooth white neck of the bird, following a faint red line that Betty knew was caused by iron deposits in the water but that reminded her of smooth human skin sliced open so neatly that she could see the line she'd need to follow to sew it back together.

Betty was still thinking about that wound and that blood when she noticed another scar: the delicate crack that split the concrete surface of Portobello Promenade, exactly in the spot where she'd placed the penny, a few moments before it was picked up by Stef Campbell.

Of all people, of all days.

It couldn't be a coincidence.

Betty had been cleaning Stef's house every Tuesday and Friday morning for four months but she'd never seen her in this context before; on a dull Monday morning, with a red running jacket and colour in her cheeks and her hair hanging loose, hiding those little silver stud earrings that she never seemed to remove. Stef had been jogging quite fast but had a funny run, as if one of her shoes didn't quite fit. If she were still at school Stef would have been teased about a run like that, and probably not picked for teams. Something else they had in common. Stef had run right past Betty then taken a few more steps and stopped dead, stared out to sea or maybe the big sky above it. Today both were slate grey, held the threat of a summer storm so severe the newsreader had apologised before he read the warning. The last week of June would be wet and windy, unseasonably wild.

Betty stared at Stef as she sat on the sea wall and took off her shoe, massaging her foot with her fingers. Her hands were exactly one ruler length from the lucky penny.

Betty knew because she always carried a ruler in her bag in case she encountered a coin in a hard-to-reach location. Sometimes she'd kneel down and scour the ground beneath vending machines, cheeks warmed by the illuminated advert on the front.

But the penny next to Stef's hand was in clear sight.

Betty willed her to see it, take it, feel the luck it held.

And then it happened. Stef finished tying her laces, then reached for the penny. Betty was mesmerised and reminded of that game at the amusements, a clunking metal hand grasping at garish soft toys piled up inside a glass case. But once the coin was in her hands Stef rubbed it clean with her sleeve then dropped it onto her palm and admired it. Betty lit up, wondered if the glow she felt could be seen.

But her world blackened just as fast when she remembered that crack on the promenade, so obvious to her now that she couldn't believe she'd missed it when she placed the penny on the ground. Everybody knew that cracks in pavements brought bad luck, not good. She tried to stay calm, tried convincing herself that the coin would cancel out the badness.

But will it, Betty? Will it?

Tears fizzed at the backs of her eyes as she got up from the bench where she'd been sitting, her gaze flitting between the crack on the ground and the red running jacket of Stef Campbell as she walked away, holding that penny in her hand. A hunch hardened into knowledge, became a red-hot stone burning in Betty's belly.

No good would come from this.

CHAPTER 3

If Andy Campbell's life had a soundtrack, it would consist of one single sound.

Sirens.

The siren that accompanied him most faithfully was the one he switched on himself every working day, whenever he was driving the ambulance. Then the police would turn up with theirs and if it was a car crash or a crushing, the arseholes from the fire brigade would roar up as well, always the latest and loudest of the lot.

Usually it was only trainee paramedics who got excited about sirens but Andy loved them because they left no room for anything else, could not be mis-interpreted or ignored. He could lose himself in the whoop and wail, the endless urgency. When they went abroad on holiday he'd listen for the foreign ones then point out the differences to Stef, who clearly didn't care despite the fact she'd worked as a paramedic for even longer than him.

But Andy's ear was tuned perfectly to their frequency. He could guess how far away they were, just by the sound, would know immediately what direction they were travelling in; if they were headed over there, or on their way to here.

Right here, now.

He lay for a few seconds, listening, before he opened his eyes. He wished he'd woken up facing the wall and the window but not this – the cold, undented sheet on Stef's side of the bed. Nausea bubbled in him, a blend of too much whisky and of something else he couldn't bear to look at; the very thing he'd drunk to forget.

He rolled over and pulled the duvet tighter. At the station they'd often make up silly mantras that matched the rhythm of the siren, all of them vying for the biggest laugh. But today he just heard that same phrase on repeat; a prayer, a desperate plea, the same wish made three times. *Don't stop, don't stop, don't stop.*

It was strange how quickly the familiar could become a threat.

He held his breath; kept holding it even when his chest started to hurt, one man battling against the will of his own body to stay alive. But the siren was upon him, a squealing heartbeat that swallowed the sound of everything else.

There was no comfort in it now, nothing that soothed.

He pulled the covers over his head and pushed hard against his ears, as if that would change anything. Tears came despite his best efforts. He hated the heat and the tickle of fabric on his skin; the nerve of it, of him. For a few minutes his whole world was a tight chest and screeching sirens and breeching tears and a thundering pulse, all wrapped up in the softness of a duvet that still smelled of Stef. But that would disappear in the wash, wouldn't it? And soon enough her body would rot, would be unrecognisable even to him.

Just then, the ambulance turned.

Andy noticed the subtle shift in the rhythm of the siren as it moved away from their street, headed towards somebody else's changing life. Still he held his body firm, resisted relaxation until the world around him became birdsong and the gentle drumming of raindrops on the window and the whisper of radiators switched on to numb the chill of a fierce summer storm.

He shoved the duvet away from his face and gulped in the thick, sleep-infused air of their bedroom; let his body return to whatever normal was now. Only then did he reach for his mobile phone.

No calls, no messages.

Something twitched in his chest but he wasn't sure if it was disappointment or relief. Either way, he knew there could be no good news; there was no way, now, to undo what they'd done. Even if they never spoke again he and Stef's sister Alyson would be forever united by this. And haunted by it.

Andy forced his feet on to the floor, walked over to the window and stared out at the orange traffic cones on the cobbled street, the rain-shiny cars that lined both sides of it, boot to bonnet. In June the sun rose at five but they were all lazy bastards on this road.

Still, they'd wake up soon enough if a siren came back this way, hiccuped to a stop outside *the paramedics' house*, of all places. He could picture them all, disguising gossip as concern, whispering as they swapped stories and theories in the bakery queue. His belly burned at the thought of it; their nodding heads and widening eyes and flickering tongues, every one of them greedy for gory details that they'd gobble up faster than a greasy sausage roll.

He checked his watch, wondered if Alyson was awake; how she was feeling.

This time tomorrow she'd be driving north to carry out the next part of their plan.

Once she got there she'd 'find' Stef, call Andy and then inform the police. Simple. Later, when blue lights came, they'd stick to the story they'd spent so many months crafting.

And they'd stick together.

If it all went smoothly they'd both be home by bedtime. But Alyson would be a sibling pruned into an only child, long before the cutting season. And what about him?

She'd convinced him this was the only way and he'd allowed it; watched those smooth, nimble hands smother his principles. He'd even started to believe it was for the best – but who for? He closed his eyes and thought of that last moment together, in the kitchen; the feel of Stef's heartbeat through the tips of his fingers. The ending seemed so completely impossible, even then; even when he squeezed her hand one last time then let her go, turned his back on that life. He and Alyson hadn't spoken since and he knew she'd offer no comfort at all. Guilt is one of those things that doesn't get any lighter when it's shared.

CHAPTER 4

Stef Campbell's doorbell was made of polished brass and when Betty lifted her finger off the button she saw a tiny trace of herself there, a smudge on the sheen that she'd remove again later with a clean yellow duster and a keen eye. When they'd given her a key of her own, Betty's skin had heated up on the inside and she'd handed it back with trembling fingers, insisting it wasn't necessary. If they were home, she'd ring the bell. If they were out, she could retrieve the spare set from their hiding place round the back, same way all their other visitors did. She told Stef it was 'easier' that way but what she meant was 'safer'. She knew only too well what could happen if keys got into the wrong hands.

Stef had laughed when she said that.

A key is trust, made solid, she replied, and Betty had never felt so loved; started dusting skirting boards so Stef wouldn't notice her eyes were wet.

But she'd still refused to take the key.

Betty stepped back when she sensed movement inside, the clump of footsteps near the door, a chain being unhooked then, finally, the rattle of the lock.

Anticipation made her body tingle, same way it did every single time she laid a coin on the ground. It was her mum who'd encouraged the habit, perhaps by accident, that day she told Betty she'd have to pick up all the lucky pennies in the world before they did any good for a child as cursed as she was. Betty had been sent to the shops to buy crisps and had spotted a one-pence piece on the way home, bright as gold in the middle of the zebra crossing. She'd stopped and looked and listened and then hunched down to pick it up, knew right away it was lucky. But when she'd shown it to her mum she'd accused her of stealing it from the change, then pressed it so tightly into Betty's palm that the Queen's face left a mark on her skin. When Betty tugged her hand away her mum said she should learn from it, that the pain she felt now was her own stupid fault.

Your fault.

She'd made the 'cursed' comment after that and Betty's wee brother had laughed, said their mum was dead right even though he usually said she was a daft cow. For years after that Betty had picked up every lost penny she saw, took her share of the luck then dropped the coin to spread it.

Those were the moments Betty treasured; seeing joy and knowing she'd caused it.

And the same thing happened every time she came to the house to clean. Stef would open the door with a grin that Betty would gladly take and match with one of her own, safe in the knowledge that somebody on earth was happy to see her. She crossed her fingers and hoped the same thing would happen now, in spite of that coin; that crack.

But when Stef's husband Andy opened the door, Betty's heart snapped shut. There was no smile, just eyes that were red and hair that was unwashed and faded pyjamas instead of his work clothes. She blushed, felt like she'd barged in on him peeing. Then he gave her That Look, the one that he usually reserved for Stef when she was doing something he didn't approve of; like going outside to paint on days of driving rain and bitter wind that soaked through skin as if it were made of paper then crept into the soft part of bones.

You'll catch your death, he'd say, but she'd ignore him and go outside anyway.

Stef was a woman who knew her own mind and listened to it. But maybe Andy wished she'd listen to him instead.

Whatever That Look meant, it filled the gap in the door.

Not fully open, not fully closed.

'I wasn't expecting you.' Andy glanced at his pyjamas then flashed Betty the kind of grin people forced for photos at weddings. 'I thought Stef had called to cancel.'

'Oh.'

'You didn't get her message?'

Betty pulled out her mobile, feeling like she'd done something wrong. She held its black screen towards Andy. 'It's been switched off,' she said, holding her finger on the switch that brought it to life with a merry beep. 'I've been having some problems with . . . nuisance calls.' She didn't say from who and was relieved he didn't ask. In fact Andy didn't react at all, just blinked a few times then turned, as if he was going back inside.

'The thing is, Stef's . . . out.' Betty followed Andy's gaze into the hall to double-check Stef wasn't there, canvas bag slung over her shoulder, waving to them as she returned from an early-morning painting session at the far end of their garden. Sometimes Betty would take her a cup of tea, balance the mug on the stump of a dead tree then wave away the thanks as if it were nothing, as if didn't fill her completely.

'Is she painting?'

Andy's eyes flicked to her. 'Aye. Some kind of art retreat.'

'Oh, she'll enjoy that,' said Betty, proud of herself for managing to put Stef's happiness before her own, even if it only lasted for a few seconds. But disappointment came all the same along with a twinge of offence that Stef hadn't thought to mention it to her when she was there last Friday. But perhaps it hadn't been planned. Maybe that was the stroke of luck Betty's penny had brought to Stef – a last-minute opportunity to attend an art retreat.

Pride swelled in her again. Sometimes she felt like a theatre director, pulling strings behind the scenes; strings that the actors didn't even know were there. But from time to time she wished she could be on the stage as well. Or at least clean it.

'I'll give the place a quick once-over since I'm here,' said Betty, then stepped forward. 'No point in wasting the bus journey, is there? And anyway, if Stef's not here I'm sure you could do with a wee helping hand.'

She forced out her best smile and Andy took such a deep breath that his shoulders almost touched his ears. He opened his mouth a few times as if he wanted to speak but couldn't, same way Betty's mum used to do after a bender, tongue stumbling over words.

'Honestly, I . . . I'd rather you . . . didn't.'

'It's no bother at all, Mr Campbell. Don't you worry.' Betty climbed the steps before he had time to say anything else and, after a few moments' hesitation, Andy stepped aside and let her through. She headed towards the kitchen that always smelled of coffee and somehow seemed to get the sun all day long. One wall was dominated by a blue Aga and next to it, a wooden sideboard loaded with piles of mail and glossy outdoor magazines with images of campervans on the front. The wall above it featured a world map dotted with coloured pins to mark all the places Stef and Andy had travelled to and next to them were dusty photos with curled corners showing them in lots of different locations. No matter where they were, they were smiling.

Betty only had one picture of Stef and she didn't really look like herself in it. Her skin was pale and her expression reminded Betty of the grumpy face her mum used to make when they got home hungry from school and tried to shake her awake. Betty treasured it anyway.

The cleaning gear was in the garage. Betty held her breath to squeeze past the blue Volvo estate parked by the storage cupboard. The car was decades old with rust around the wheel trims and cracked leather seats and Stef's name on a leather tag attached to the keys that were hanging on a hook by the door. She turned with a start when Andy appeared in the doorway. He was pinching his nose, as if he could smell something Betty could not. She inhaled discreetly, wondering if the stink came from her.

'You really don't need to stay,' he said. 'I'll pay you for coming – and call you a taxi to get home quicker.'

'I'll finish what I've started,' said Betty, dry mop in one hand, empty bucket in the other as she walked towards him. He didn't budge.

When she came to clean on Tuesday and Friday mornings Andy's car would be in the driveway, ready for his imminent drive to work, and Stef's Volvo would be in the garage. That's why she took the bus to theirs. Finding a parking space nearby was time-consuming and expensive and anyway, if she brought her own car she'd miss out on the lift home with Stef after her shift; the chance to sit near her in that Volvo.

Conversation always flowed, felt easy.

But on the rare occasions she was alone with Andy her tongue would go dry and words would stick to it then come out all wrong. Sometimes she'd rehearse lines in her head before she spoke them out loud and if a question was involved she'd imagine Andy's answer and, depending on that, would change her mind about asking in the first place. Even though it was Andy who'd organised the interview then offered her the cleaning job, she often had the sensation that he'd like to pick her off his life and flick her away.

But still she tried.

'So when did Stef go gallivanting?'

Betty chose the word 'gallivanting' on purpose, hoped it would lighten the mood, prove she was just making conversation as opposed to being nosy or accusing or worried or all three. Andy whipped his eyes back to where she stood, then let her through.

'Yesterday evening.'

'Somewhere nice?'

'Somewhere . . . remote. No phone signal, that kind of thing. Her studio organised it,' he said, then shrugged as if to say *you know Stef* and Betty felt blessed, and the need to respond.

'Explains why she didn't take the banger,' said Betty, expecting Andy to smile when she used his nickname for Stef's car, same way parents laugh when children copy adult phrases. When he didn't respond at all Betty wondered if she'd annoyed him, overstepped the mark.

She started to speak then changed her mind, turned words into a cough.

'Sorry, did you say something?'

Betty flushed. That phrase was too familiar.

'Nothing important,' said Betty, desperate to make her voice sound carefree. 'Stef's car's here so I just asked how she got to the retreat.'

'Richard.'

'Sorry?'

'Richard took her.'

'That's her teacher, isn't it? The one with all those mad ideas?'

Andy didn't seem to register her question. Betty wanted to ask again but didn't want him to think she was prying. She didn't want to give too much away, make him suspicious. To Andy she was just the cleaner, wasn't she? She swept and mopped and scrubbed and hoovered and polished and took two sugars in her tea and was paid in cash and smoked a cigarette with her first coffee of the day just so Stef would remind her every cigarette shaved twelve minutes off her life and, with those words, prove she cared. Andy didn't know what had really happened between her and Stef; but Betty knew that was why Fate had brought her here.

Andy had put an advert on the Portobello Pals Facebook page four months ago, in February, and Betty was one of a few locals who'd applied for the job. But it wasn't until Andy called and gave her the address that Betty realised where life was leading her.

She'd been to Stef's house two or three times before that, on the days she followed her home from the ambulance station. But back then she'd only seen it from the outside; sandstone walls and a bright yellow door and windows that she wanted to be on the other side of. Andy had interviewed her at the kitchen table on a rainy afternoon, explained his wife had been on sick leave from work since Christmas and was feeling *a wee bit delicate* – which is why they needed an extra hand around the house. Betty had offered references, was relieved when Andy said it wasn't necessary. Questions would have been asked.

But right now, Andy was silent.

'I best get started,' said Betty, and Andy flinched, as if he'd forgotten she was there. The big vein on his forehead looked fatter than ever, ready to pop. Betty wondered what would happen if it did, pictured a power hose with a puncture, shooting out blood.

But it held, for now.

Andy went back into the kitchen without a word and Betty followed, noticed right away that her payment wasn't where it should be. Stef always left two twenty-pound notes on the table, folded over once and held in place by the packed fruit bowl. Betty never took it until she was finished and never asked for more even on the days she stayed for longer. But today there was no money there. Betty felt embarrassed asking, was opening her mouth to speak again when Andy looked at his watch, winced.

'God, I really need to get ready for work,' he said, then disappeared upstairs.

Betty stayed where she was until she heard the front door closing a little while later, then went to the hall window and watched Andy unlock his car and drive off.

She usually cleaned the kitchen first, chatting to Stef as she lifted every single plant pot from the wide wooden window sill on to the worktop before she dusted, so Stef could see she did things thoroughly and wasn't one of those cleaners who'd wipe around the edges and hope nobody noticed. No. Betty was a mover of furniture, a lifter of bins, a shifter of tables and chairs. She even polished the light switches, just before she left.

She liked to replace things a few centimetres to the left or right of where she'd found them, left clearly visible a dent in the lino or the carpet, a stain ring from overwatered plants; something that would serve as proof that Betty had been there and done a good job. Even if it wasn't commented upon, she knew they'd notice and that was reward enough.

She returned to the kitchen to get started but it felt different without Stef and even the sun that always shone there was missing so she decided to break yet another tradition and begin with the bathroom. If Andy was here on his own it would need a good scrub, even though he'd clearly not bothered shaving this morning.

Betty pushed open the bathroom door, breathed in the reek of bleach. Andy had probably cleaned the loo and not flushed it, left splashes of sticky blue all over the bowl. When she stepped inside she saw ghostly tracks on the floor tiles; the hangover of inefficient mopping. Betty always mopped in a figure of eight but whoever had cleaned here had slopped the mop from side to side and hadn't changed the water often enough.

Betty rolled her eyes, pushed up her sleeves, and got to work.

There was something deeply satisfying about cleaning; coming face to face with the soiled remains of others and removing all the waste, the toxins, the bad bits; staying with something until it gleamed again. Stef once said it wasn't so different from being a paramedic and Betty held on to that thought as she worked.

She'd heard about people in big offices who spent entire days doing nothing apart from walking between the photocopier and the water machine and the cafeteria and the smokers' shelter and the printer and then back to their desk to shuffle papers and start all over again. That wasn't for Betty and it wasn't for Stef. They both transformed bad to good, didn't they?

And that's what she'd done in Stef's bathroom this morning.

All bad smells were gone. The floor and wall tiles gleamed. There were no more toothpaste splashes on the mirror. All that remained was the light switches and door handle and the job would be done. She'd already cleaned behind the door – another spot that was often overlooked – but it was only when she hunched down to polish the chrome surround of the door handle that she noticed the part she'd missed. There, on one of the wall tiles, was a dirty mark that she should have seen earlier. She leaned closer to the wall, finger pushed into the underside of the damp cloth, ready to rub. Close up she could see it wasn't just one spot of dirt, but a splatter of them. And once the moisture of the cloth breathed colour into what had been dry, she realised it wasn't dirt at all. Right there, three tiles from the floor in Stef's bathroom, was a spray of blood.

CHAPTER 5

The letter came the same day as the funeral; made solid the warnings that had been whispered for weeks. Stef Campbell was halfway down the stairs when it was pushed through the front door, landed on a scattered pile of sympathy cards and early Christmas post, delivered yesterday but deliberately ignored. She half-walked, half-wobbled towards it in shiny black heels that would deform her toes by noon and a black dress she suspected was too tight for the occasion. She'd bought the dress from a charity shop years back. Posh brand, rarely worn, hers for a fiver. Its grimy origins made compliments all the more satisfying although they came in a wild flurry any time she ditched her jeans. The fact she was wearing a dress at all was usually enough to widen eyes and induce a predictable flow of dull comments about her scrubbing up well. The surprise in their voices stung, sucked the pleasure out of being momentarily adored by someone other than Andy. Then Andy would turn up and hand her a pint and she'd thank God she'd chosen a man who saw who she really was and loved her anyway.

Anyway, folk didn't tend to comment on clothes at a funeral.

She picked up the letter and headed to the kitchen, glanced at the clock then flipped on the kettle. They'd have time for a quick cup of tea before they left. For a moment she stood at the window and stared out over their garden, searched for her favourite robin. Andy took the piss when she went on about it, asked how she could possibly know it was the same one. But she just did. She'd tried painting it a few times but it was hard to paint life that wasn't yet stilled. Give her a tree trunk or a mountain ridge or a cliff any day of the week and she'd get it on to canvas with a few flicks of the wrist. Job done.

A breath was harder to capture.

She dropped two teabags into the pot then sliced open the envelope with the paper knife she'd bought during one of their campervan trips to Spain. Inside was a single sheet, folded twice. She leaned against the kitchen worktop to read it.

The page was half empty, a big bright stage for a few dark words.

An ultimatum, just for her.

She heard Andy on the stairs, shoved the letter between two hardback cookery books, seconds before he walked into the kitchen. She was still holding the paper knife in one of her hands, its rounded tip pointing in the direction of the door.

'You help me with my tie, love?'

She put down the knife, pushed a smile into place.

Andy looked odd in a suit. They'd picked it up last week in one of those awful strip-lit stores next to the twenty-four-hour supermarket, filled the boot of the car with loo roll and Fairtrade bananas and red wine then popped next door and bought a black suit which he'd refused to try on for size, insisted he'd only be wearing it once – and only because his mum had requested it from her deathbed. He'd agreed; one final attempt to win her over.

But he'd snapped at Stef when they were at the till, annoyed when she'd asked the shop assistant about the refund policy if it didn't fit. The woman had glanced at Stef as she folded the trousers into a noisy paper bag, flipped her easy smile into something that was tight-lipped and simpering and never welcome anywhere, ever. Pity. Stef let it go.

She'd had more than enough pity at work recently, whenever Vicky Steele was mentioned. Vicky was clinical team leader at the station, so her name came up a lot; but even the gobbiest of her colleagues would mutter apologies when that woman *slipped into conversation, as if they were the one who'd broken a vow and a heart to touch her.*

It only happened once, Andy had said, as if that would stop Stef's mind conjuring up images of an urgent, drunken kiss between him and Vicky at the Halloween party and of the inevitable fumbles that would have followed. Vicky Steele, taking her place and pleasure in it. Stef knew better than anyone where Andy's mouth would have led his hands. It sickened her, the thought of blood rising in the pair of them when their touches were no longer accidental or easily excused. But in reality the pity of others was worse than the act itself.

That, and the whispered accusations that had coated Andy's apology.

She'd been distant, he said, and he was right. Stef had been edging away from him for months, little by little carving out a space between them in the desperate hope that he wouldn't notice her slurs and her stumbles. Sometimes life looks better from a distance.

Maybe Andy's suit would as well.

Stef pushed herself on to the pointed toes of her funeral shoes, flipped up the collar of Andy's shirt then tugged the tie into the right position. That was another thing Andy was adamant about. No ties, ever. Hence the help. He'd have managed if she'd not been here but she knew that what he really wanted was this: her hands gently on him and their faces close. She thought about kissing him but didn't, the instinct flattened by the thoughts of that loose, slippery tongue in his mouth.

'There,' she said, then tapped his chest with her palm and stepped away.

'If I didn't know you better I'd think you were trying to choke me,' said Andy, tugging at the collar, fingers fumbling behind the fat knot until he'd managed to undo the top button of his white shirt. 'God, I hate these things.'

She wasn't sure if he meant the tie or the suit or the funeral, gave his arm a squeeze anyway.

'Tea?'

'We got time?'

'We'll make time.' She held the pot with both hands when she poured, somehow managed to fill them without spilling a drop. Andy stared at his mug when

she held it out to him, tried to blink away tears. It had been a Christmas gift from his mum, years ago.

She sipped her too-hot tea to break the silence; welcomed the sound of the doorbell.

'That'll be the car,' said Andy, not moving. 'I really wish we'd just taken our own.'

'It was what your mum wanted,' she said, moving past him into the hall. She opened their front door and nodded to the driver. He tilted his hat. The car was absurdly shiny, far too big for just the two of them. She waited by the door until Andy came through, pinching his nose between his fingers and taking a big sniff before he spoke. 'Let's get this over with,' he said, then took her hand and let her lead him down the steps.

Andy stared out of the side window for the short drive to the church but Stef's gaze was fixed on the hearse and the woman it held. Not for the first time her mind spat out images of wide eyes inside a coffin; the terror of waking up, locked in.

She thought also of those little humans who'd died in the warm darkness of her rounded belly; years of ambulance work proving useless when her own body turned against her. But mostly her mind took her to that letter and the person who'd written it. There was *so much power in those words and so much potential for damage. Every part of Stef that could burn, started burning. But by the time the hearse pulled up at the church she knew what would have to happen next, even though Andy would fight it, to the death.*

The time had come to leave him.

CHAPTER 6

Betty stared at the smudge of blood on the tiles until her thighs got sore then heaved herself up, using the door handle for support. Part of her wanted to spray it with bleach and rub the tile with her damp cloth until there was no trace of rusty red on white but at the same time she wondered if she'd be destroying evidence in the process. But, evidence of what?

She kneeled down again and studied the splatter.

If it had been there on Friday she'd have noticed it – and that meant someone had bled here over the weekend. But who, and why? And did it actually mean anything was wrong?

No, Betty, it does not.

And yes, Betty, you're being ridiculous.

That's what her mother would say if she could see her now and maybe she'd be right.

If Andy said Stef was at an art retreat, that's where she was.

Betty straightened up, forced her eyes away from the blood but she'd been looking at it for so long that when she blinked she could see the splatter in negative. She tried to ignore it, along with the creaks and groans and rumbles only heard when a house is empty.

It was unusual for her to be there on her own.

Andy usually left for work around the same time she got there but Stef was almost always at home. She'd never told Betty directly why she'd been signed off work but Betty knew the signs, had been brought up by a fragile woman who'd used most of her energy trying to pretend she wasn't. Some days nobody would answer the doorbell and when she let herself in using the spare key she'd find a note from Andy on the kitchen counter, telling her Stef was Having A Bad Day and should not be disturbed. Those were the days Betty would choose to deep-clean the upstairs landing; would polish radiators and wipe down lampshades, whatever task allowed her to linger closest to the room where Stef was taking refuge. One day she'd put her ear to the door, thought she heard sobbing.

She'd knocked, gently, used a recently boiled kettle as an excuse for being there.

Tea was offered, silence the only reply.

But mostly Stef was downstairs and chatty and seemed happy to see her, to have someone there who'd listen without asking questions. Sometimes she'd tell Betty quite pointedly that she had An Appointment, then be gone most of the morning and when she returned she'd seem a little bit sad; would grab her painting kit and go to the garden without a word. Betty would watch Stef tramping across the grass into the shadows cast by trees. She carried her kit in a little yellow bag she'd made from one of Andy's old shirts and if he happened to be there when she came inside he'd insist on washing her brushes for her; would stand at the sink and whistle as he unclogged the hairs with warm water and his thumbs, colours swirling and blending before they disappeared down the plug-hole. Stef would let him clean her hands too; would hold her sticky fingers under the hot tap and let him rub them with his. It made Betty's eyes well up because if she looked at Stef in that moment she could tell she loved him more than anything, anyone.

A fist formed in Betty's throat at the thought of it.

She ached almost as much when Stef's sister Alyson visited. The siblings would sit side by side on the back-doorstep; mugs steaming, thighs touching, voices hushed. Betty would have loved to have joined them. Instead she'd stay as far away from the kitchen as possible so they wouldn't think she was eavesdropping or know she longed for so simple and complex a thing as human touch.

But she'd find none of that today. The only thing she'd hold was the brush.

Betty went to the kitchen, knew that if she swept the floor she'd see toast crumbs and individual oats and a few of Stef's long hairs in the pan. But for once she ignored the dirt, stared instead at the sideboard and the one thing that should not be sitting on top.

Stef's painting kit.

Betty picked up the bag and unzipped it and rubbed the pad of her thumb against the dry paintbrushes. She'd worked for Stef long enough to know she rarely left the house without her kit. Why would she have left it here if she'd gone to an art retreat? Betty's mind bubbled with answers but logic popped them before they'd fully formed. Stef would be fine. She was at an art retreat with a different set of paints and a shaving cut on her leg and a lucky penny tucked safely into her pocket. Betty needed to finish her job and mind her own business. But then she thought again about that penny sitting on that crack.

Your fault.

She had to make wrongs right.

Betty pulled out her phone and scrolled until her thumb hung over Stef's name and number. She took a few deep breaths then pressed the call button. Her eyes flitted to the fruit bowl, rested again on the place Stef usually left her money but this week had not. If Stef answered the call, she'd say she was phoning about the payment. And what if she didn't? Her brain was already shooting out theories when the call connected; and then it came, a sound she didn't expect. Here, now, in this house, she heard the muted vibration of a ringing mobile phone.

When she looked beyond the kitchen table and through the door that led to the utility room she could see Stef's bright red running jacket, hanging in its usual place. And when she walked through and touched it, she could feel a vibration against her fingers. With one quick look she knew it was Stef's mobile phone – and that something was wrong.

CHAPTER 7

The reek of a filthy microwave seeped into Andy's nostrils the moment he opened the door to the mess at the ambulance station. Sure enough, Amechi was sitting on the sofa with a steaming bowl of porridge. He smiled at Andy. 'Thought you'd done a runner on me.'

'What?'

'You're late,' Amechi said, scooping up another spoonful of slimy oats. 'Well, late for you.'

'Busy morning.'

'Sounds ominous.'

'Don't ask.' Mostly when folk said that, they meant the opposite. Andy did not. God, he couldn't even look at the lad. He'd studied himself in the car mirror before he came in, trying to work out if his eyes were puffy or not; if the redness had subsided. The tears had been threatening to flood him since he woke up; he'd pushed them back with forced coughs and hard, sticky swallows.

But they'd finally swamped him when Arthur's Seat came into view on the drive to work. How many times had he and Stef climbed it? Far too many to remember but now, never again. He'd flipped on his hazard lights, pulled into a lay-by, let himself cry. Head in hands, chest on fire, mind replaying the jumbled, stuttering answers he'd given to Betty.

He should never have let her in the house.

But at least he'd learned from it; had practiced telling the story he and Alyson had spent so many months weaving together. Better to mess it up with Betty than someone in uniform.

But from now on, he'd say nothing.

If anyone asked why he looked so rough he'd say he'd eaten some dodgy mince, had the shits; say something people wouldn't want to ask about. And if anyone asked why he was checking his phone so often he'd invent a story about a leaking roof or a burst pipe, one of those things he used to think mattered.

He and Alyson were both working today, on purpose.

It had seemed like a good idea when the plan was still theoretical; something that may or may not happen. Not a fact. Not what was happening, *right now*. But today, the ambulance would be his alibi – and Alyson would have dozens of them.

She'd packed her estate agency schedule with viewings, would spend the day showing credit-checked clients around semi-detached villas and swanky flats with sash-and-case windows; trying to convince them that happiness increases in direct correlation with how much stuff you've got. But a fiver said she'd be thinking the same thing he was.

You leave it all behind when you die, don't you?

Their first callout was a road accident; a fight between a tree and one of those wee cars that are great for parking in the city but not so impressive on the country roads after a summer rainstorm. A young dad with a crap beard, bleeding from his chest and asking about the wee baby strapped in the back, thankfully screaming its head off. They'd be fine, except for his drink-driving charge. Twat. Next up was a home visit, some old dear who'd slipped on a wet step and almost bitten off her own chin. Total mess. But she'd be fine as well. And so the hours went on, a whirlwind of saving lives and stitching people back together and those moments when they knew they'd done everything they could, but that life had gone and left anyway. It's one of those jobs that the careers service will tell you is never the same two days running; and they'd be right. But they won't tell you about the days that stay with you long after the date has changed. Amechi was too soft, had spent half the morning lamenting some wee druggie who'd died on his previous shift.

'Lesson one – *again*,' said Andy. 'Don't take this job home with you.'

'Easier said than done.'

'Aye.'

'There must be some patients that stay with you,' Amechi said. 'In all the years you've been doing it.'

'A few, maybe.' They were stopped at traffic lights. Andy kept his eyes fixed on the red light but he could tell Amechi was looking at him, wanting more. 'But you toughen up, learn to disconnect from it. You have to.'

Before he started the job Andy hadn't realised how big a part death would play in his career. Stef asked him what he *had* expected and he'd told her what he told everyone else. He wanted to save lives, end of story. He'd not thought so much about the many times he'd lose one, or how he'd feel when he did.

The first patient he'd ever lost at work was a woman in her sixties who'd choked while she was eating her lunch. When Andy arrived she was convulsing on her dining room floor next to a fork still loaded with food. Andy had driven past the house later, pulled up across the road and wondered about knocking on the door. He'd pictured the woman's husband, setting the table for one. Andy had stayed there for ages, hoping he'd have to move his car when relatives and friends of the couple arrived to bring the man flowers and ready-meals and suitably sad faces. But none came. Andy left when he saw the curtains close and the lights go off upstairs. And he realised then that life just goes on.

'Vicky said your wife struggled a bit?'

'With what?' Andy's cheeks were burning.

'The deaths. Vicky said that was why she got signed off. How long's that been now?'

'Six months or so,' said Andy, anger sparking in his chest. 'There's something else you'll need to learn, pal – and quickly. Don't trust everything Vicky Steele tells you. I know she's a team leader but she's also a total liability.'

Bloody Vicky. What did he ever see in that woman? When he'd confessed to Stef he'd blamed the free bar at last year's Halloween party. Stef had missed it because she'd been working the late shift but even before Andy had taken a single drink he'd sensed the longing in him. The sad reality was this: there had been a few lingering looks between him and Vicky long before that party. But it wasn't really *her* he'd been needing, was it? It was someone who didn't flinch when he touched them; who offered a kiss instead of excuses.

Regret still gnawed at him, remembering how graciously Stef had forgiven him.

In fact it was Vicky who wouldn't let it go and now she was spreading nonsense about why Stef was off sick. She had no bloody right. In fact, nobody did. Especially now.

'How's Stef doing anyway? I'd love to see her.' Amechi sounded like he meant it, was someone else who'd miss her. 'She said she'd pop in one day, but she never has done.'

'She's . . . fine. Painting a lot.'

'Landscapes, isn't it?'

'Aye.' Andy thought of that peak, that ridge, that woodland, that bothy, and the soft earth that would hold her. Would her body be cold by now? He pictured her blood, now useless, settling in the parts of her that touched the ground; a low tidemark on her skin. 'You mind if we talk about something else?'

'No problem,' said Amechi, then launched into a monologue about the pros and cons of the vegan diet. Food was probably the biggest topic of conversation on paramedics' shifts, mainly because there was rarely time to actually eat any. It was also reliably safe territory, kept their mouth and minds well away from what they were dealing with.

Andy ended the shift in exactly the same way he'd started it, boiling the kettle. He filled and flipped and waited, flicked through the city paper while the water rumbled to boiling point. He'd often see names and faces he recognised; a few of the many lives he'd passed through. A person becoming a past tense. Today, he couldn't bear it. He closed the paper, tossed it towards Amechi on his way out of the door. 'All yours, pal. But it'll just depress you.'

'Can't be any worse than spending a shift with you,' said Amechi, then blew him a kiss. The sound of his laughter followed Andy out of the door and into air that felt thick and heavy and damp, held the threat of a storm. It was far too chilly for an evening in June. But it would be much colder in the hills, assuming you were alive to feel it.

He drove home the long way – the scenic route, Stef called it – past Arthur's Seat and over the hill to Duddingston, catching glimpses of narrow cobbled streets and that old graveyard he and Stef often wandered through on their way to or from the Sheep Heid Inn. After that the road sloped down towards the coast; all big skies and calm sea backed by the rolling hills across the water. A good day offered views of the three bridges that stretched across the Forth and always brought them home. Tonight the sky was clear but all Andy could see was Stef's sagging body; a loose tongue and a floppy neck and heavy arms and useless legs. His Stef, a dead weight; impossible to push out of his mind.

He was astonished he'd made it through that shift.

He took the turning for Musselburgh then stared for a while at the harbour and the memorial benches that stood, sad and still, with their backs to the sea wall. Painted fishing boats bobbed on the dark water while he breathed in salt and seaweed, gulping in the familiar bitterness of it. From there it was a short drive along the coast to Portobello and to the house that was theirs, yet now was not. He parked then stood, staring at his front door and at the roses Stef had planted just after they'd moved in, fifteen years earlier. More than once those thorns had caught the sleeve of his jacket or the tanned part of his arm. He touched that morning's wound as he stared at the roses, traced the soft pads of his fingers over that delicate red line, raised above the hairs and already hardened into a scab. His body was already repairing itself and that was it right there: the greatest and simplest of all life's miracles. That was the reason he drove an ambulance every day.

The conversations with Amechi looped in his head. It was true that he'd trained himself to disconnect, to leave the names and faces at work with his uniform. Washed, dried, stain-free. But every patient came with a world attached.

He was a master of looking the other way but the technique failed spectacularly when he shared the same name as the dead; when the weight of loss was crushing his own family; and when the fault lay with him. A lifesaver, taking lives.

Until now the worst had been the first.

His dad had been at work and his mum had been bathing his wee sister upstairs when the doorbell rang and he'd run through the hall in his Batman pyjamas and shouted up the stairs, asked if he was allowed to answer it. He'd pulled back the pink roller blind on the glass front door before he answered, came face to face with the drooping heads of two pheasants, gripped firmly round the neck by the woman standing on their doorstep. The gamekeeper's wife, dressed in green wellies and a brown body warmer, one of his mum's patients, bringing the two dead birds as a gift of thanks. She did it every year and Andy knew from bad experience that she had no qualms about handing the corpses to wee boys. He remembered the weight of them in his hands, the way he'd tried but failed to keep his arms outstretched while he walked through to the kitchen to make sure their still-warm bodies and the long colourful feathers in their tails wouldn't brush against him.

That was why he'd dropped the blind into place that night then raced up the stairs and begged his mum to go and answer the door; touch the dead instead of him. She'd lifted a handful of bubbles from the bath and placed a big crackling blob on his nose.

You watch your wee sister, she'd said, then gone downstairs.

Andy had only left the bathroom for a few seconds and only because he'd heard a song he loved, coming from the radio in his mum and dad's room. He wanted his wee sister to hear it, ran through, struggled for a few moments to find the volume button in the dark. But then it was blasting out, that song from the charts that they'd all sung along to in the car and his wee sister had laughed, kept repeating one of the only words she could.

Again, again, again.

But when he got back to the bathroom she wasn't saying anything at all and even if she had done, he wouldn't have heard her because her face was under the water and her mouth was facing the bottom of the bath and the music was so loud that even when his mum came upstairs and her mouth curled and stretched in a way he'd never seen before; even then, he couldn't hear anything except that cheerful chorus of that song in the background, the singers shifting up an octave and repeating again, again, again.

His mum had pushed him so hard that he hit his head on the bottom corner of the bathroom cabinet then dragged his wee sister out of the water and on to the blue mat and started pressing and prodding and squeezing her little body in lots of different ways that, back then, he didn't understand. He'd just stood there with bubble-splashed pyjamas and one hand on his bruising head and the knowledge that he'd done something really wrong and the desperate wish that he could go back in time just for two minutes, or even just one, so that he could change what he had and hadn't done and the look that had darkened his mum's eyes forever after that, no matter how hard she tried to hide it.

And he'd wished that stupid song would end.

Now, back inside, home was far too silent.

He ordered pizza then opened the beer he'd been thinking about all day; downed it. He opened a second, had just drained it when the doorbell rang. He padded through the hall and unclipped the security chain as noisily as possible so the delivery man knew he was there. His hand was on the Yale and he was about to pull the door open when he heard sounds he didn't expect from the other side. He stopped, heart thundering in every part of his body. When the noises came again the strength drained from his legs. He steadied himself against the door frame, wishing he was somewhere else; somebody else.

A radio beeped. Static fizzed. Then somebody knocked on his door and said one word, far too loudly.

'Police.'

CHAPTER 8

Stef caught Andy's eye and held it, a millisecond before tears blurred her view of that hole, that coffin and his mum, nailed inside. He'd done well, so far. First funeral he'd attended in almost forty years, ever since he was old enough to have a choice in the matter. It didn't take a genius to work out why Andy's first funeral had been his last one, until today. Nine years old and he'd been dressed up like a wee man in a Marks & Spencer suit, expected to act like one when they put his little sister in a wooden box and burned her until all that was left was an urn packed with ashes and a mother, drained. He'd been too wee to help at the time but he'd carried the weight of her coffin ever since. Would it lessen now his mum was gone?

She looked at Andy but this time he didn't look back.

Stef's mind wandered as well, took her back fifteen years to that afternoon in that woodland. She'd held that box like a baby tucked into the crook of one arm, tight against her body. They'd chosen the spot together but she'd walked behind Andy on purpose, slowing her pace whenever he did so there was no possibility or need for a conversation. He stopped when they reached the hole she'd dug alone the previous night.

Stef had hiked out there after dinner cooked on their camping stove, couldn't bear to sit with Andy while he repeatedly checked the empty wine bottle for dregs she'd already downed. Every one of his tuts was an accusation, a judgement.

She could see now that the hole she'd dug was far too big for the box but she'd found it hard to stop digging once she started. The ache in her shoulders helped distract from the pain that gripped the rest of her.

She kneeled down, used both hands to place the box in the bottom. It weighed almost nothing, contained only a tiny white outfit that still had the factory folds.

She looked up at Andy. 'Should we say something?'

Andy made a face that was almost a sneer then pulled a letter out of his jacket pocket. When he placed it on top of the box she watched his lips move but heard only the outline of his words.

'I thought we'd have said something together,' she said. 'Something from both of us.'

Andy sighed and stood up, stared over her head into the thick darkness of trees that would be stripped bare before too long. 'You really think words can capture it?'

'I don't think anything can,' she said, then looked where he was looking, saw shivering leaves clinging to branches, somehow holding on despite the breeze that shot up from the river, carrying with it the nip of winter that made her cheeks red and tight and cold, the opposite of tears. Above them the evening sky was already sucking up the colour from the world, leaving only blackness. And what about the darkness in them?

Three times she'd got pregnant and three times, they'd lost the baby.

She stood up, reached for the spade, offered it to Andy. When he shook his head she wanted to hold him but didn't, knowing now how jagged he became under a soft touch.

The sound of earth on wood blocked out all other sounds as she filled the hole. Stef wished for a whisper or whistle of wind, a bird singing at the wrong time. No other sound came and neither of them spoke until she had finished. Stef gently patted the earth with *the spade, then kneeled down; laid a few leaves and branches on top.*

'What now?'

He shrugged. 'Home.'

'I mean with us,' she said, sighing. 'Our family.'

Andy made that sound he always made just before he would cry, a breath pushed out too hard and too fast. 'We'll go back to work, Stef. We'll do what we tell everyone else to do. Carry on.'

'And that's it?'

'We've already spoken about this.' He started walking away, carefully stepping around that spot of flat, fresh soil. No part of him touched it, or Stef.

'I want to try again, Andy.'

He stopped, turned, stared at the place the hole had been; at the earth that now swallowed that box. When she got closer she could see his tears. But his hands didn't shift from his pockets. 'There can be no more loss,' he said, and only then did he reach for Stef, held her so tightly and so close to him that she could feel his heart thunder through all the layers he wore to keep the cold far from him.

He reached for her again, now, as they walked away from his mother's grave to the hotel, coat collars pulled up against the breeze that greeted them every time they crossed one of the roads that led to the beach. Their fingers were intertwined, their palms pressed together.

For a moment she felt only love and she convinced herself that this latest betrayal – hers, this time – wouldn't change things. But the moment was like a match struck in the rain, a fizz of flame and then it was snubbed out, twisted out of shape, ready to drop. Stef's eyes blurred with rain and tears and she stumbled when she stepped up on to a pavement. 'Bloody heels,' she said and Andy held her tighter. But the distance between them remained the same, carved out by those losses.

And now, by lies.

CHAPTER 9

Andy forced a smile when he opened the door. There, on his doorstep, was Detective Inspector Farida McPherson. Her name was Syrian, as was her mother. Her accent was not. Brought up in Glasgow, her words had sharp edges, could burst an ego in one minute flat. Her eyes scanned Andy like those machines at the airport and to be fair, if she'd demanded he take off his shoes and belt and watch, he'd have done it. He knew her only from crime scenes at work. But now he had beer on his breath and guilt on his conscience and lies already forming on his tongue.

'You're not here to bring me pizza, right?'

'Afraid not,' she said, not a trace of humour in her voice. 'Could we possibly chat inside?'

Andy opened his mouth but no words came.

'I appreciate this is a little . . . unorthodox,' said Farida, and for a moment Andy sensed a slight uncertainty in her that he'd never seen before. 'But I'd appreciate guidance with something.'

God, she knew how to work a room. Make the plebs feel useful and they'll let you in, do as you please. Today of all days, he could do without this, her, here, now. But on an ordinary day he'd happily help. It was vital he acted as if that's exactly what this was.

'Sure.' Andy stepped to one side and ushered her in, smile pinned in place. 'Sitting room's on the right. Excuse the mess. Can I get you a drink, or—'

'That won't be necessary.'

'I'll be right back.'

He went into the bathroom and locked the door, then hunched down with his head in his hands. *She can't be here. This is not happening.* He squeezed his head between his hands and wished for a different ending, an easy way out. He pulled out his phone and typed out a message to Stef's sister. Deleted it. Then typed it out again. He was about to press send when he heard a cough from the sitting room, knew it was forced and aimed at him. He stuffed the phone in his pocket then flushed the loo, made a show of drying his hands on his jeans when he reached the sitting room. Farida was still standing.

'Shall we sit?'

She took the couch, left Andy with Stef's armchair; the cushion still dented from the last time she'd sat in it, a dark smudge on the cloth where her head usually rested. Andy perched on the wooden arm, crossed and uncrossed his legs; desperate to look relaxed.

'Actually,' she said, clearing her throat and turning it into a drum roll, 'it's Stef I really like to speak to. Is she here?'

Andy's tongue was sandpaper. Lying to the cleaning lady was one thing but Farida was the police. This was exactly the situation they'd wanted to avoid.

'Art retreat,' he said. Verbs failed him.

Farida tilted her head to one side. 'So she's not here?'

He shook his head. 'Be gone a week or so. In the Highlands. She's thinking of visiting friends afterwards so I'm not sure when she'll be home.' He forced the kind of quip that would have made Stef roll her eyes. 'The luxury of being an artist, eh?'

'And when did she leave?'

'Yesterday evening.'

'Have you heard from her since?'

Andy shook his head. 'No signal up there. Deliberately. That's a selling point for some folk.'

'I see. In that case . . .' Farida sniffed, pointedly, then reached into her bag, pulled out a carefully folded piece of paper. 'I don't wish to alarm you, Andy. But there's something you need to look at.'

Don't wish to alarm you. Jesus. When would folk learn that saying those kinds of phrases produced exactly the feelings they were designed to avoid?

Farida kept her eyes on the page while she spoke.

'Police were called to the home of a . . . known criminal . . . last night, following reports of disturbance. We received several calls from concerned residents of neighbouring properties and, given the history of this particular individual, I decided to attend the scene.'

She looked up, caught his eye.

Andy did everything he could to keep his breath calm, swallow the panic that was creeping from his heart across his chest and into his limbs, making them tingle and twitch. He had to stay focussed, couldn't mess this up now, after everything they'd been through to get there. He forced his face into the expression he wore at work. Interested but unshocked, regardless of the horror he faced if he was first on the scene.

'Go on,' he said, as if he wanted to hear it.

'The front door of the property had been forced open but there was nobody inside and after a full search, we found no obvious sign of wrongdoing. I can't say more as it's still under investigation. But officers did bring to my attention a few unusual items at the property. I'm here because I wanted Stef to have a look at a photo I took at the scene – but in her absence I'll ask you to confirm its authenticity.'

She glanced at the page in her hand then held it out towards him. They both leaned forward, arses off seats, arms outstretched, fingers almost touching like a poor re-enactment of a Michelangelo painting. For a few seconds he kept the paper as it was, folded, safe, dormant. He felt sick. Farida's eyes were on him as he unfolded the A4 page and studied the black-and-white photo printed on it. And there it was. Stef's face, looking straight back at him.

'Andy?'

'Where did you say this was found?'

'On a mantelpiece, in that . . . criminal's flat. But I'm unable to reveal the address.'

'But why do you think it was there?'

'Your guess is as good as mine. Perhaps now you'll understand why I'm keen to speak to Stef. Can you confirm it's an authentic paramedic ID card? And that it's Stef's?'

'Looks like it.'

'Has she reported it lost or stolen?'

He shook his head. 'She's not mentioned it to me. But . . . she's been off work for months so there's a chance she—'

'Can I stop you there?' said Farida; as if she'd not already barged her way into his sentence, chopped it in half. 'Why has Stef been off work?'

'Stress.'

Farida gave him a look that suggested it was his fault. 'How long for?'

'Just over six months.'

'And is she . . . making progress?'

Folk always asked that question and Andy never knew how to answer it. His mouth was still open from before but he snapped it shut, worried the truth might slip out before he could swallow it.

'It's a complicated process,' he said, knowing fine well that meant nothing to anybody, but usually ended the conversation.

'Of course,' said Farida, and Andy noticed a softness in her voice that hadn't been there before. 'Either way, we'd really like to speak to her.'

'I could try calling but . . . but if there's no crime, what does it matter?'

'If I think it matters, it matters,' she said, all soft edges retracted. 'Now if you'd kindly give me your wife's number I'd appreciate a word with her.'

Andy forced himself to nod then pulled his phone out of his pocket, swiped the screen to bring it to life. This is how a normal husband would act in a normal situation, wasn't it? They'd give their wife's number to the nice policewoman who was, after all, here to help. He scrolled through the contacts, slowly, as if he could somehow delay or avoid what was about to happen. When he reached Stef's number her face appeared in a little circle at the top of the screen. He loved that photo; had taken it one day in the woods, a selfie, though he was now edited out of the image. 'Here we go,' he said, then read out the number. He stared at the screen while he did it but it was just a way to avoid looking at Farida. He knew Stef's number off by heart – and he knew there was no way she was going to answer Farida's call.

He and Alyson had seen to that.

She read it back to him then typed something into her phone – Stef's name, presumably. Andy willed her to stuff her phone in her pocket, to test the number later, somewhere else; anywhere else. But instead she stared at her screen, nose twitching as she sucked in air, a short, sharp inhale. She had a flight of sniffs, that woman, one to perfectly match every type of awkward situation. But what had triggered this one?

Blood drained from his cheeks when Farida put her phone to her ear. If she sensed the anxiety in him, she didn't show it, but she didn't shift her gaze either. Andy counted the seconds to distract himself, speculating what Farida could hear and how quickly it would go to voicemail and if she'd leave a message and if so, what she'd say. But then he heard it; the faintest of vibrations, coming from another room in the house. He'd muted the ringer on Stef's mobile but not switched it off. How could they have been so stupid? Andy faked a cough, hand cupped over his mouth, forcing it out in bursts that matched the rhythm of a ringing phone. Then Farida hung up, sat her phone on her knee.

'No answer,' she said. 'I'll keep trying. And if she should contact you I'd appreciate it if you ask her to call me. You'll understand that I can't reveal further details and I'm hoping there's a logical explanation – but there is some cause for concern.'

'Concern for *what*, exactly?'

Farida looked at him for a few seconds before she spoke again.

'For your wife's safety,' she said.

CHAPTER 10

Worry had kept Betty awake ever since she'd dropped *that* penny on *that* crack on Portobello Promenade on Monday morning. Now, as Tuesday night became Wednesday, old paranoias crept into her mind, added a sprinkling of menace to ordinary moments.

She'd finished her cleaning shift at Stef and Andy's house by Tuesday lunchtime then spent the rest of the day doing DIY and scrubbing every inch of her own home.

As she worked her mind churned out wild theories about the blood on Stef's bathroom wall and the mobile phone in her jacket pocket and the dry paintbrushes in that little bag and the penny on the crack and what good luck or bad luck it had inflicted on Stef, the Finder. She dreaded a knock on the door, finger pointing right at her and a booming voice telling her she was to blame for all of this.

Your fault, your fault, your fault.

It didn't happen but the fear stayed with her, followed her to bed and lay down beside her. She had to make sure Stef was OK. When her curtains changed colour, signalling sunrise, she dragged herself out of bed and into a decision that surprised even herself.

She'd drive to Stef's art studio and innocently ask about the retreat, settle her mind and her nerves in one fell swoop. So here she was, sleep deprived but driving anyway.

She flipped the indicator then glanced in her rearview mirror, wondered if the driver behind had noticed the hand-painted sign for Green Den Studios a few minutes earlier. It was only ten minutes' drive inland from Portobello but most people didn't even know it existed. It was a world of its own with trees for walls (those were Stef's words but Betty liked to pretend she'd said them first), hidden from the city and the motorway by tightly packed pine trees and a driveway that looked fit only for tractors. But in fact there were a few rambling country houses within walking distance, including one that Betty used to clean.

The lady who'd lived there would often visit exhibitions at the studio and tell Betty all about them while she watched her dust chandeliers and polish brass ornaments in her hall. But she never asked Betty if she'd been or wanted to go, probably assuming that *people like her* didn't appreciate art.

But in fact Betty had spent a lot of time in museums and galleries when she was wee because their mum would dump them at the big ones in Edinburgh city centre then go to meet pals in the Grassmarket pubs. Before she left, her mum would kneel down so they were looking directly into each other's eyes. She'd pinch Betty's cheek and tell her to look after her wee brother and not get up to nonsense, then make her repeat the line she was to give to security guards or anyone with a lanyard around their neck. If anybody asked, her mum had just popped out to meet their granny at the bus stop and would be back very soon.

She never was, though.

They'd still be there when the lights inside the display cabinets were switched off and most parents were shooing their children towards the cloakroom. Betty and her brother would follow them and wait by the front door with their jackets zipped to the top and their gloves on and the story on their tongues and tears stinging their eyes when the main lights clunked off, stripped the yellow off the walls and made the whole world grey again. Eventually someone would lead them into the security guards' office and give them a snack and when their mum arrived she'd be given a telling off instead of a biscuit and told this wasn't a bloody day-care centre.

Her mum would put on her posh voice and tell them she was perfectly aware of that, thank you very much, then she'd skelp Betty around the ears as punishment for running off and telling lies to the nice man and in the end Betty would hang her stinging head and apologise, though she was never quite sure what for.

Betty had rarely been to galleries or museums since her mum left them, mainly because she carried within her the fear that somebody wearing a jacket with a name badge attached would tap her on the shoulder and ask her what she was doing there on her own.

And that Wednesday morning, when Green Den Studios came into view at the end of the long and winding access road, Betty started to ask herself the very same thing.

Stef usually came for an art lesson on a Tuesday afternoon, would come straight here after she'd dropped Betty at home. She'd often said Betty should come and have a look around the studio and Betty's heart would fill up and she'd want to say *yes* but would always find herself saying *no* instead, then spend the afternoon regretting it.

When she reached the car park she drove to the far side to be sure she couldn't be accused of stealing anybody's space. She got out, tugging her black fleece down over the waistline of her jeans so nobody would notice the missing button that she kept forgetting to replace. She pushed her hands into the deep pockets, squeezed a penny for luck as she headed for a blue door with a sign above it that said Main Entrance in curly letters.

She pushed open the door and stepped into a tiny reception area that was unlit and unmanned and dominated by a scrap-metal sculpture taller than she was, depicting two identical pigeons that appeared to be pecking out each other's eyes. Ragged pieces of tinsel had been wrapped around their necks, too tightly. The pigeons would be one of Richard's creations, probably. Stef had told Betty he tried very hard – *too hard*, she said – to be Big In The Art World, was forever trying to create things that nobody had ever made before, or thought of.

Betty didn't like the pigeons, turned her back on them.

There was another door to her right, half open. She held her breath and listened, hoping she'd hear Stef's voice; that the retreat was over and that she'd popped to the studio on her way home. But all she heard was a man on the phone, talking too fast and laughing too loud.

Betty pushed open the door anyway.

The room was vast, with exposed stone walls and varnished wooden beams that stretched across the ceiling, all the way to a set of double glass doors at the gable end.

A woman with bright green glasses and a fuzz of grey hair looked up from her easel and smiled at Betty when she stepped inside. 'Can I help you, love?'

For a moment Betty just stood, hands in her pockets, gently running the pads of her fingers back and forth over the cold metal edges of the Queen's face as she tried to wish Stef into the room, to safety, to a place no threat could reach her. But Stef wasn't there and when the fuzz-headed woman asked again if she could help, Betty smiled and said she really hoped so. The woman smiled too when Stef's name was mentioned.

'I'm a family friend,' said Betty, as per the script she'd prepared for herself on the drive over. She'd been worried she wouldn't get past that line; that they'd take one look at Betty and wonder why on earth Stef was friends with a woman like her.

If only they knew. If only anyone did.

But in fact the woman said her name was Ellie then continued smiling so Betty kept on talking. 'She told me I could pop in and see her at this art retreat she's gone to,' she said. 'Gave me the address for it on a Post-it note before she left but I can't find it anywhere. Checked my handbag eighteen times but it's nowhere. You know how it is.'

Ellie laughed when she said that, as Betty had hoped.

But that was the point where Betty envisaged the woman would have got out a pen and scribbled down the location of the art retreat and tell her to say hello to Stef from her; maybe even feel a twinge of jealousy that would show in her eyes when she handed over the address, expose the fact she wished she was as close to Stef as Betty was.

But when Ellie stopped laughing she said she had no idea what retreat Stef had gone on, then shouted to the bald man who'd been talking on the phone. He was now standing on a table staring at a flickering bulb and tugging the tip of his greying beard.

'No idea,' he said, introducing himself as Hamish. 'She never mentioned any art retreat to me. You sure you got the right dates? Almost everyone from the studio has gone to an art fair this week, held at some stately home near Cumnock. They're hoping to flog their paintings before the holidays. Not that you'd know it's summer, eh? And it's going to get worse. If the weather forecast's right we're due a proper storm any day. Four seasons in one day and then some.'

Hamish smiled when he said it and when Betty looked back at Ellie she was smiling too so Betty forced one into place even though the insides of her felt like the direct inverse of what a smile should mean. Andy said Stef had gone on retreat. Andy, with blood splatters in his bathroom and puffy red eyes. Stef, who'd left her car and her mobile phone and her painting kit at home, her brushes dry as old bones on the kitchen shelf.

Betty squeezed the penny in her pocket, wished for words that didn't come.

The silence that came instead was uncomfortable and clearly Betty's fault so Hamish glanced at the flickering bulb and Ellie picked up her paintbrush and words rushed about in Betty's mouth like ants in their nest. But then they fled, surged out of her.

'I can see you're really busy but I just wondered if there's someone else you can possibly ask? I'd be awfully grateful.' Betty felt rude asking, was sure that the moment she left they'd say she had *pure cheek* and conceded they'd probably be right. 'Maybe her teacher? The one she meets on a Tuesday?' Betty was glad she knew the day of Stef's lesson because it proved they were friends, that she knew her better than most.

Betty liked to hear stories about the studio but Stef would change the subject if Andy came in because he'd make snide comments about her teacher and call him silly names. Stef would get annoyed when he did that and Betty would feel that knot inside of her loop into something that was even bigger and harder to do undo, wondering if Andy had a nickname for her too.

'You mean Richard?' Hamish raised his eyebrows. 'You seen him around today, Ellie?'

Ellie shook her head. 'Nope. That doesn't mean he's not here, mind you. He's quite often holed up in the office, isn't he?' She glanced at Betty. 'He's the owner of the studio, you see. Might be worth knocking on his door. It's possible he told Stef about some retreat that the rest of us didn't know about. But like Hamish said, almost every artist from the studio is at that art fair. And thinking about it, Richard will probably be there too. He wouldn't miss a chance to promote himself.'

Betty frowned. 'But Andy – Stef's husband – said Richard was driving Stef to the retreat, so he won't be here, will he? Unless he dropped her off and came back?'

'That's . . . possible?' Ellie looked at Hamish. 'I've certainly not heard a peep from either of them since the end of last week.'

'Me neither,' said Hamish. 'Maybe that's what they're calling their *rendezvous* these days. "*Art retreats*".' He let out a laugh after he said that but it wasn't a friendly one.

Ellie cleared her throat. 'Did you say you're a *family friend*?' She gritted her teeth when she said the last two words and looked at Hamish with big wide eyes, even though the question was meant for Betty.

'Yes, I'm . . .' Betty hesitated, hadn't invented a history beyond that phrase. *Family friend*. Her blood started churning, getting ready to betray her by creep creep creeping towards the surface of her skin. 'Perhaps I'll go and check Richard's office, if that's all right? If he's there I'll ask him directly. And if he's not then maybe I can leave him a note, ask him to call me if he knows the location of Stef's retreat.'

'Sounds like a good plan.' Ellie motioned over Betty's shoulder. 'Head to the main entrance, past the pigeons and into the annexe. Richard's name is on his door.'

Betty thanked them and set off, but before the door closed she heard Hamish laugh and Ellie shush him. She always left laughter in her wake, a bitter slipstream.

The lights in the corridor clunked into life when she pressed the switch, accompanied her footsteps along a modern corridor that reminded her of a school or hospital; something built to be practical rather than beautiful. There were three doors on each side, all of them with a little window in the top half. One was a small gallery, one was a little kitchen and two were set up as classrooms with whiteboards on the wall and rows of plastic chairs filling the floor space. A small artist's studio held two chairs in front of an easel and a big window that overlooked woodland. That would be the place Stef got her lessons on Tuesday afternoons; the place she should have been yesterday and maybe would have been if she hadn't picked up Betty's coin from that crack on the promenade.

But if the fault was hers, it was also her duty to set it right.

She knocked on the last door, knuckles inches from the wooden sign that said *Richard Owens* in bright blue letters. He'd pulled a blind down over the little window so Betty couldn't see inside. No answer. She tried again. Nothing. She pushed her face close to the door and said his name, addressing him like a teacher so he'd know she knew he was boss.

'Mr Owens?'

Silence.

She glanced up the corridor just as the automatic lights went out, filling the whole space with shadows that the silence seemed to cling to even more eagerly.

And then, she opened the door.

CHAPTER 11

Andy opened his eyes on Wednesday morning and for a few seconds he forgot about Farida's visit and the photo she'd shown him. In the silence between one raindrop and the next, his mind and heart and body and marriage and world and morals were still intact.

But the rain kept coming.

A summer storm had been battering against the bedroom window for hours but his thoughts were wilder than anything nature could throw at him. Now, fully awake, his mind kept replaying Farida's evening visit. She'd come, dropped a bomb, then left. He'd done his best to get a few more answers out of her before she made it to the front door but she wouldn't budge, just kept churning out that same line about concern for Stef's safety.

But one question kept clattering around in Andy's brain, a tin can caught in the wind.

Did Farida somehow know about him and Alyson?

Maybe she'd come to him under false pretences; had worked out more than she was letting on and wanted to catch him out by distracting him with some other story about things going wrong. Where Andy saved lives, Farida read minds; was famed for it.

But surely there was no way she could have guessed their plan.

He could barely believe it himself but every time he closed his eyes he saw the same thing.

Stef; stilled, stiff, silent.

For a while she'd just look like she was sleeping but he knew how quickly death took over a body; that the stillness on the surface masked the storm raging underneath the gradually greying skin. A body turns on itself; ruptures, blisters, bloats. The skin that his own had always been drawn to would loosen and liquefy; become a stain.

He wished, now, that she was in bed beside him but instead he forced himself out of it, did the things that usually made mornings feel normal.

But all routine did was highlight the fact he was doing it alone. He switched on the radio, boiled the kettle, made toast and spread it with butter, cursed the empty room when he realised he'd forgotten to take out the paper bin. At least that one wouldn't stink.

When the early morning news came on he turned up the volume and listened to a woman with a posh-Scot accent reel off the stories she'd been told to tell. When she laughed and handed over to the lad on the sports desk Andy's hard, hunched shoulders dropped from his ears. There was no mention of a body being found. That was good news, of sorts.

He and Alyson had agreed to avoid contact but he wanted to tell her about Farida's visit – and her unexplained concern for Stef's safety.

Arse on the radiator, eyes on the screen, he typed out a message with his thumbs, telling her about the news report and about Farida's unexpected arrival. He read it over a few times but something told him not to send it. He'd deal with this alone.

Farida had refused to tell him where Stef's ID card was found or why the location was so relevant. But he needed to find out, had to know if Farida really was on their trail.

Think, Andy, think.

If Stef's paramedic ID card had been lost or stolen she'd have reported it to the area service manager, Bert Forsyth, even if she was totally exhausted after a hard shift. No swipe card meant no access to medical supplies, so it was vital every paramedic carried one with them. Andy would call Bert first – though the man's main hobby in and out of work was scratching his arse so the chances of him picking up before breakfast were slim at best. Andy called anyway, tutted when it switched to a newly recorded voicemail message reminding all callers that Bert was on a training course and would only take emergency or urgent calls.

He hesitated, then hung up.

Who else could help?

He vaguely knew a few of the lesser-ranking police officers but doubted any of them would be willing to tell him much, knowing Farida was leading the case. The word *respect* was often used when folk spoke about Farida but as far as Andy could see it was fear, plain and simple. The only man who ever dared take her on was Sandy Hamilton, a news reporter from one of the Edinburgh papers. He was past retirement age already, didn't give a shit if someone threatened to ruin his career because he'd already completed it; was only at the office because he was an addict; saw potential stories every single time he left the house.

They'd chatted a few times at murder scenes and car crashes and once in a classic Edinburgh pub. They'd sought them out, those dimly lit places with heavy mirrors hanging precariously off wallpapered walls and wildly patterned carpets underfoot that you wouldn't even sniff for a dare. They were places made for drinking and talking and that was it. You'd get a wee bag of Scampi Fries if you were lucky but ask for avocado toast and you'd be escorted out with a boot up your arse and a taxi hailed for some wanky bar in the New Town.

They'd bumped into Sandy about a year ago in a tiny pub hidden down on a long, steep staircase that leads from the Royal Mile to Market Street. Even there, dressed in his weekend clothes and three pints in, he'd held a pen in his hand, clicking it on and off, as if he expected the next big news story to happen at any time.

Stef had spent much more time talking to him than Andy had – turned out they'd both done art classes with Richard Owens and shared an affinity for shifting light in forests that they'd never tire of speaking about even if everyone else in the room was long since bored by the conversation. They'd even said they'd go and paint together some day, but never had – at least, not as far as Andy was aware. But he remembered her taking Sandy's number for that reason. It would only take a few seconds to fetch Stef's phone, punch in the passcode then scroll through her contacts list until he found it. But they'd decided her phone shouldn't be used at all once the plan was in motion. He hated having it here, muted. It was like some awful metaphor for what was happening to Stef, right now. His wife, silenced. He should have given the phone to Alyson, let her deal with it.

He'd taken it upstairs last night so he didn't have to look at it – and to ensure there was no repeat of that episode with Farida. He'd been lucky she didn't hear it vibrate when she'd dialled Stef's number. He'd have been behind bars by bedtime if she had.

If he wanted to speak to Sandy Hamilton he'd go via the newspaper offices.

The receptionist picked up on the second ring and sounded genuinely delighted he'd given her something to do at the start of her shift. Click-clack, and he was passed through.

'News desk, who's calling? '

'Sandy? It's Andy Campbell. Stef's husband.'

He clicked his tongue. 'Any more clues?'

'We're both paramedics. Met one night in the Mara Bar?'

'The artist?'

'That's the one.'

'We never did arrange that painting date. Tell your wife I'm ready and waiting.'

'Will do,' said Andy, even though he wouldn't; couldn't, now. 'She's actually the reason I'm calling. To cut a long story short, her name's come up as part of a police investigation and I need someone to tell me what the hell's going on. It's a long shot but—'

'I'm master of the long shot,' said Sandy, and Andy heard a pen being clicked on and off; a notepad page being turned. 'But let's start with the basics. First of all, why are *you* calling me instead of your wife? She's got my mobile phone number, wouldn't need to go via the treacherous gatekeepers. Don't tell me she's gone and got herself arrested.'

'No, nothing like that. She's . . .' Andy's jaw tightened as he scrambled for the right words. It was as if his own body was fighting him, trying to stop the lies in his head from being released into the world, presented as truth. But they came. His line about the art retreat in the Highlands had grown arms and legs, was running free.

'And you definitely can't get hold of her?'

'No signal.'

Sandy tutted. 'That's worth a story in itself. It's absurd that whole communities up there are ignored by technology companies. Sometimes I think they assume the savages up north are happy with messenger

89

pigeons. Anyway, on with the story in hand. Tell me everything.'

Andy explained about the impromptu visit from Farida McPherson the previous night and, as predicted, her name merited a heartfelt tut.

'So let me get this straight,' said Sandy, once Andy had finished explaining. 'You're sure your wife is safe and sound at some art retreat up north. Meanwhile, Farida McPherson finds her ID card at the home of some nameless criminal – but says there's no actual crime at the scene. And yet Farida insists Stef's in danger? Why? It doesn't add up.'

'It's something to do with the address where the ID card was found – which is why I'm calling you. I wondered if you had any way of finding out *where* the police were called to on Monday night? Farida wouldn't give me the address but she told me neighbours had reported a disturbance – whatever that means – and that the front door of the flat had been forced open. Surely there wouldn't be too many calls matching that description?'

'You'd be surprised. Police brand most things "a disturbance" before they have full details so this one may be lost in a sea of minor crimes. But I'll certainly put some calls in. The police press office tends to be pretty useless but in theory they're obliged to tell me the details of every incident they attend, if and when I ask for it. But tell me, what do you intend to *do* if I get the address? Go round there? Ask the occupants why they have your wife's ID card? I'm not Farida McPherson's greatest fan but if she's concerned for your wife's safety I'd certainly advise against you sticking your nose in.'

'I suppose I'm just hoping the address will mean something to me – or to you – and explain why her ID card is there.'

'And that should snuff out Farida's *concern for her safety*, yes?'

'Exactly.'

'So you *are* concerned.'

'No, I'm just . . . I'm sure Stef's fine at her retreat.' Andy sighed. 'I suppose I'm just . . . confused.'

'That makes two of us,' said Sandy. 'Leave it with me. I'll call you once I've spoken to the police and we can take it from there. Agreed?'

'Perfect. And, thank you.'

'Anything to annoy Farida,' said Sandy, then hung up.

Andy went to the kitchen, ate a floppy piece of buttered toast which had long since gone cold while he waited for the kettle to boil. Pot filled, mug out, milk carton sniffed, tea poured.

He was blowing on the surface when his phone rang again. Unknown number. Could it be Sandy already? He put down his mug and answered, hoping he sounded calmer than he felt.

'Well, that was easy.' Sandy sounded both chuffed and disappointed. 'Press office triumphed.'

'So you've got the address?'

'Yes, unfortunately.'

'Unfortunately? Why?'

'Because I know it, and its occupant. Been there dozens of times,' said Sandy. 'And because of that, I'm afraid I now quite understand Farida McPherson's concerns.'

'Why? Who lives there?'

'Have you ever heard of a man called Alex Mitchell?'

'I don't think so. Who is he?'

Sandy sighed. 'Are you sitting down?'

'No.'

'Then find yourself a chair,' said Sandy.

CHAPTER 12

Richard Owens's office smelled of overly ripe bananas. When she stepped inside Betty glanced into the bin beside the door, expecting to see the floppy, blackening skin of an old one in there but it was empty apart from a few pieces of paper, scrunched up into balls. A big window behind the desk overlooked the woodland that surrounded Green Den and Betty felt that familiar tightening of her nerves, like someone or something had just wound a handle inside of her, stretched them to their limit. She'd never *ever* sit with her back to a view like that one.

She liked to have a wall behind her, something solid that nobody and nothing could creep or rush out of. For a moment she imagined deer and foxes standing at the treeline; ears pricked, shiny black eyes staring through the window at the back of Richard Owens's head. At least animals would freeze then flee if you turned on them.

Sometimes humans were a different story.

She shivered, forced her thoughts away from woodland and her eyes away from the window. There was plenty to look at inside the office anyway. It was chaos; no surface without something on it. The banana would be hidden in the mess somewhere, no doubt; caught between bulging files of bash-edged papers and unopened mail and plastic boxes filled with curled-up tubes of paint and filthy jam jars loaded with brushes and pencils and scissors that needed a good sharpening.

Betty would soon get it sorted; her fingers tingled at the idea of restoring order to the chaos, of hiding outside in the woods and witnessing Richard's surprise when he returned again to the office and found it transformed.

What else would she see happening in this room if she were out there, looking in?

She turned to the desk. A red light on a landline phone was blinking on and off and next to it was a framed photo, its picture covered by a large brown envelope. Betty glanced over her shoulder into the corridor, then back to the window. It was strange, to feel like the watched instead of the watcher. Every time she dropped a lucky penny then sat nearby to wait for a finder she'd experience that same surge of power, of knowing she was witnessing actions people assumed would go unnoticed. But people are everywhere, even when you can't see them – always with one eye on their own life and one eye on yours.

Betty moved the brown envelope to one side then picked up the photo frame from the desk and held it towards the window so she could see the faces in natural light. The picture had been taken somewhere far away and hot with palm trees and skies so blue it was hard to believe they'd ever seen a single cloud. A couple stood in front of a swimming pool, holding hands and laughing as if one of them had just made a really good joke.

Was this Richard Owens and his wife?

The woman had a ginger bob that looked as if it could be clicked on and off like the jagged-edged hair of a Playmobil figure. The man beside her had grey hair and grey skin and grey eyes and Betty wondered if Richard made wacky art to compensate for the striking lack of colour he'd been born with.

But was he the one person who could tell her where Stef was? Betty cursed herself for not getting a phone number from Ellie and Hamish.

But his number must surely be here, in the office, somewhere.

She set down the frame in exactly the same spot she'd found it and shifted the envelope back to its previous spot as well, covering the photo. The scene looked untouched. Richard clearly didn't care too much about privacy if he'd left his door unlocked but still, Betty didn't want anyone to know she'd been in here uninvited.

She straightened up then spun slowly on the spot, scanning the office.

One wall was dotted with framed photos of Richard standing next to odd sculptures and paint-splattered canvases and plastic boxes filled with coloured lights. He wore the expression in every single photo; it reminded Betty of the one that shaped her face when she witnessed the joy of a Finder. Lucky pennies were her gift to the world and maybe strange art was Richard's. Saying that, Andy sometimes said Richard seemed to think *he* was God's gift and Stef would tut and tell him to shut up and grow up but instead he'd get up and leave.

Betty turned again, came face to face with an overloaded noticeboard; a mess of letters and flyers and posters and business cards, one on top of the other, precariously held in place with a plethora of little plastic-topped pins. It didn't take her long to find

Richard Owens's home address on one of the letters. She took a photo then decided to dig a little deeper, see if there was anything else of interest. She lifted the bottom edge of a letter and peered at the papers underneath, scanning for any mention of art retreats in remote places; the place Stef should be. But her mind dragged her to darker places and for a moment she imagined finding Stef there, pinned to the cork noticeboard alongside everything else; tiny points of sharpened metal pushed through her palms.

Behind her, in the corridor, a door slammed.

Bang – and her pulse was off, racing.

She heard a voice. Laughter. A man. Was it Hamish? Or Richard Owens? Footsteps, now. But in what direction? She moved to the door, mouthed a little prayer the way her mum used to do when the doorbell rang late at night. Not that it ever helped. Betty's dad would just let himself in if her mum didn't answer. The only thing he'd never given up on was the key to the house and *My Legal Right As Your Husband*. That was the phrase he'd come out with on the days he'd go into her mum's room without asking and close the door behind him with a slam and make her cry.

Betty prayed anyway; ears to the corridor, eyes to the office.

As she stood there she scanned the places she'd touched. It was only then that she noticed that the envelope had fallen over and was no longer covering the photo frame. Now it was lying face up on the desk so the front was facing outwards, exposing the word on that side. Richard's name, in Stef's familiar handwriting. She'd used the same red pen that deposited blotches of ink on the To Do list she left for Betty every Tuesday and Friday.

The sight of it made Betty's heart thunder so loudly she could barely tell if there were still voices or footsteps or doors banging. Thud, thud, thud. She held her breath, heard a car horn toot merrily, then an engine rev, the way only men and learner drivers do. And then, finally, silence.

Betty didn't hang around; she poked her head into the corridor then scuttled along it as quietly as she could manage. And clutched in her hand was that brown envelope, folded over twice, with Richard's name on the front. It could be anything – fees, bills, an invoice, hate mail, love letters, a confession, a threat. Whatever it was, it was Betty's now. And wherever Stef was, she would find her.

CHAPTER 13

Andy stared at the stains on their kitchen table, let his eyes blur while Sandy told him horror stories. The story from the press office matched the outline of what Farida had told him – two patrol cars were called to an Edinburgh address on Monday evening after receiving a call from neighbours about a disturbance at that location. When officers arrived the door had been forced open but the flat was empty. They entered but found no evidence of any crime – and the press office story ended there. But the address they'd been called to had a long history.

'The press office wouldn't give me the specific flat number, but as soon as they said *Hartfield Court* alarm bells started ringing in my head,' said Sandy. 'It's one of the bleakest high-rises in the city, made even more notorious thanks to its most vicious resident, the one and only Alex Mitchell. I've sent one of the reporters down there to knock on a few doors, confirm the police activity was at *his* flat on Monday night but I'm pretty sure my hunch is right. It would certainly explain Farida McPherson's involvement. She's far too senior to attend a random callout like this one. But she's worked on several cases involving Alex Mitchell so it makes sense she'd be alerted if there was any suggestion of further wrongdoing on his part.'

'What kind of "wrongdoing" are we talking about?'

'For a long time he was into petty crimes like shoplifting, break-ins; the kind of thing I like to call necessity crimes. Need money? Steal it. Simple as that. In short, he was a regular pain in the arse for society as a whole, but I wouldn't say he'd ever been considered a danger to anyone.'

'I sense an "until".'

'Aye, it's coming.' Sandy paused for a breath, and effect. 'He skidded spectacularly off the rails after his mum drank herself to death – at least, so say the social workers in court when they're trying to mitigate his sentences. He started by beating up a girlfriend, somehow got away with a fine that time. Shortly after that he was jailed for a nasty and prolonged attack on his ex-girlfriend's mother. That was his first time in prison and he wasn't liked, got a few sore beatings. But he behaved himself after that, bagged himself early release and became a model ex-con. Did volunteer work, signed up for courses, got himself a few wee jobs here and there. Barely heard a squeak from him for years until last Christmas when he assaulted a woman called Melanie Best, manager of the McDevitt Bar. She refused to serve him, got a fist in her face for her efforts. Given his violent history he was jailed, awaiting trial. Stayed there for six months, until his case came up on Monday.'

'And they believed his not guilty plea?'

'No chance,' said Sandy. 'He was ruled guilty as charged and sentenced to six months behind bars. But – and this is key – it was backdated to when he was jailed at Christmas, which is why he walked free from court on Monday afternoon.

'Seems mad to me,' said Andy. 'But if that case is done and dusted, why is Farida McPherson still taking an interest?'

'That's where it gets really interesting,' said Sandy. 'Enter Maureen Aitken, aged eighty-four. May or may not suffer from dementia. Only daughter lives in Dubai.'

'Jesus. Please don't tell me he's a granny beater as well.'

'That's the big question. Maureen Aitken was registered as missing in the New Year, not long after Alex

101

was shipped back to his cell. She lived alone, rarely left her house except to walk her beloved poodle. But she had regular video calls with her grandkids in Dubai and her daughter grew concerned when she failed to log on. Police were called, found an empty house. There was no body, no blood, no evidence of wrongdoing. But Sophie wasn't there either.'

'Sophie?'

'The poodle.'

'Jesus, he killed a dog as well?'

'That's the question. Nobody knows what happened to them. Our crime reporter got some great background detail and a few wild theories from neighbours but there's still no trace of her. A few folk claimed Maureen had dementia so one theory is that she wandered out of the house with her dog and got lost. And I'm sure you remember the horrendous weather we had last winter. Coldest temperatures on record, snow up to your armpits, ice so thick it was bulletproof. She wouldn't have stood a chance, might well be buried under a lingering snowdrift in her dressing gown and slippers, they said. But a few other folk linked her disappearance to a handyman she'd paid to do a few odd jobs around the house. Re-enter everyone's favourite ex-con, Alex Mitchell.'

'But didn't you say he was back in jail when she went missing?'

'No – I said he was back in jail when Maureen was *registered* as missing, when her daughter got worried and contacted the police. But she could have been dead for weeks by that stage. Nobody knows *precisely* when she disappeared. Is it possible that Alex Mitchell killed her before he was jailed for the pub landlady attack? Yes, it is. But the police need hard evidence and so far, they don't have it – not even a body. But from what I've heard Farida McPherson is totally convinced Alex Mitchell has something to do with it.'

'Where is he now?'

'No clue,' said Sandy. 'But I'm sure the police are keeping a close eye on him. If Farida can't pin Maureen's disappearance on him she'll be determined to get him in court for something else – which is why she'd have attended the disturbance at his flat on Monday night, and why she'd be worried to see an image of Stef there. He always targets women. When did you last see Stef?'

'Monday night.'

'Ah,' said Sandy. 'That's an . . . unfortunate coincidence.'

'Aye,' said Andy, thinking again of the last moments he'd spent with Stef; the last look she'd given him.

Again and again he asked himself – could he have stopped what happened next?

'Andy? You still there? I asked when Stef is due home?'

'Sometime next week. She's planning to visit some friends after the retreat but she's not sure how long she'll stay away.'

'She'll call at some point, though?'

'Not necessarily.'

'Really? Then surely there's a landline where she is? I can understand mobile phones being out of signal but there must be some way of getting in touch, in case of emergency.'

Andy's mouth went dry; his mind was blank. He should have known better than to call a man who asked questions for a living. He gently placed his palm over the mouthpiece so Sandy wouldn't hear his breath, getting faster. *Calm down, Andy. And act like you'd normally act.* 'I'm sure Stef said there's no landline either, to give them peace. It's crazy, isn't it?'

'I'd call it irresponsible, actually.' Sandy swallowed a sigh, but Andy heard it anyway. 'So be clear – you're telling me that your wife has buggered off for a week and you don't have any way of contacting her at all? And that you don't even know where she is?'

'I am.'

'I can only dream of such freedom with my wife. Ex-wife, I should say. For that reason. You're a lucky man. You clearly trust each other. One final thing, Andy – and perhaps I should have asked this at the outset. But I don't suppose you know of any possible connection between Stef and Alex? Through her job, maybe? Or at the art studio?'

'I'll ask.'

'What about checking patient records?'

'I can't access that system,' said Andy. 'I'd need to be logged in by one of the station managers. But it's worth an ask. I'm off today but I'll head over later.'

'If I were you . . .' Sandy cleared his throat, as if he was sorting through all the words caught there and deciding which ones would inspire the least amount of panic. Andy held his breath. His lungs were fit to burst by the time Sandy finished his sentence. 'If I were you, Andy, I'd go right now. Chances are there's a logical explanation for this. Maybe Stef lost her card and this scumbag found it. Or maybe he stole it from her on purpose, wanted to get his hands on her drug supply. Whatever the reason, if there's even the remotest chance this man has Stef on his radar you have to make sure you reach her before he does. I'd advise against googling him – it doesn't make happy reading. First things first, find her.'

'What are you suggesting, Sandy?'

'That you get your arse into work, that's what. Call me when you know more.'

Sandy hung up but Andy stayed where he was, staring straight ahead but seeing nothing.

He could understand, now, why Farida was worried about Stef's ID card being found in the home of a man with a history like Alex Mitchell. It was Farida's duty to protect the public and she wouldn't rest until she knew for sure Stef was safe or until she had a logical explanation for her card being in that man's flat. But Andy desperately needed to get her off their trail. The last thing he and Alyson needed was a woman like Farida sniffing around, asking questions about Stef that they couldn't possibly answer. Not truthfully, anyway.

He checked his watch, again.

He'd promised he'd wait for the call, that he'd trust Alyson and stay calm; but never had patience tried so hard to beat him. Heart in his mouth, he wrote her another message, then deleted it. Started again, then deleted. The link to Alex Mitchell wasn't something that should be told in a text message. It would just frighten Alyson unnecessarily. He was about to close the app when the screen refreshed and told him Alyson was writing *him* a message. He waited, willing her to press send. A few times the words disappeared and he guessed she was doing the same as him, reading and revising and deleting and doubting. Eventually the phone rang.

He jumped then answered quickly but she didn't say hello or make any room for his. Instead she said words that no amount of planning could have prepared him for.

'I can't do it,' said Alyson.

Andy closed his eyes, wished he could black out what she'd said just as easily. He'd have to tread carefully. Stef and her sister were alike in many ways but Alyson lacked the calm determination that he so admired in his wife. 'Yes, you can. And . . . you have to.'

'Can you come?'

'No, I can't. Not yet. Jesus, Alyson, how many times did we talk about this? We've been planning it for months and you insisted – absolutely insisted – that you'd be OK.'

'And I'm not allowed to change my mind?'

'Ask that question to Stef when you see her, will you?'

'That was uncalled for.' She sighed, breath quivering. But if she was looking for reassurance, she wouldn't get it from him. This wasn't a bloody hair appointment they were talking about; it was life and death, a future made of choices or one spent locked in a room you could never escape from. You can't just change your mind about things that matter as much as this.

'It's the only way, Alyson. You hear me?'

Silence.

'Alyson?' He could tell she was crying. That was both a miracle and a worry. Normally the woman had a fist in her chest instead of a heart. Part of him wanted to comfort her but did not, could not. The rage would not allow it.

'I just want it to be over and done with.'

'Don't we all?' Andy felt dizzy, blinked a few times to settle his head. This was exactly the situation they'd wanted to avoid; exactly the reason he should never have trusted Alyson to do what he should have been man enough to do himself. It was *her* that had talked him out of it but he should have been stronger, insisted.

'I don't know what to do.'

'Just follow the plan.'

'We can't just—'

'Yes, we can. What else can we do? Call the police? I don't bloody think so.'

They both went silent, knew there was no plan B. 'I need you to tell me that you'll go,' said Andy. 'I need you to get in the car and drive north, do what needs to be done.'

'OK,' she said and for a moment Andy felt relief but it crumpled when he thought about Alyson, alone, leaning over the body of her sister. He pushed away the image but then his mind spat out a picture that was even more disturbing. Alex Mitchell, holding Stef's ID card. His wife's face, stilled, and clutched in the hands of a killer.

CHAPTER 14

Betty stopped in a passing place halfway up the drive, then twisted round in her seat and looked back towards Green Den. From here she couldn't see the studio or the car park or any trace of humans at all. And *hopefully* that meant she couldn't be seen. She locked the car doors then pulled the brown envelope out of her pocket.

She was proud of herself for resisting the temptation to rip it open the moment she found it, regardless of who was coming and what they'd say if they discovered her in Richard Owens's office, opening letters addressed to someone else for the first time in all of her life.

But she'd waited. She was good at waiting.

Adrenalin fizzed in her chest when she slipped one finger under the seal but when it came unstuck with no effort she realised it had already been opened by somebody else. The paper was torn a little and it wasn't of her doing. Plus, it weighed nothing.

She tutted to herself then gently pushed the sides to widen the slit and allow her to see inside before she reached in with her fingers.

She held the envelope towards the window for better light but it didn't help.

The woodland was so thick here that barely any sunshine got through. Even from here Betty could see the struggle of the smaller plants that grew in the spaces between trees; stalks and trunks bent towards the light that reached the road, like children with their chins held high, trying to avoid being trampled or plucked, roots and all, out of the one place they belong.

She switched her gaze from the blackness of the woods to the envelope's opening then turned it upside down and tapped the end. A handmade card fell onto her knee and she knew right away it was Stef's creation. The drawing on the front was a small version of the mountain landscape that featured in so many of Stef's paintings; a mountain peak and a craggy ridge and a squat stone bothy in the valley at its feet. Inside, the card was blank except for a short, stark message, also written by Stef.

All yours x

Betty tapped the envelope again to see if anything else came out and when it didn't she tore it open. Nothing. No clue.

She turned the card her hands. What did Stef's message mean? And what part of herself she was giving to this man? Questions bubbled in Betty's brain, but they all burst at once when someone rapped the car window – then Ellie's face appeared on the other side of the glass. Betty gasped then shoved the card and envelope into the door cavity.

Ellie motioned for Betty to open the door but she lowered the window instead, just a few inches; wide enough to let air flow, but not a big enough gap for arms to reach through. Ellie hunched over so her mouth was closer to the gap.

'Sorry if I gave you a fright!' She laughed after she said that, stopped when she realised Betty wasn't joining in. 'You've not broken down or anything, have you? I always go for a wee walk in the woods at this time of day but when I noticed your car on the drive I thought I'd come and check you were OK.' She seemed to remember the cigarette in her hand when she said it, took a long drag before she spoke again. 'I'm glad I caught you, actually, so I could apologise for Hamish's comment earlier, about Stef and Richard. He was out of order and I'm sorry if it sounded like we were gossiping about her, which, I suppose, we were.' She shrugged. 'But I'm embarrassed about it, knowing you're friends.'

Betty smiled when she said that.

'Forgiven?'

'Forgiven,' said Betty, amazed how easily the word came to her. It was probably the first time she'd said it; definitely the first time she'd felt it. She made sure the envelope was out of sight, then got out of the car. 'Easier out here, isn't it?' said Betty, as if she often stopped on roadsides and talked with strangers. 'Just so you know, the door to Richard's office was wide open. In case you think it was me.'

Betty hoped her words would cover her tracks. Surely that was something only an honest person would say, not someone who'd just stolen a letter from someone else's desk. Her cheeks burned at the thought of it. 'You just never know who's lurking, do you?'

'Richard's the biggest lurker of the lot,' said Ellie, and smoke puffed out of her mouth when she laughed at her own joke. 'Sorry, you must think I'm awful, speaking badly of him. He's really not such a bad egg. He'd just . . . different – quite challenging to work with at times. It's beyond me why Stef chooses to spend so much time with the man, but needs must. I suppose she wants to make the most of her "career break".' Ellie made inverted commas with her fingers when she said that. 'It's odd – you'd have thought her artwork would improve, given the fact she spends *more* time painting now than ever before.' Ellie sighed. 'She had her first solo exhibition just before Christmas and we all thought she was destined for great things. But . . . she's seemed a little . . . *distracted* since then. She's had some . . . issues with her husband and with her job and . . . well, there have been rumours about how well she'd been coping with all of that.'

Betty nodded, lips pulled tight, pretended she knew was Ellie was talking about.

'She used to talk to me about these things but then I stuck my nose in where it wasn't wanted and she's been distant with me ever since. But I was just worried, you know?' Ellie opened her mouth to say something else but then she hesitated, took a draw on her cigarette instead. 'How close are you two?'

Betty felt her blood switch direction in her veins and creep towards her skin. 'Close.'

Ellie flashed her eyes between Betty and the tiny orange glow at the end of her cigarette. 'And did she ever tell you what I said to her? After the exhibition?'

Betty shook her head. 'I don't remember her saying anything, no.'

'Believe me, you'd remember,' said Ellie. 'But look, if Stef wanted you to know, she'd have told you herself. It's not my place, is it? You'd think I'd have learned after all these years to keep my big mouth shut and my nose out of other people's business. But, no.'

She stubbed out her cigarette on the sole of her shoe after she said that and Betty sensed the beginning of a familiar feeling; the biting sensation that people were trying to break away from conversations with her, finding excuses to leave. Usually it was both an insult and a relief. But she didn't want Ellie to leave, not yet.

'I'm probably being silly but . . . I'm worried as well,' said Betty, and immediately felt like she'd said too much. She didn't want to say any more or be asked questions; anything that might expose the real reason she knew Stef. People wouldn't understand, never did.

'Is that why you're really here? Because there's no retreat. I checked, out of interest, and there's nothing in the diary this week except for that big art fair. So unless Stef's buggered off somewhere on her own then she's been lying to you as well.'

Betty flushed, sensed betrayal. 'As well?'

'Same way she lied to me.'

It was rude to ask. Nosy. Not her place. But the question came anyway.

'What about?'

Ellie took a breath that filled her whole chest, then held it, and Betty's gaze. Above them, blackbirds sang, shadows shifted, trees branches creaked and rubbed against their neighbours. When she exhaled she released the reek of tobacco and two words were spoken quietly, as if that would somehow help contain the violence of them. 'Her bruises,' she said.

CHAPTER 15

The scattering of mourners followed them through town like the Pied Piper's rats, coated in black. Stef barely recognised anyone apart from their colleagues from the station. She'd noticed Vicky at the cemetery, dolled up to the nines and huddled against that Italian lad she'd snared online. He called himself Izzi and ran a trendy grocer's in the Old Town; would use phrases like eco-crusader without even the tiniest bit of irony. Amechi had popped in as well, before his shift started; was getting more sideways glances than anyone else there on account of the fact he wasn't white or dressed in black. Stef wished he'd turned up in the ambulance, sirens blaring, light pulsing some life into death.

Andy would have loved that, on any other day.

He tugged the sleeve of her coat, nodded to the front door of the Comelybank Arms. It was the kind of place that aspired to host French kings, but laughably failed. When they'd popped in to confirm the booking last week the manager told Andy his mum had arranged the funeral tea years earlier; had chosen the food and drinks and which room she'd like it to be held in. The only missing detail was the date.

After that Stef and Andy had gone together to see the lawyer and he'd talked them through the will, then pushed a page across his desk with all the details of the hymns she wanted at the funeral and the poems that should be read, and by who. She'd not requested Andy read anything and Stef had felt relief on his behalf until she noticed his jaw pulsing the way it always did when he was hurt but too proud to say it. He'd picked up the page, sucked his lips inside his mouth as he read it. 'She doesn't even trust me to organise a funeral tea,' he'd said, then handed Stef the page with a tiny shake of the head that would have been easy to miss but which she'd seen before. A flinch, the only sign of the tremor beneath.

A fat man with a beard took their coats in reception, was almost out of sight when Stef realised her cardigan had slipped off as well. She dashed off to catch him, felt his eyes linger on her bare arms when she reached out to tug free her cardigan from the pile in his hands. She covered herself then rushed to Andy moments before a woman wearing blue eyeliner and too *much perfume ushered them into the function suite through the back, its alleged sea view consisting of an occasionally shimmering square of grey framed by the harled wall of the car park and the big yew tree hanging over from the garden next door.*

They took their place at the entrance, spent fewer minutes than expected shaking hands and thanking people for coming and doing their best not to make eye contact. The manager nodded to them when the last ones were through, made a show of returning to the main entrance and looking around in case anybody had got lost in the three metres between there and here. 'That's your lot,' she'd said, pulling a face at the half-empty room that Stef imagined was supposed to be sympathetic but looked more like pity. The difference was subtle but key; a caress or a slap, a regular kiss or one of the Glasgow variety.

Andy didn't seem to notice, or ignored it if he did.

The manager bowed her head then she closed the double doors behind her, left them to it. Andy stared at the doors for a moment, as if he was contemplating making a run for it. Then he mouthed something to himself before he turned and faced the room. She'd seen him do the same when they were out on the ambulance, taking a moment backstage, with himself, before he stepped into the spotlight and became the unflappable actor that their job required.

Most folk had drifted towards the bar already so he started there, accepted a pint from an uncle who'd retired to Mallorca and was making sure Andy knew he'd come just for this. He liked a good funeral, he said, as if Andy would be chuffed. But that was the Scottish way. His mum had requested seating for eighty, urns instead of teapots. Stef did a quick head count at the bar but got lost at thirty, guessed there was a handful more.

Enough that they wouldn't notice her absence.

She used the excuse of a full bladder to escape a dull conversation about the price of Scottish prawns then slipped out a side door; found a sheltered spot near the wall of the car park then checked her phone. Alyson had left a voicemail, raging about queues on the Edinburgh bypass and saying she'd be there as soon as possible. Even her annoyed voice was a comfort, but Stef suspected her tale of heavy traffic was an excuse to avoid the funeral service and the memories it would have pushed to the surface. It was twenty years since their own mother had died, and twenty-five since she'd stopped being wholly herself. Towards the end it had been hard to believe that she was still the same person, that the stories she'd always told were still inside of her, somewhere. The absence of words weighed more than anything else, made the air in her room so thick that Stef had avoided being alone with her.

It was only later that Stef had wondered how her mum must have felt in those moments, noticing the changes in herself and her children; knowing it would damage them.

Stef shivered. She was cold but would wait outside, would rather face rough weather than fresh grief – and the air inside was heavy with it, stung eyes and throats like pollen.

She leaned against the wall, staring at that little square of sea and listening to the sounds that drifted up from Portobello Promenade. It would be packed with the after-school crowds soon, squealing kids on scooters trailed by rounded mothers with ponytails and full prams; runners with thin wrists and huge watches darting between them, wishing they'd chosen a different time. There would be dogs tearing along the sand and chasing bobbing balls in the water alongside those gloriously mad old women who swam all year without a wetsuit then took a warm shower at the public baths.

Life and death lived side by side.

She knew Alyson had arrived when she heard heels on tarmac, walking faster than necessary to prove she cared about being late. Stef opened her eyes then her arms, pulled her into a hug.

'How's Andy?'

'Coping.'

'And you?'

'Fine.'

'Who are you trying to convince?'

Stef eased herself out of the hug, leaned against the wall again. It was hard and cold but at least it didn't patronise her. 'You know what would be really nice? If once – just once – you let me deal with things in my own way.'

Alyson glanced at Stef's empty whisky glass for a few seconds too long. 'As you wish.'

'Meaning?'

'Andy told me about the complaint at work.'

Stef's soft skin became armour. 'It wasn't a complaint,' she said. 'Just some exaggerating arsehole telling the boss I'm past it because I filled a needle four seconds slower than normal. It was minus eight degrees and dinging it down but apparently it's a crime for paramedics to have cold hands these days.'

'And that's it?'

'Aye, that's it.' Stef stared into her glass, pinching her bottom lip with her teeth. 'And anyway, since when have you and Andy started talking behind my back?'

'Don't be like that.'

'Like what?'

'Like this. There's no shame in asking for help when you need it.'

'I'm fine, OK?' Stef tipped back her glass, let the melting ice cubes clatter against her teeth and the vaguest trace of whisky flow momentarily over her tongue. She wanted another one, even though she'd be judged for it. Mainly by herself. 'You got a cigarette?'

'Is the Pope Catholic?'

Alyson pulled a packet from her handbag, lit one for Stef. 'And don't worry, I won't tell.'

She winked as she handed it over, was one of the only people Stef knew who could pull it off without looking like a pirate or a total prick. It was her secret weapon, so ridiculous it always made Stef smile. She took a draw, body turning to water when the tobacco reached her toes.

Stef only smoked once or twice a year, and only ever with her sister.

Alyson had picked up the habit where their mum left off, literally. Her hands had been too weak to grip her own cigarettes towards the end so Alyson would wheel her out to the garden and light one up, hold it to their mum's lips while she took a pathetic inhale. After a while Alyson got into the habit of smoking the rest of it. It was something to do, a distraction from the ache of watching their mum disappear in front of their eyes.

'Thanks for coming, Al.'

'Pleasure's all mine, Stef. How's the fag?'

'Awful.'

'That'll teach you,' she said, puffing smoke between them when she laughed.

Andy would tick Stef off when he smelled the tobacco on her breath, would gently remind her she'd agreed to climb every Munro in the country; and they only had eighty-two to go. They'd bagged their two-hundredth peak last summer, near a wee village few folk visited or had any reason to. Lewistown. But Stef and Andy knew it well, had often admired the mountain but never climbed it until that day. When they reached the summit Stef had placed three little stones on the cairn at the top, then Andy had produced whisky.

'To us,' he'd said, then they'd clinked their plastic cups and she'd drunk it far too quickly, hoped the burn of it would be enough to drag her mind away from the lies she'd told him on the drive up. They say that if you practise something for twenty-one days in a row it becomes a habit, something that can be done without thinking – but she'd been lying to Andy for much longer than that and still her own mistruths tormented her.

And at the end of day, what's the point?

Lies don't make the truth disappear. Or the bruises.

CHAPTER 16

Betty made excuses when Ellie suggested they go back to the studio to chat about Stef over a nice cup of tea but in the end she relented, partly because she was thirsty and partly because that's what a caring friend *should do* but mainly because she hoped Ellie might help her work out what Stef meant when she wrote *All Yours* in that letter to Richard. She hoped it wasn't the reason she thought.

The driveway had grass up the middle and potholes on either side. Betty drove more slowly than usual so Ellie would think she was relaxed. When they reached the car park, a small square of flattened ground, she was relieved to see that it was completely empty, exactly as Ellie had promised. Everyone else had already left for the art fair.

Ellie made tea for the pair of them then led Betty to an area of mossy decking around the back of the studio, directed her towards a bench fit for firewood.

Then she sat on the ground and pulled her knees to her chest.

'I noticed the bruises at the launch party for Stef's first exhibition so that must have been . . . what . . . six months ago now? Just before Christmas. She's never been one for getting dolled up, has Stef, but she turned up in a woolly jumper and trousers despite the fact we always have the heating cranked up full. I didn't expect her to wear a dress, obviously – I think she's allergic to them – but it seemed odd she wouldn't have worn something a little more elegant. Anyway, I dismissed it, got on with the party. Stef seemed to get pretty drunk early on which wasn't unusual for her – but when she slurred during her speech, Andy stepped in, made some excuse to get her off the stage. It was a bit embarrassing for everyone, to be honest. I certainly wouldn't want my man telling me what to do, and definitely not in public. It was her big moment – her first ever solo exhibition. She had every right to celebrate. But it was obvious to everyone there was tension between them. We'd all heard rumours about Andy having an affair with some young manager at his work. But there were whispers about Stef and Richard by that point as well, not helped by the fact he followed her around all night. If she was getting praise for her exhibition, he wanted to be right there making sure people knew *he* was her teacher and that *he* owned the gallery. It was obvious to everyone that Andy didn't like the man . . .' Ellie shrugged. 'Personally, I don't think Stef would even look at a someone like Richard, but people talk.'

Betty nodded. She knew that more than most.

'Anyway, I stayed at the end to help Stef wash up. Andy was loading the car and everyone else had long since left. She seemed a bit distracted, kept dropping cups and plates. Broke my favourite mug, but I didn't say anything because I could tell her mind was elsewhere. I got her chatting eventually, reeling off some nonsense story about my wee boy Harry and his antics – and she relaxed a bit, laughed that laugh of hers.'

Betty felt a tweak of sadness; had hoped it was a laugh reserved only for her.

'For a wee while she seemed more like her old self, ' said Ellie. 'And that was when she rolled up her sleeves. I'd noticed they were soaking wet but didn't bother telling her, figured she just didn't care. But then all of sudden she pushed them up, one then the other, then carried on washing the dishes. We were mid-conversation but

I got flustered when I saw her arms, all black and blue and yellow. *Covered* in bruises. She asked me what the matter was and I said I was about to ask her the same thing, asked her what had happened.'

Ellie took a long drag on her cigarette, closed her eyes as she pulled the tobacco deep into her lungs. 'She tensed up again, started telling me she'd had a fall, skidded on bathroom tiles or something. Tried to laugh it off but *that* laugh was totally forced, nothing like her real one. Needless to say she tugged her sleeves down and made her excuses to leave pretty sharpish. I didn't have any reason to think she was lying but that, combined with her botched speech and Andy trailing her like a gun dog . . . it just didn't sit right with me. Next time I saw her she acted like nothing had happened so I tried to forget about it, put it down to my overactive imagination. Until I saw more bruises.'

'On her arms?'

Ellie shook her head. 'Legs, this time. I walked in on her while she was taking a pee – the blooming lock's been broken for ages. I didn't hang about, obviously, but those few seconds were long enough for me to see the bruises on her legs. I waited outside to apologise for walking in – then I asked her about it, straight out.

I said I was worried about her – and concerned about Andy's behaviour – and asked if she needed help.'

Ellie paused, shook her head.

'She was absolutely raging, defending Andy to the last and accusing me of sticking my nose in where it wasn't wanted. I managed to keep my calm but everyone in the studio heard her. And . . . a few folk thought she sounded like she'd been drinking that day as well. All of it was just so out of character – but the angrier she got and the more excuses she gave me for having those bruises, the more I became convinced she was hiding something. It's human nature, I suppose. When something touches a nerve we lash out, don't we? Anyway, to cut a very long story short, she apologised later and told me she'd been a bit low since she got signed off. But we've barely spoken since.

'She's still been coming here for lessons with Richard and for meetings about yet another one of his wacky projects – but she avoids the rest of us like the plague. The others think she's just embarrassed about losing her temper but I can't get the image of those bruises out of my head. I've been there, you see. In that position. Suffered in silence for years so I know how hard it is to escape from it, especially when your man's the picture of a perfect husband.'

She sighed, shook her head. 'I hope I've not crossed a line, telling you all of this. I'm sure you know Stef and Andy much better than I do but . . . och, I've been needing to tell someone. I just hope she's got someone she can talk to, feel safe with. Sometimes I wonder if that's why she and Richard spend so much time together. I think maybe she confides in him. Like I said, I don't buy all these rumours about an affair. They're friends and fellow artists, end of story.'

But was it?

Betty had come here hoping for something to settle her mind but instead her theories had bred, spread like a plague. Now when she thought of Stef's tight, tanned skin she pictured it turning black and blue instead. And when she tried to think of innocent reasons for the blood splatters in their bathroom – a skelf or a shaving cut or a slip on wet tiles – her brain filled with scenes she wished she could unsee.

Betty thought again of Stef's words in that card to Richard. *All yours.* Part of her wanted to tell Ellie about it, see if that toppled her theory about the true nature of their relationship. But she couldn't tell her without admitting she'd stolen his letter, so she kept it to herself. And anyway, a tiny selfish part of her liked having a secret to hold on to, access to a part of

Stef that most other people didn't know about. Apart from the person who'd opened that letter before her. Chances were it was Richard, but if Betty had managed to walk freely into his unlocked office, it was possible somebody else had as well.

What if Andy had seen it? How would *he* react to that message, those kisses?

Betty shuddered, knocked over the remains of her tepid tea when she stood up to leave. Ellie told her not to worry about it and Betty wished for a life where that was possible. Back in the safety of her car she locked the doors and belted up then pulled a lucky penny from her pocket. She passed it from one hand to the other, over and over, same way folk from the Catholic church played with rosary beads. But while believers thought about Jesus on a cross, Betty was thinking about Stef and her bruises.

When she first started the cleaning job she'd noticed traces of blue on Stef's forearms and when Stef noticed Betty looking at them she'd laughed, branded them as an 'occupational hazards' which Betty thought was odd because by then she no longer had an occupation.

Were those the same bruises Ellie had seen?

Could be. The exhibition was held just before Christmas and Betty was offered the job in early

February and bruises could last a few weeks, couldn't they? Hers did, at least.

The only other time she'd noticed bruises was that icy day in March when Andy called her mobile from work and said Stef would be in bed when she got there because she'd slipped on a frozen slab, hurt her hip. Andy had asked Betty if she could check on Stef when she arrived and Betty had felt like Someone Responsible and part of a proper family.

She'd taken the early bus to Portobello and once she was inside Betty had gently knocked the solid wooden bedroom door then pushed it open. It whooshed on the new grey carpet then jammed on the thick pile – but the gap was wide enough for her to squeeze her head through. Stef was fast asleep in bed and, for a few minutes longer than she should have, Betty watched her. She'd never seen her asleep before, her face so completely relaxed. Both her arms were lying on top of the pale blue duvet, palms up, bruised undersides exposed like the curved bellies of dead fish. Betty had assumed she'd bashed them when she slipped on the ice, like Andy said, but now she wondered if that was an easy excuse; man blaming nature for his sins. She felt guilty, thinking badly of Andy, but the idea wouldn't shift.

She sat there for a long time in her car, hoping for guidance. It came in the form of a little robin that flew down from the trees and sat momentarily on her bonnet, head cocked to one side. It was Stef's favourite bird, one she'd often tried but failed to capture in paintings. In the end Richard Owens had painted one for her instead, gave her the framed canvas as a gift last year when she turned forty-four.

If Stef had been with her, she'd say it was a sign, life telling her that's where she should go. Betty had his address, she had a car, she had time, she had a reason. All she had to do was find Richard Owens and ask him for the location of Stef's art retreat. Simple.

But it wasn't her place.

She couldn't just go to a stranger's house and ask questions as if she was somebody from the papers or the TV – and he'd know right away that she wasn't, even if she got dressed up in her best clothes and put on the same accent her mum would use at parents' nights and disciplinary meetings with the head teacher.

But if Stef trusted Richard, maybe Betty should too.

Betty read the card again, triple-checking it was Stef's handwriting. *All Yours*. Then she pulled up the photos on her phone, copied Richard's address into the map app and pressed *Go* before her brain churned out more reasons not to. But one question stalked her as she drove, tight as the shadows on her back.

If Stef had offered him every part of her, what was he giving in return?

CHAPTER 17

The garage was noticeably colder than the rest of the house, smelled of bleach. Andy saw Betty had upended the mop in the blue bucket so it would dry more quickly, exactly as Stef had taught her. She was nothing if not keen, which was probably why Stef had such a soft spot for her, same way she was drawn to limping pigeons and stray dogs.

He made a note to himself to call Betty, make sure she didn't turn up again on Friday. He shouldn't have let her stay yesterday morning either but Stef must have forgotten to cancel and it would have looked suspicious if she'd sent her away.

Anyway, Betty was harmless.

Andy patted his pocket, searching for his car keys, but they weren't where they should be.

He retraced the steps he'd taken after work last night – he'd been so stressed after his shift and so desperate for a beer that everything else was a blur.

And after Farida's visit all his thoughts were on Alex Mitchell and Stef's ID card and how the two of them were connected. The keys could be anywhere.

He closed his eyes and when he opened them the answer was looking him right in the face. He'd switch cars, take Stef's old blue Volvo. He'd not driven it for years but the smell of it was familiar as ever; Stef's minty air freshener, the faint scent of paint stripper. He was probably the only man in the world whose heart would swell with love every time he got a whiff of the stuff. Keys in, engine on, belt fastened, and he was off.

He wasn't due to work today – and Alyson wasn't either – but on Sandy's advice he'd head for the station anyway, get a favour from Vicky that she'd make sure he didn't forget to return. Meanwhile, that phone call with Alyson played on loop in his mind.

I can't do it, she'd said.

But she had to; would make today one of those dates they'd never forget.

He felt bad hanging up on Alyson when she cried but tears didn't right wrongs, did they? Andy had learned that lesson the hard way. He tried not think about it but his mind dragged him back thirty-five years in less time than it took to drive out of the garage.

Him at the hospital with his mum and dad, staring at his wee sister's tiny bed and the screens of those machines that kept beep-beep-beeping. When he'd cried his mum had glared at him and Dad had taken him out of the room, told him Tears Won't Help. His dad didn't tell him what *would* help so he'd been figuring that out for himself ever since.

Right now he needed to stay busy – and more, he needed to find out why Stef's ID card was at Alex Mitchell's flat so he could eliminate all thoughts of that man from his brain.

He'd start at the ambulance station, would phone Vicky on the way so she knew to expect him.

When he tried to stick his phone holder to the heating vent it fell off and slipped into the footwell. He tutted and stopped the car, dragged his fingers over scratchy carpet and ancient fluff and the sharp edges of the seat runners until he found his mobile, fished it out of the darkness. The dashboard was curved, so that wouldn't work. He sat his phone on his knee but it slid off, into the passenger footwell this time. He cursed the car then set off anyway, was halfway along the street when he noticed the perfect outline of a circle on the middle of the windscreen that didn't shift when he passed the wipers over the spot. The mark was on the inside; it looked like it had been made by a sucker. Had Stef finally given up on her old road map and invested in a satnav? Surely not.

He pulled over, opened the glove box, and there it was.

She was the proudest of old-school drivers, refused help from him when they drove together and often said she wouldn't even contemplate receiving help from a machine. Instead she'd open her tatty road map on the bonnet or the back seat before she set off, jot down or memorise the road numbers and junctions that would lead her to where she needed to go. If she ever got lost she'd pull out the map again and locate herself; try to solve the puzzle before she'd consider asking a local for help. But here she was, using a satnav after all, too proud to tell him she needed help from time to time.

Typical Stef, to the end.

When he reached the ambulance station he parked on the street then texted Vicky to make sure there was nobody else around. He hadn't explained why he needed urgent access to old patient files but he'd told her to keep it quiet, knew she couldn't resist the lure of a secret. She texted back right away, told him to meet her at the fire escape. She greeted him with a conspiratorial wink then led him upstairs to Bert's office, opened it with a swipe card. When she ushered him through their bodies came within a hair's breadth of touching. Andy's mind flashed to an image of the pair of them in here after the Halloween party last year, coming upstairs for an entirely different reason.

Vicky closed the door behind them, softly, then motioned for Andy to sit down. The office was cold and smelled of a pound store. It was home to an over-sized desk and a computer with a massive monitor that existed mainly for the grand task of gathering dust.

The only staff authorised to access patient report forms were team leaders like Vicky and the area service managers for each station. Here it was Bert, a former paramedic who was always on holiday, on sick leave or on such a massive dose of antidepressants that even though he'd make it into work, he wasn't really there at all. As a result Vicky knew the systems far better than Bert did and Andy knew she'd be far more willing to help – especially since it was him doing the asking.

'Make yourself at home,' said Vicky, signalling for him to sit on the black chair sprinkled with a thin layer of Bert's dandruff. Andy plucked a hankie from the desktop box, brushed the flakes on to the floor and then sat down, adjusting the height of the chair as he pulled it in. As well as having a flaky scalp, Bert was a short-arse.

Vicky brushed Andy's leg with her shoulder when she reached under the desk to switch on the harddrive. When it whirred into life she logged in with her team leader ID. All patient report forms were logged online and every time they were accessed the username was recorded and sent to head office. There was no way Andy could do this without her, and she knew it.

'All yours,' said Vicky. 'Maybe you can take me out for a drink sometime and tell me what it's all about?' She winked again, same way she'd done *that night*. Then, he'd laughed and let himself be led. The fault was his. But what had so briefly tempted him now turned his stomach. He hated her knowing she'd had that power over him; hated her thinking it could happen again. 'I appreciate your help, Vicky. You're a pal.'

Her smile deflated. 'Hope you find what you're looking for,' she said, then left.

When Andy had started his career all the records were kept on paper. Any checks of previous patients required a quiet afternoon, a large dose of patience and sufficient charm to convince the station manager that the search was really worth their time and effort.

He was thankful the system had finally been updated about a decade ago, making it relatively easy to track down past cases. But he had to do this quickly.

Teams working early shifts had just left the station but chances were they'd return before too long. All it took was a puker or a pisser or a bleeder and they'd be back to change their uniforms and restock supplies. In theory they were supposed to return to the station for breaks – two twenty-minute rests per shift – but the reality was very different. In all his years work-ing the ambulances that had happened approximately twice. If he had time between callouts he'd track down one of those speciality coffee shops and spend half his wages on caffeine and fancy foam. It was unlikely any of the paramedics would choose to go to Bert's office on their break – but it wasn't impossible.

He couldn't be caught in here on his own.

When Vicky had left he opened the database she'd directed him towards and typed Alex Mitchell's name and the address Sandy had given him. Hartfield Court. The screen froze for a moment then the wheel at the top started spinning, round and round and round. His thoughts were doing the same thing. The screen flashed. Andy blinked. And then a new page appeared on the screen, showing the results of his search. There were no direct matches, meaning Alex Mitchell had never been treated at Hartfield Court. That in turn meant there was no reason for Stef to have been there, with or without her ID card.

How else could Alex Mitchell have got hold of it?

Sandy had given Andy the name of the old woman who'd disappeared – Maureen Aitken. He hadn't said much more about her, except that Farida suspected Alex was connected to her disappearance.

Did Stef have some connection to her? Or to Melanie Best, the pub landlord that Alex Mitchell had attacked?

He checked her file first but it was another dead end. Stef hadn't attended. He then typed Maureen Aitken's name into the search box. One file came up, dated a few weeks before Christmas. The patient was eighty-four, just like Sandy had said. Andy could see right away that Stef hadn't attended that job but he read through the file anyway, wincing at the details of her injuries. He pictured a wrinkled face made smooth by the swelling, soft white skin turned purple; eyes like slit plums. The notes suggested she'd had a fall, but given her disappearance a few weeks later and her connection to Alex Mitchell, could her injuries be the result of something more sinister?

Andy hated when the fragile were targeted. Just when he thought he'd seen every kind of case something like this would come up and show him yet again that, sadly, the world was even sicker than that. Some wee boy's granny, a mum's old mum, battered.

What kind of man could do that to a wee old woman?

The kind of man who kept Stef's ID card on his mantelpiece.

He went back to the search box, typed in Alex Mitchell's name *without* his address, heart sinking when dozens of files appeared on the screen. Half the men in Edinburgh seemed to share the same name. He'd just started trawling through them when Vicky popped her head around the door, made him jump. 'Jesus Christ, I thought you were Bert.'

'That's definitely not a compliment.' She closed the door then moved so close to Andy that he could smell her perfume. Usually she went for fruity ones but today she was drenched with incense, reminded him of the way Stef used to smell after yoga class.

'Any luck?'

He shook his head. 'Not really.'

'Sure I can't help?'

Andy sighed. Vicky knew the files better than anyone. But how could he tell her what he was looking for without explaining what was really happening? 'I can't go into details but . . . I'm trying to find out if Stef treated a particular patient. I've done multiple searches but according to the system there's no connection between Stef and this man.'

Vicky straightened up, stepped back from the desk. 'And why exactly do you need to know? It's one thing for me to sneakily give you access to the system for a work-related issue – but I'm not so keen on the whole jealous-husband-hunts-wife's-lover idea. The shit will hit *my* fan if you're caught, remember. And actually, if you suspect Stef's having an affair, I'm not sure I'm the best person to help you expose it, given our history.'

Andy sighed. 'It's nothing like that.'

'Then what is it?'

For a few moments they stared at each other and Andy was tempted to tell her, have someone else share the burden of it. But she'd never help him again if she knew.

'You just need to trust me, Vicky.'

'Easier said than done.' She rolled her eyes but there was a smile on her face when she did it. 'Don't ever say that I'm not good to you.'

'I wouldn't dare.'

'So how can I help?'

'I need to know if Stef's ID card was ever registered as lost or stolen. That possible?

'Of course.' Vicky hunched down beside him, brushed his hand when she reached for the mouse. 'May I?'

She minimised the case files, clicked her tongue as scrolled through numerous drop-down menus on the screen. Andy's hope surged every time she opened a file, flopped just as quickly when she closed it. 'This is a waste of time, isn't it?'

'Anyone ever tell you patience is a virtue?' Vicky clicked back to the main folder, scrolled down and down and down; was almost at the very bottom of the list when the sound came. Two voices. A man and a woman in the corridor. Getting closer.

'Shit.' They both shot up. There was nowhere to hide. Vicky leaned over the desk and started click click clicking shut all the folders and files then pressed Shut Down. The screen flashed a couple of times then a message box popped up, saying one or more files had not yet properly closed. A timer appeared beneath those words, counting down from thirty.

'For fuck's sake.' Never had time passed so slowly. Andy willed the countdown towards zero as the voices got louder, closer, easier to recognise.

The timer had just reached five seconds when they reached the other side of the office door, two soft grey silhouettes tattooed on to the frosted-glass window. Four seconds, the handle rattled; three seconds, it turned. There were two seconds to go when the office door was pushed open and one when Andy met Bert's surprised gaze. With a click and a gentle buzz, the computer screen switched off.

For a few moments nobody spoke or moved. Two men and two women, standing in each other's places. It should be Andy and Vicky out there in the corridor, looking in. But instead it was the bulk of Bert and next to him, his polar opposite: Farida McPherson.

CHAPTER 18

Richard Owens lived outside Edinburgh in a modern housing scheme that looked as if it had been peeled off a computer screen and dumped in a field. Every house was identical; a white box with a double garage and a square of lawn and approximately four inches between its side wall and the one belonging to its neighbour. The entrance to the scheme was guarded by a huge billboard showing visitors an image of the place they were about to enter and telling them exactly how much they could expect to pay if they wanted to live there. Betty didn't love where she lived but she'd never move to a place like this because it would mean she'd have to take the car if she wanted to drop pennies, otherwise all the luck she held would be contained within five perfectly matching streets and the families who lived inside them. She'd soon get spotted or bored or sore legs because there were no benches to sit on apart from one beside a tiny playpark that was silent and still smelled of fresh paint.

There was a parking space there too, so Betty left her car there and walked the short distance to Richard's house. Number 18. All she had to do was knock on his door, ask a question, find out the address of Stef's art retreat. Easy. She slowed her step as she got closer, cast a few glances that she hoped would be classed as casual, should they be seen and assessed.

The garage door was open and inside sat two cars, one red, one blue. To the right of them was a table loaded with jars of paintbrushes and little pots of paint and numerous rigid cardboard tubes for rolling canvases. A little further back she could make out a wooden sculpture far taller and wider than she was but she couldn't tell what it was supposed to be. In front of that was a rusting green lawnmower and a bin liner that was stuffed full and stretched to its limit like an overfilled water balloon.

Betty's brain spewed out an image of Stef, rolled up like an old carpet and pushed inside that black plastic bag. She knew it was personal sabotage, her mind creating reasons to run. But it worked. She walked on, trying to calm her mind and slow her pulse and find her courage.

The rush of adrenalin she'd felt on her way here suddenly slowed, stuttered. She was a tractor filled up with rocket fuel, dreaming herself to death.

Who did she think she was, coming here?

Betty circled a tiny roundabout at the end of the street, desperate to look casual, as if that had been her intended route all along. Then she headed back towards Richard's house, trying but failing to convince herself she was brave enough to do what she'd come to do. All she had to do was knock that door and ask that question: where is Stef?

But when she reached his house the scene had changed.

The bin liner was now sitting on the driveway, behind the open boot of the red car. Above it, a cloud of flies swarmed, bumping into each other as they fought to get closest to the neatly tied knots that kept it closed. Then came sound; the crunch of gravel underfoot and a snort that reminded Betty of the noise her mum used to make when she drank too much and passed out on the floor. A bark followed the snort; then a big brown dog raced towards Betty, out of the gate and across the road, nudging the backs of her knees as she hurried away. Her hand brushed its wet nose when it started poke poke poking her pocket and

Betty tried to remember the last time she'd touched or been touched but could not. It would have been Stef, no doubt, but she couldn't place the moment. Her heart swelled then ached.

Poke poke poke.

Betty stopped and looked into sticky eyes and for a moment she wondered if the dog would follow her to the car then climb in and come home with her and spend the rest of its days faithfully at her side, even after she died; another Greyfriars Bobby like that statue in the Old Town that tourists swarmed around and rubbed with their fingers for good luck.

'You got a bag of mince in your pocket?' A hand came from nowhere and grabbed the dog's collar and when Betty dared raise her head she was staring into the face of the ginger woman in Richard Owens's desk photograph. She didn't look as friendly now as she did on glossy paper, trapped under glass. Betty wasn't sure how to answer her question about the mince so she said nothing apart from that she really had to go, then she lied and said the dog had very lovely eyes. It was on its hind legs now, tugging to get free, choking itself and baring yellowish teeth as the woman tried to drag it home. Betty moved away and it was only then that she noticed the car boot was closed and the red reversing lights were on and the bin bag that had been sitting behind it was no longer there. Betty heard the crunch of a handbrake being pulled on in a rush; then Richard Owens – she recognised him from the photo, too – got out of the car and slammed the door and shouted to the woman, said he'd walk the daft beast before he left if she was really too bloody lazy to do it. He ducked into the garage, came out with a green dog lead wrapped around his shoulders like a scarf.

Betty shivered, imagining the loose ends, tugged tighter; the damage it could do.

The woman dragged the dog towards him and once the lead was clipped into place they both turned and looked at the garage, to the spot where a cloud of flies still darkened the air, like noisy crowds lingering in the street long after the pub's closed.

Richard said something that made his wife step away from him and shake her head. She glanced at Betty then and asked if she wanted a photo or to bugger off and Betty chose the second option. When Betty got to her car the woman was marching away from Richard and he was standing in his driveway, shaking his head. Beside him the dog was wagging its tail and licking its hairy lips. Richard kneeled down and held its face between his hands, gently, as if it were a child.

When it barked he laughed then stood up and started walking, thankfully in the opposite direction to where Betty stood with her hands caressing the copper face of the Queen. It took her less than a minute to retrace her steps and drop the penny at Richard Owens's front gate. She kneeled down on the pavement and deposited a 2016 penny exactly in the spot that Richard had just walked over.

That part was no different from any other day. But Richard would be a different kind of Finder; one who'd been chosen on purpose. Was that allowed? Betty wasn't sure, even though she'd invented the rules.

But the decision was made. She'd wait, watch, let Fate be her guide.

If Richard Owens walked past the coin she'd left for him, Betty would go home and forget about all of this, tell herself that Stef was fine and not in danger and that all the hateful images in her head were based on a misunderstanding.

But if Richard Owns picked up the coin?

Then for the first time in Betty's life, she'd follow a Finder.

CHAPTER 19

'Speak of the devil,' said Bert, sausage fingers rolled into fists on his meaty hips; eyes bright but tiny against the bulk of his cheeks, like sticky raisins pressed into uncooked dough. 'Vicky. Out. Andy. Sit. On *the other side* of the desk, eh?'

Bert clearly loved the chance to show off his authority, especially in the presence of somebody who held significantly more power than he ever would. Farida stayed quiet, arms crossed, eyes trained on Andy.

After Vicky had left, Bert stepped into the corridor and held out an arm to let Farida enter the office first. 'After you,' he said, then came in behind her and closed the door, puffing with effort when he pulled an extra chair towards his the desk. The pack of cigarettes in his shirt pocket was the only tight line on him.

'Andy, I believe you've met DI Farida McPherson? We were just talking about you, actually, so you've saved me a phone call.' Bert avoided looked at Andy, flicked through some printed A4 pages he'd pulled from his bag. 'But first, can you tell us what you and Vicky were doing in here?'

Andy stared straight ahead.

If his eyes went to the computer screen, theirs would as well. He was sure he could still hear the occasional buzz of static as it cooled down, whispers of evidence caught in the spaces between words. 'We were just chatting.'

'And I'm the Queen of Sheba.'

'Nice to meet you.'

Bert scowled. 'Is that really the best excuse you've got? *Chatting*? I hope you came up with a better line than that when Stef asked about the "incident" in here at Halloween.'

Andy glared at him. 'That's got nothing to do with . . . *this*.'

Bert snorted. 'Whatever you say.'

He started to protest but Bert butted in, cut him off.

'Let's get to the matter in hand. We all know the rules. You more than most. You're the one who drums them into all the newbies, doing your best to keep them on the straight and narrow. That's why all of this is so bloody ironic. And why it's so hard to believe. I still can't, to be honest. But it's all here in black and white.' He tapped a tobacco-stained fingernail on the printed page in front of him. It was a mixture of words and numbers, but Andy couldn't read it from where he was sitting. 'I've checked and double-checked. But there's no doubt, no room for excuses – and absolutely nothing I can do except report this to a higher level. She was always going to get caught in the end.'

Rage blazed in Andy's chest. He should never have involved Vicky, had known fine well she'd let her feelings overrule her head.

'The blame's mine, OK?'

'Very noble of you, Andy, but it's obvious something's been wrong for a while. I kept hoping I could nudge her in the right direction but she seems hellbent on self-destruction. Such a shame, really. She was one of the good ones.' He tutted, shook his head. 'But she's taken it too far now. I'm only glad I got the phone call from DI McPherson when I did, or she'd have milked us dry.'

'Milked you dry? Of what? I told you, me and Vicky were just chatting.'

Bert's shifting eyebrows signalled confusion. 'Don't get daft with me, boy. We're not talking about Vicky any more. It's Stef we're speaking about. And it's Stef

I'm worried about, getting mixed up in this kind of thing, with those kind of people.'

'You've lost me, Bert. What's all this about?'

Bert clasped his hands together. 'I'm sure DI McPherson will explain it better than I can.'

Farida took the baton. 'As we recently discussed, your wife's ID card was found at an address known to police and that this caused me some concern.'

'Alex Mitchell's flat,' said Andy. 'Hartfield Court.'

Farida flinched, but it was barely perceptible; the way teacups wobble when a magician whips out the tablecloth from beneath them. 'I don't recall telling you that name when we spoke. Or the address. I'd be keen to know how you got hold of such sensitive information.'

'Contacts.'

'Then perhaps they can help us *contact* your wife,' she said. 'As I was saying – when you were unable to provide a logical explanation for Stef's ID being at Alex Mitchell's flat, I got in touch with Bert to confirm whether or not your wife's card had been reported as missing. The good news, in some respects, is that Bert was able to track a missing card report. Stef's card was registered as lost around six months ago, shortly before she was signed off.'

Bert nodded, looked chuffed. His chins wobbled, silent applause.

'The less good news is that during his investigations Bert discovered that while a new card was issued immediately, the old card was not deactivated. A significant oversight for a swipe card that gives access to restricted drugs, I think we'll agree?' Farida sniffed. Bert stared at his desk, said nothing. 'It seems the system automatically records the name linked to each card, not the individual card itself. So while the system recognises that Stef's card is being used, it can't distinguish if it's the old card or the new one. This is most inconvenient given the fact that there has been some unusual and . . . worrying activity connected your wife's profile. If you'd like to continue, Bert?'

Another nod, another wobble.

He picked up the pile of paper and turned it in his hands, tapping every edge against the desk until they were all perfectly in place. 'There's no easy way to say this . . . but . . . we're missing drugs, Andy.' Bert paused, a moment of dramatic silence to let the words sink in. 'And whoever took the drugs used Stef's card to open the safe.'

'There must be a mistake.'

'I don't remember asking for your opinion.' A bead of sweat trickled from Bert's hairline to his temple then worked its way through the stubble that poked through his ruddy cheeks. 'As I was saying, Stef's ID was used to open a safe on board one of the ambulances, late on Monday evening. Obviously Stef's not been at work for six months so she had no reason to be anywhere near any of the vehicles – and someone would have noticed if she'd just strolled into the station, wouldn't they? They'd have been delighted to see her, no doubt. We all would. But clearly she didn't want to be seen; went for the ambulance that's in the mechanic's workshop, out of sight. And now, out of drugs.'

'That's . . . impossible.'

'Impossible?' There was almost a laugh tagged on to the end of Farida's voice. 'Please do correct me if I'm wrong but yesterday you told me that your wife left home on Monday evening – and that you've had no contact with her since? If that *is* really the case, I'd say Bert's theory is *entirely* possible.'

Andy's tongue felt like it was made of old carpet. He tried to remember the precise details of what he'd said to Farida about Stef's departure to the art retreat. If she had a theory about what had happened to Stef, he knew what question was coming next.

Why?

He was right.

'I've got a question,' said Farida, then whipped the spotlight on to Bert instead. 'If the ambulance was in the garage, why was it loaded with drugs? It seems a little . . . irresponsible?'

Bert's face became a beetroot.

'That particular ambulance has a wonky door that's due to be fixed but it can still be used as and when required. All vehicles remain fully stocked unless they're going to be out of action long-term. Why? So they're ready to go at short notice, if required, and also to minimise the movements of controlled drugs. We do a stocktake on all safes every day but if an ambulance is with the mechanic and hasn't been used, we're not as rigorous. That's why the discrepancy wasn't noticed until you got in touch.'

When Farida raised an eyebrow, Bert hung his head.

'But facts are facts,' he said, moving the attention back to Andy. 'God knows what Stef's doing with the drugs, but—'

'Is this actually a joke?'

'Trust me, I wish it was. I'll be strung up for it as well, especially if the press hear about it.'

Farida's eyes burned on Andy's face so he held it as still as he could manage, hoped the rest of his body wouldn't betray him. Arm uncrossed. Face unmoving. *No lies here, officer.* He had to gather his thoughts, reason his way out of this office and the accusations it held.

'Let me get this straight,' said Andy. 'First, you have a record of Stef's ID card being lost but not cancelled six months ago and a new one being issued to replace it. Second, police find Stef's ID card at Alex Mitchell's flat. Third, you find out that Stef's ID card has been used to access drugs from the station on Monday night. But we do *not* know which of the two cards was used or who was holding Stef's ID card, do we?'

Bert shook his head. Andy looked at Farida until she looked back.

'And please do correct me if I'm wrong, Farida – but yesterday *you* told *me* that Alex Mitchell walked out of court on Monday – and didn't you say he hadn't been seen since?'

'Correct.' Farida sucked her lips inside her mouth, skin tight against her teeth.

'Which means the drugs were taken on exactly the same night Alex Mitchell walked free. It's hardly rocket science, is it? Surely the logical explanation is that Alex Mitchell stole Stef's card and somehow realised he could get his fill of drugs without paying a penny. End of story. Stef's only crime is losing her card, or having it stolen.'

Bert winced. 'That was my first thought, Andy. I know Stef. Respect her. I'd never have dreamed of pinning something like this on her. Even now, I struggle to believe it. But then . . .'

'But then what?'

Bert looked at Farida, got the nod he was looking for.

'But then we checked the CCTV,' said Bert.

CHAPTER 20

Betty rarely noticed the cars behind her when she was driving but she was convinced that Richard Owens was watching her in the rear-view mirror as he turned off the main road on to a smaller one with grass verges and hedges instead of pavements and traffic lights. If they'd been in the city she'd have lost him right away but out here in the countryside it was easier to hang back and still keep him in sight. There were no cars between them, just lumps of dried mud that had fallen off giant tractor tyres and the occasional mound of horse manure. She glanced at her petrol gauge, wondered how long they'd be driving for and how she'd get home if her tank ran dry in the middle of nowhere. He drove more slowly than she'd imagined, especially given how angry he'd looked when he returned from his walk and discovered his wife had locked him out of the house – instantly dissolving the smile that had filled his face when he'd found Betty's lucky penny on his own garden path.

He'd thumped the front door for a while then tied the lead to the handle and left, moments before the dog hunched over like an old man and deposited a shit on their step. When Richard drove past the playpark where Betty was parked their eyes met for a millisecond. Then Betty looked away and vowed to keep a bigger distance between them for the rest of the journey. He headed towards the coast and for a while Betty thought he was heading to Stef and Andy's house in Portobello but he turned off just after the beach came into view. A few minutes more and Richard's car turned inland on to a road lined with trees. There was no signpost to tell Betty where it went and the trees were so tall on either side that she could barely see what lay beyond the first twenty metres. But Betty knew where they were, used to come here all the time.

They were heading for the back entrance of the Green Den estate, close to that house Betty used to clean twice weekly; a Victorian villa with pink sandstone walls and a rotting conservatory used by the owner to grow fat tomatoes and skinny grapes. Even when the old lady had lived there the house looked derelict and she'd once told Betty she kept it that way on purpose so that she wouldn't attract thieves, used flaky paint and chipped windowsills as her gargoyles.

Now it was empty, it had become the kind of place teenagers went after school to drink cheap spirits and call on dead ones.

Betty sped up when she drove past the house, slowed again when it was out of sight. She took every curve like a learner driver in case Richard's car was waiting . for her on the other side; kept picturing his parked car, a dead end, and absolutely nowhere to turn. But when she reached the back entrance of the estate she couldn't see any trace of him at all. She'd lost him, failed Stef.

What now?

Betty pulled over, opened the door and listened. She could hear crows calling and wind bending branches and then, somewhere, the thud of a car boot being slammed shut. Then she saw movement through the trees in front of her.

She'd be easily seen if she walked on the road so she headed for trees, stepped from hard tarmac on to a woodland path that had no definite edge and seemed to move with the weight of her, like walking on sponges. She stopped after a few steps, hesitant. The light and the temperature and the sounds of the day had changed all at once. The woods held a different scent as well. More than anything she could smell the trees but when a breeze came it brought a few other scents – cut grass, fumes from the road, the trace of something burning. Always when she smelled smoke or heard a fire engine Betty wondered if it was her own home that was ablaze, would picture charred doors and melted white goods and collapsed beams and books reduced to ash and a firefighter with blackened cheeks salvaging her jar of lucky pennies from the smoking ruins.

She stepped further into the woods, glancing towards her parked car before the path took a sharp left and sloped gently downhill toward a shallow brown stream and a wobbly bridge made out of a wooden palette. She'd just crossed it when she caught sight of Richard Owens up ahead.

He was standing in front of a squat, thick-walled stone outhouse with a corrugated iron roof and tiny blacked-out windows. It must have been a store at one time, or maybe a shelter for animals. Whatever it had been, there was no sign anybody used it now.

Except for Richard Owens. He stepped up to the door, pressed an ear to the wood.

Betty held her breath, heard a low humming sound that she couldn't quite place. A fridge, maybe, or a generator; nothing that she could see from here.

A sunbeam broke through clouds and pushed over the outhouse roof, splitting into edgeless rays that made Betty's skin glow. That was the kind of light that Stef liked to capture in her paintings, hands gripping that delicate paintbrush, stilling the life on her page.

If Stef *was* here, maybe that was why.

Maybe the bin liner Richard had dragged from his boot was full of painting supplies and blankets and something special for Stef to cook on her little camping stove.

Betty clung to that thought as Richard tugged a stretchy running scarf over his mouth and nose, covering most of his face. Then he pulled out a pair of latex gloves, blew into them before wriggling his hands inside and tugging the tips of the fingers until they were wrinkle-free. Finally he took a bunch of keys from his pocket, unlocked the door and slipped inside with that bulging bin bag in tow. He shut the door behind him.

Betty waited, cold copper growing warm in her hand as the minutes dragged on. She pictured herself storming out of the woods and throwing open the door, demanding answers and getting them. But she stayed where she was; unseen.

When Richard came out ten minutes later he ripped off the gloves and pulled off the scarf and muttered to himself as he made for his car, head down, trailed by flies. He glanced at the outhouse before he got in and Betty was sure she saw him shudder.

She held her breath, waited until the sound of his car had disappeared completely before she dared let it go. What now? She heard a tractor engine ticking over, somewhere far behind her.

She could run to the farmer but what would she say?

She didn't know for sure that anything was wrong and what if it was? A familiar fear stalked her; stopped her in her tracks. If something was wrong they'd think it was her fault. They'd give her that look reserved for people with A History and bundle her into a van then a cell and she'd deserve it and not be missed by anybody that really mattered.

But Stef would be missed, already was.

She thought of blood splatters on tiles and dry paintbrushes and the discarded mobile phone and bruises on arms and *those* hands, on her. She couldn't leave until she knew what was inside. Every tiny sound in the woods became a threat and she twitched inside tight skin as she crept towards the outhouse.

In her belly, nausea swirled. And in her face, flies did.

She gripped a lucky penny and headed for the door.

CHAPTER 21

The day after the funeral Stef got up before the sun, tucked the duvet around Andy's shoulders so he wouldn't feel the cold and wake up. The room smelled of him; fermenting whisky and sweat, a hangover in the making. He'd suffer but, for once, Stef was glad he'd overdone it because it meant he'd sleep longer than usual. And that meant she had time.

When she got downstairs she locked herself in the bathroom and read that letter one last time before quietly ripping it up into tiny pieces and flushing it down the toilet, scrap by scrap until she was sure it was completely gone. Still, that name lingered; a bad smell that wouldn't shift no matter how many times she flushed or squirted bleach into the bowl.

She pulled out her phone and typed the name into a search engine, felt sick when her screen filled up with newspaper articles written with one purpose. To frighten the readers, to make them glad none of this was happening to them or the people they loved; and to sell more papers. Terror captured an audience.

All the articles followed the same formula, photos of smiling strangers of all ages who were all given the same label. Victims. Stef hated that word but read on, wondering if one day her face would appear on a printed page that others would read over breakfast or on the train to work and if they'd feel as invincible and untouchable as she always had; if, like her, they'd quietly judge the victims, safe in the knowledge that somehow, it would have ended differently for them. Every single one of them believing they'd be The One Who Got Away.

Those were the words on her mind when she heard a creak upstairs; Andy was on his way down, probably dreaming of coffee and some buttered toast and a brisk walk in the bitter cold to wake himself up.

She flushed the toilet one final time then closed window after window on her phone as she crept from the bathroom to the sitting room. She lay on the couch, pulled their old blanket over her legs and plastered a smile on her face in the hope it would cover the cracks in her.

Andy's his face lit up when he saw her. He'd hide his tears, that man, but when it was love he felt it gushed and roared, could not be held inside.

He pushed open the sitting-room door then stood there in his navy-blue dressing gown, hands on his hips, tired smile on his face, patchy stubble darkening his chin.

'Couldn't sleep?'

She shook her head. 'But I've been researching summer holidays.' That'd please him because all she'd done lately was avoid the topic. She wouldn't be going anywhere – at least, not with him.

'And?'

'You were right,' she said, knowing how to play him; all the ways to make him feel relaxed and think everything was exactly as it should be. 'Catalonia looks brilliant for campervans, like you said. I'm up for it if you are.'

'Excellent. I'll investigate, get a few quotes for the van rental.'

'Definitely.'

'But thinking about today – you fancy climbing Arthur's Seat? I know we're due another shedload of snow but I could do with a walk to clear my head.'

'Hike then pint? Might help us get into the Christmas spirit.'

'Perfect,' he said. 'You know me too well.'

Stef was glad breaking hearts could not be heard. 'Deal.'

'But first, coffee?' He was already turning away. He'd be thinking of caffeine; not terror and torture and escape and the best time to flee. She stayed where she was, body tight, heart racing, willing him to leave, but he was eyeing the clock. 'What time did you get up anyway?'

She shrugged. 'It was still dark.'

'Early bird,' he said, then smiled; she smiled back but in her head all she could see was a soft, slippery worm, clamped in a beak, desperately trying to wriggle free. But it could not.

CHAPTER 22

All conversation stopped when Andy pushed open the door of the mess, as if his feet had triggered a mute button. Vicky put down her mug and leapt up from the sofa but then her gaze drifted over his shoulder, checking if the coast was clear before she asked any questions.

It was not. Farida followed, a missile on his tail.

She walked beside him once they got outside, put a hand on his back and directed him towards the bike shelter to escape yet another summer shower. It had been drizzling on and off all morning but this one looked like it would persist. Farida glared at the rumbling sky.

'Shall we talk further in my car?'

'I'd rather not.'

'The talking part isn't an option,' she said. 'Officially this is an informal chat between two members of the emergency services. Paramedics assisting the police, same as ever. There will be no record of it. But I warn you, we won't be discussing the weather.'

Silence stalked them as they walked towards Stef's blue Volvo.

When they climbed into the car Andy slid the keys into the ignition then adjusted the wing mirror and opened the window an inch on his side. He'd happily have fidgeted all day but Farida had different ideas.

'Where do we go from here then, Andy?'

'Home, hopefully.'

'You know that's not what I meant,' she said. 'We need to talk about the CCTV.'

Bert had played the full recording to both of them, twisted the computer monitor round on his desk so they all had a decent view of someone sneaking into the mechanic's workshop after hours then disappearing inside one of the ambulances for more than a minute. The CCTV footage was grainy and jerky and recorded by a camera mounted high on the garage wall, but Bert was clearly convinced it was Stef. Plus the date and time of the recording perfectly matched the date and time her card was used to open the safe.

'I'm sure you're aware it's an extremely serious offence,' said Farida. 'She'll be struck off from work permanently, I'd imagine – but that'll be the least of her worries. This could potentially lead to a jail term, Andy. Or at the very least, a significant fine.'

He couldn't look at her.

'This whole thing will be less painful for everyone if we can speak to Stef directly. I've been trying her phone number repeatedly but no to avail. I'm aware that husbands want to protect their wives but you need to tell me where she is.'

'I've already told you she's at an art retreat up north.'

'And you still expect me to believe that, even now?'

Andy glared at her.

'Can you remind me *where* this art retreat's being held?'

'No, I can't. I didn't have the address yesterday and I don't have it now. I've not spoken to Stef either.'

'Inconvenient, isn't it? Or convenient, depending on which seat you're sitting in.'

Andy's jaw tightened. 'I've told you everything.'

'I think we both know that's not the case,' said Farida. 'Which is why I'd like to ask you a few more questions. First of all, I've been reliably informed that several staff members raised concerns about Stef's conduct at work, prior to her sick leave.'

'Bert had no right to tell you that.'

'I didn't name any names,' said Farida. 'But from what I've heard at least two colleagues suspected she was under the influence of drink at work. Or drugs.'

'Don't even go there.'

'I'll go wherever I want to, Mr Campbell. It's my job.' Farida paused, stared at him until he looked back. 'I've also heard rumours of a romantic relationship between you and your team leader, Vicky Steele; the woman who helped you access those files today.'

'And like I said to Bert, that's done and dusted and totally irrelevant.'

'*Irrelevant?*' Farida sniffed. 'I'd very much like to ask your wife if she agrees. Yet another question to ask when she responds to my calls. In the meantime, can you tell me the real reason you and Vicky were in Bert's office today?'

Andy lowered the window further, sucked in some cool air. 'I was just confused about why Stef's ID card had been found at Alex Mitchell's flat, especially once I realised who he was. When I couldn't get her on the phone I tried contacting Bert but he didn't pick up either. That's why I called in a favour with Vicky, asked if she'd give me access to the patient report forms. I was just trying to settle my mind, hoped to find a case file that proved Stef had attended an incident at Alex Mitchell's flat. But there's nothing on record. As far as I can see there's no evidence of any contact between them at all.'

Farida cleared her throat before she spoke again, an actor sweeping the stage before she stepped into the spotlight and delivered her line. 'That's where you're wrong.'

Her words were like a cold key, dropped down the back of his shirt. 'What do you mean?'

'Your wife phoned Alex Mitchell's landline on Monday afternoon.'

'What? How can you possibly know that?'

'I'll come to that in a minute,' said Farida. 'But in case you've forgotten, Monday is the day Alex Mitchell walked free from court and headed home to his flat. It's also the day you last saw Stef and, of course, it's the day the drugs were stolen from the ambulance station using your wife's ID card – potentially the same ID card I photographed at Alex Mitchell's flat that same day. So while you didn't find a direct link between Stef and Alex on the station computer, my investigations suggest there's plenty of evidence elsewhere. And before you ask, I don't believe in coincidences.'

'I do.'

'What about phone records – do you believe in them?'

Andy twisted round, eyes wide. 'You've been tracking her calls?'

'Not exactly. But when I was a trainee in Glasgow my boss taught me to check the landline the moment I enter a crime scene, to identify the last person to call that particular property. It's rarely proven useful but I do it automatically these days. And when I entered Alex Mitchell's home on Monday night I did the same. The number meant nothing to me but I saved it on my phone. And when you gave me your wife's number yesterday I realised the two numbers matched. So while I can't give you a reason at this stage, I can confirm without any doubt that somebody used your wife's phone to call Alex Mitchell's home that day. Perhaps now you'll understand my increased interest in the case.'

For a few moments there was silence. Why would Stef have called that man?

He couldn't sit back and take Farida's word for it.

He'd go home, get Stef's mobile, check for himself.

'I need to go,' he said, then turned on the engine. The radio controls lit up, plus a symbol telling him he needed more fuel. Typical. He pulled out Stef's secret satnav, searched for the nearest petrol station then opened *Frequent Destinations* and scrolled down, looking for their home address so he could add in the route home from the garage.

Farida got out, slammed shut the door so hard the car shook. Andy barely noticed.

He had one hand on the steering wheel and both eyes on that illuminated screen. Listed halfway down the *Frequent Destinations* list on Stef's satnav were two words that made all the other dots join, that made the picture complete. Two words. *Hartfield Court.*

Alex Mitchell's home address.

CHAPTER 23

Flies covered the window; a swarm so thick that from outside it looked like drawn curtains. It took Betty a while to realise the black behind the glass was moving, like a TV with no signal and the volume turned down. The sound she'd thought was the hum of a fridge or a generator was coming from them. Betty stared at the writhing mass of black on the glass, tried to focus despite the endless movement of bodies she knew would bleed red blood if she squashed them with a book or a rolled-up magazine or, on a brave day, her fingers. They reminded her of those optical illusions from the Sunday papers; digital images that looked like wallpaper but if she stared at them for long enough she'd see a panda or a bicycle or a bonsai tree. But these were definitely just flies.

How many were there? Hundreds? Thousands? It would be impossible to count them unless they were dead – and death was the only thing that would silence them. But right now they lived, they breathed, they flew, they clung to smudged glass and they made *that* sound.

The word *rasp* came into her head but that made her think of her tongue against a blade of thick, waxy grass, the kind that grows at the far end of Portobello beach. She couldn't bear the idea of her mouth anywhere near those flies so she dismissed the word, quickly, ignoring nausea. She edged closer to the window, ear turned towards the glass but not touching it. Flies weren't magicians: they couldn't and wouldn't force themselves through the glass and into her ear, little feet padding merrily through wax. Still, for a moment she pictured the flies swarming into her body via her conveniently awaiting ear, squeezing into the space between her brain and her skull and rushing into the squelchy places between her organs and gasping for air in the tubes that needed to be clear so she could breathe.

Betty Stevenson, drowned by flies.

They loved death, thrived on it – and she knew that from personal experience. One time when she was doing a forest walk she'd accidentally sat and had her lunch close to a sheep carcass, kept getting whiffs of a bad smell as she chewed her cheese and salad cream sandwiches and it was only when she stood up that she saw it. Stiff limbs and a bloated belly, its stilled face being greedily devoured by beings a thousand times smaller than it was. Would she find something similar here?

Betty stepped away from the window and went to the door, glanced over her shoulder before she tugged at the cold metal handle. It was locked, barely moved an inch even when she used her whole weight to push against it. She looked over her shoulder again then knocked on the door, firmly, the way people do in films when they've got something really important to say.

She put her ear to the door, couldn't decide if she hoped to hear a voice or not.

'Stef?'

But only the woodland answered. The gritty screech of crows, the gentle creaks of branches, the occasional buzz of a bee or wasp as it raced past in search of colour. Somewhere further away was the toot of a horn and the merry chug of a diesel engine.

She walked right around the building, found a tiny deep-set window on the gable end. It reminded her of those little niches in the walls at church, the places believers would leave statues of saints then light tiny candles that gave them a magical glow but blackened their faces. She hunched down, peered into the darkness holding her breath as she reached into the hole. Relief and disappointment came in equal measure when her fingertips touched glass. The whole place was locked up, its contents locked in.

She returned to the blackened window at the front, watched the flies lift and land and crawl and creep across the glass. But then she saw something she hadn't noticed before; a tiny crack in the bottom right corner. She pulled the sleeve of her jacket over her hand and stepped up to the wall, pushed the little triangle drawn out by the split in the pane. Nothing happened at first so she tightened her hand into a fist and pushed harder, using the middle bone of her middle finger, the one most people use to be rude. When that little corner broke with a sudden snap the whole window cracked and Betty was just as surprised as the flies were. Her hand slipped forward with the force, skin catching on the splintered edges of the hole. The blood came before the pain did. She snapped her hand away, squeezed it under her armpit as the flies on the other side of the glass lifted off the surface and, just for a moment, gave Betty a view of the inside. All she could see were more flies. On the walls, the floor, the ceiling, and everything in between. When the flies from the window returned to their previous spot a few found the hole and little by little they started filtering out like waking bats fleeing their cave at sunset.

'Stef?'

A few flies brushed Betty's lips when she opened her mouth to shout. She bowed her head and waved her good hand in front of her, trying to get a better view of what lay behind the swarm; and of what kept them there. And it was there, as she stood at the edge of the woodland, pushing against a tide of flies, that she heard the roar of an approaching car engine. She ducked into the woods, batting buzzing flies from her hair, then fled.

CHAPTER 24

The little car park close to Holyrood Palace was packed when they got there so Stef drove a little further on, parked on the road close to the ruin of the wee chapel that overlooked a loch on the path towards the summit. They sat together on the back bumper of the car, elbows knocking into each other as they leaned over and tied the laces of their walking boots.

'Ready?' Stef opened her favourite hiking app, the one they used to find and record hikes even in the wilderness of Scotland; places a phone signal would never reach. Stef had scoffed when Andy first suggested they download it, convinced GPS technology wouldn't work in remote places, that a mobile phone could never replace a map.

Andy had laughed, said she'd learn to love it. And she had – although she wasn't quite as obsessed as Andy was. He'd started timing everything since he turned forty and was automatically propelled into a different age category. He'd assumed he'd scoop up all the records since he was probably one of the youngest in that group but the crowns and medals didn't come as often as he'd have liked.

Still, he'd come home beaming when the app told him he'd done well and if they weren't together he'd take a screenshot photo of his result, text it to her. Before his mum succumbed to dementia she'd told Stef that he did the same to her, was forever sending her news of his tiny victories. They'd laughed about it at the time but later Stef felt sad, suddenly seeing the wee boy in Andy that still so desperately needed his mum's approval. He needed to know she was proud of him; proof, somehow, that he'd been forgiven for what happened to his wee sister. That would have meant more than all the gold medals and speed records put together.

But it never came, and now would not.

She locked the car and followed Andy up the tarmac path then on to the lumpy line of trampled grass that led to the edge of the Salisbury Crags. She walked more slowly than he did on the best of days but Andy never seemed to mind, would reach the highest point of any path then find himself a plinth to stand on, push himself a little closer to the sky and take in the *view from there. Today was no different. The ridge was busy but she spotted him right away, standing atop a rock with his hands on his hips facing the Old Town, streets strung with garish Christmas decorations that would be switched on later. From time to time he'd turn his head to the right and she knew he'd be looking for the beach promenade at Portobello, would count the streets back from the end until he saw the roof of their house.*

She wanted to be up there with him, to hold out her hand and let herself be warmed by the heat he radiated, whatever the weather. But today she was dragging her feet, taking twice as long as usual.

'Slowcoach,' said Andy, when she finally reached him. Then he winked and hauled her onto the rock beside him, groaning as if she weighed ten times more than she did. Either that or the dread that filled her chest could be measured in grams and kilos.

For a while they stood in silence, watching birds swooping and soaring, wings spread wide against invisible currents. When the breeze brought goosebumps to their skin they set off for the summit of Arthur's Seat. Stef scrambled for conversation, spoke only the obvious. 'Stairs or slope?'

Andy shrugged. 'Is there actually any difference?'

'Not in metres. But I suppose it's the difference between a sprint or a stroll.'

'Then let's sprint it,' he said, glancing at his watch and setting off up the stone steps, taking two at a time. He stopped when the path switched back on itself and he was directly above her, but out of reach. He grinned and shouted down at her. 'Last one up buys the first drinks!' She could hear him laughing to himself as he continued uphill. He'd expect to see her next time he turned round, taking a short cut, clambering over rocks and sprinting over clods of moss and lichen-covered rocks; Stef, reaching the summit mud-caked and ruddy-cheeked and gasping for breath, whatever it took to make sure Andy was picking up the tab.

But that's the trouble with expectations; the higher they rise, the greater the disappointment if they aren't met.

When she eventually reached the summit she looked for Andy on the concrete pillar that marked the highest point. It was selfie capital of the city these days and there was often a queue for it, folk lining up with their backs to the view and their eyes on the digital version of themselves, working out which angle would catch them at their best. But right now there was only a handful of people left and all of them were in proper *hiking gear. Hoods up, head down, no doubt making jokes about the Scottish weather as they gazed over the city and the castle and the rock that it clung to; the sea with its royal yachts and cargo ships and rowing boats and paddle surfers and brave swimmers and mad dogs; the sky with its clouds and that promise of blue that never ever lasted long enough.*

But Andy wasn't there.

The sky rumbled and the lowering clouds brought with them a spit that hung in the air, threatening proper rain, the kind that would jab at your eyes and drench you to right the bone in less than two minutes flat. Stef zipped up her jacket then picked her way over the rocks at the top. She watched her breath swirl in the cold air and become part of everybody else on the summit; sucked in by sniffs, pushed around by sighs and coughs.

'Stef?'

She whipped her head round, eyes wide. It couldn't be him. Not here, now.

But there he was.

'Thought it was you.'

Stef's hood rustled in her ears as she tugged it down, screwing up her eyes as the swirling wind snapped at her cheeks. She tucked her hair behind her ears, knew it wouldn't stay and hoped he wouldn't either. He pulled his hand out of his jacket pocket and held it out to her but she didn't budge; just stood in silence in the wind, staring at his outstretched fingers. She knew his intentions and all the ways she'd suffer if she did what he said.

'Come on. You know I don't bite.' He let out a sound that was carried off by the wind before she could work out for sure if it was a laugh. How dare he.

Stef took a step back and up, wrapped one arm around the trig point as she searched for Andy. There was no sign of him on the summit. But was he watching them from further down the hill? He couldn't see her talking to this man.

She'd been with him in secret last week while Andy was working and he'd urged her yet again to come clean.

Just tell him.

He'd ache less once he knew for sure he'd lost her.

Not yet, *she'd said.*

She didn't want Andy to know about all the times she'd met this man when he was at work or climbing a hill or enjoying a daytime drinking session with folk from the station.

It was not fair but she was not ready.

Stef fled. She pulled up her hood then clambered over the wet rocks, stumbling on moss and long grass as she moved down the steep slope on the other side of the hill. She saw Andy after a few minutes. He started clapping, whooping when she slipped on a patch of mud carved out by far too many boots. He pulled her up and kissed her, both of them soaked, hair plastered against their heads, Andy laughing and Stef's heart breaking when she glanced towards the summit and saw that man, still there, looking down at them.

'I'll never grow bored of this,' said Andy and for a while they stood together up there between mountain and sky, the rooftops and spires and bridges and squares of the city at their feet. If Edinburgh was the place Stef called home, Andy was where she felt it.

They'd built that together, on trust; but she'd pick it apart all by herself with those lies leaking out of her every single day, leeching into their very foundations. She looked up at Andy, both wishing he could read her mind and dreading the idea of it.

If he looked inside of her now he'd see the threat held in that letter and the images from those newspaper articles and the memories of unspoken moments spent with that man from the summit when Andy thought she was alone, at home. And if he kept looking he'd see her, his wife, reluctantly lie down on that thin mattress, letting her eyes blur as she stared at pale green walls and lights that were far too bright for the size of the place. He'd see that man's face above her, looking down and smiling even though both of them knew what was coming. Stef, trapped and whispering for help; stilled by a tightening grip.

CHAPTER 25

Alex Mitchell's flat was twenty minutes away, according to Stef's satnav. There wasn't much traffic but the lights turned red every time Andy got within two metres of them. Drive, stop, drive, stop, drive, stop. It was infuriating.

His body was half fear, half adrenalin; a bitter cocktail that made his mouth dry and his thoughts swirl and his heart thunder far too fast for comfort. Why had Stef been *frequently* visiting this man, according to her satnav? And more to the point, why had she never mentioned those visits to him?

Sandy Hamilton had warned Andy not to search for information about Alex Mitchell online and he'd resisted, until now. But he pulled out his phone at a particularly slow set of traffic lights, typed the man's name into the search box. Within seconds he was looking at dozens of articles detailing Alex's numerous court appearances and disturbing criminal record.

Beating up his girlfriend, torturing her mother, then attacking the landlady of that pub – Sandy had given him an outline but had spared him the more horrifying details. None of the papers had made a direct link between Alex Mitchell and Maureen Aitken's disappearance – but that didn't mean a thing. Newspapers would be breaking the law if they openly made that connection before the police did, could even stop the case going to court if judges felt jurors would be unable to give him a fair trial because of sensational press reports. Until he was charged and found guilty, the papers were gagged.

Andy took one last glance at Alex Mitchell's face then stuffed his phone into his pocket.

He looked for distraction, found the solid green hulk of Arthur's Seat.

Wherever he drove in Edinburgh he'd search for glimpses of it between the houses. He could just make out the path and the lumps of rock at the top that, from a distance, looked like outlines of people standing on the summit. There would be a few folk up there, no doubt, despite all the warnings about a storm. You had the runners in the early morning, drinkers up there at night, trying their hardest to last until sunrise; and in between was a mixed bag of tourists and dog walkers and students with their pals or their parents or maybe a novel so they could sit up there and feel like a proper intellectual, overlooking the city with a book in their hands.

The cheerful man locked inside the satnav told him to turn left.

'You sure, pal?' Andy knew the area well, had attended dozens of cases at Hartfield Court during his career. But he'd never been there off shift, out of uniform. There was even a chance he'd treated killers in the back of the ambulance, but he'd never gone looking for one.

His mind crept again to the headlines and the photos of Alex Mitchell from the newspaper articles. He looked like an ordinary man. But killers often did, didn't they?

If he dared look in the mirror he'd get the answer to that one.

Andy slowed, spotted a space between a white van and a BMW that was almost as old as he was. He unclipped the satnav and hid it in the glove compartment. As much as he defended folk from the estate and as much as he wanted to see through the smog of prejudice that lingered, the sad fact was that more stuff got nicked in these places than anywhere else. He locked Stef's Volvo then set off towards Alex Mitchell's flat.

It was as grim as the prospects of the folk living inside it. Only eight storeys, this one; it looked like the stunted half-cousin of the flats that towered over it. Harled grey walls were streaked with black mould that stretched down from the flat roof to the dying grass beneath; as if a massive bird had sat on the roof and taken an almighty shit. A bony girl with a rash around her mouth watched Andy approach while her obese Jack Russell lifted a stubby leg and pissed against a bike chained to the railings by the door.

Andy stepped around the puddle and into a poorly lit entrance hall.

He decided the lift wasn't worth the risk, headed for the stairs. Alex Mitchell's flat was on the sixth floor and there were only four doors on each level so it was easy to find.

He rang the bell then stood back and waited.

He could hear a few TVs and someone laughing and somewhere higher up, music blaring. Folk who'd always lived in detached houses had no idea how lucky they were; had never suffered the torture of thin walls and noisy neighbours. He and Stef had been there, done that, got the earplugs. But their house in

Portobello was a different story. It was all birdsong and rustling leaves and, if you got up early enough, the whisper of rolling waves. When he got home from work there would be eighties songs on the radio and Stef, asking him how his day had been. He dreaded the absence of those ordinary moments.

Here, it was the Alex Mitchell who was absent.

He rang the doorbell again, nerves twitching.

There were three more flats on this floor. Should he knock on their doors as well, start asking questions? He wasn't a news reporter or a policeman, had no right – and no experience either. He spent most of his working life in stranger's homes, but he was invited in. They'd be standing on the street or in the corridor by the time he got there, would hold open their front door and usher him in and thank him for coming. He'd never had to ask, convince or persuade anybody to let him in. If you're wearing the right uniform, you'll get through the door. He doubted his chinos and hiking shirt would have the same impact but if he didn't try, he'd never know.

He pressed the doorbell for the flat across the corridor. No answer. He moved to the flat at the end, heard the click of locks being turned, a security chain being unclipped. That was a good start, at least. Andy stood the same way he did at work, hoped it gave the same impression. Friendly, trustworthy, in control.

The woman who opened the door was wearing a bright green Hibernian football top and holding a screaming baby on her hip. 'You here about the leaking windows?'

'Afraid not. It's your neighbour I'm looking for actually. Alex Mitchell?'

The girl's face darkened, same way a hillside turns from green to grey when shifting clouds cover the sun. 'Jesus Christ, are you from the papers? 'Cos I'll tell you something – I'm sick to death of you lot, trying to schmooze your way into this building so you can write some horror story about that sick bastard. I don't know him, all right? So you can fuck right off.'

She slammed the door, had already clunked shut the locks and bolts by the time Andy could react. He rang the bell again and when she didn't answer he ducked down, called through the letter box. 'I'm not from the newspapers, all right? I'm just looking for my wife.'

He heard footsteps, deliberate stomping. And then a shout from the other end of the hall. 'You won't find her here, pal.' He was about to shout a reply when he heard the sound of an explosion followed by squeaky voices. She'd turned on the TV; a cartoon, volume on full.

Andy straightened up with a sigh then pressed the bell of the fourth and final flat on this floor, was rewarded with the rattle of keys in the lock. The woman on the other side held her face so close to the door that he could only see half of it. A few wiry grey hairs floated skyward as if someone had just rubbed a balloon against her head.

Andy forced a smile, got the same empty gesture in return. 'I'm hoping you can help me,' he said. 'I'm trying to find Alex Mitchell.' There was a definite flinch, like someone on the other side of the door had zapped the woman with a cattle prod. 'I'm not from the press, OK? And I'm not his pal. I just need to speak to him, so if you've any idea—'

'Who the hell are you, then?'

'Sorry?'

'If you're not the police and you're not his pal, who are you?'

Andy pulled out his paramedic ID, held it out to her. She stuck a bony hand through the gap, snapped it from his fingers the same way seagulls swipe chips from outstretched hands at the beach. Her eyes flitted from Andy's face to the card and back again.

'Are you here to beg forgiveness, then?'

'What for?'

'For saving that bastard.'

'Alex Mitchell? I've never met the man, never mind saved him.'

The woman stared at him through the gap, slowly munching her fat tongue. He could hear the stickiness of the saliva in her mouth as she swallowed, too often. 'But *would* you?' She handed his ID card back.

'Every life counts.'

'Even if they're cunts?'

'It's my job.'

'My job, my arse,' she said. 'Anyone with half a brain knows that man's a bad egg, rotten to the core. They might not have found a body yet but I'd swear on my mother's life that he's involved with the disappearance of that old lady. But *still* you lot saved him.'

'What do you mean, *saved*? There's no record of that. I've checked—'

'You can fuck off with your records. I was here. I *saw* them. Watched two paramedics hold him down and stitch him up, even though he was roaring his head off, telling them not to. Slitting his own wrists was probably the only way he could escape the guilt of whatever it is he's done to that poor old woman – and the only way he'd escape jail. Job or no job, I wouldn't have wasted an ounce of energy saving the life of a man who'd sinned like he had.'

The woman paused for breath, crossed herself.

'I've known him since he was wee. That mother of his drank herself to death, left the weans to run feral. He used to run away all the time and I swear to God his mother didn't even notice. He'd creep back, hoping they'd missed him. Fat chance. But he did exactly the same thing this week, so he did. Turned up here fresh from court on Monday, off his head on something, banging his front door so hard I could feel it through *my* walls. I think he was expecting a welcome home party. I was terrified, called the police before he banged down my door instead. The lad's not had it easy but I can't forgive him for doing the devil's work. He can burn as far as I'm concerned.'

She nodded after she said that, firmly, like she was drawing a big fat full stop with her forehead. Andy could sense his time was running out.

'Do you remember what the paramedics looked like? The ones who saved him?'

'Why? You going to have a word?'

'I might do, aye.'

201

'I'd like to give them a few words myself – and they wouldn't be pretty, that's for sure.' She shook her head, muttered something Andy couldn't hear. 'As for what they looked like? It was months ago now – before Christmas – but I remember they were both women, even though I could only see the arse of one of them, sticking out of the lift. She was on her knees, treating Alex, and the other one was wanting to give her a hand but the one in the lift lost the head, kept telling her she didn't need help. We all thought she was a bit rude. There were a few of us there, you see, being nosy buggers. Can barely wipe your arse in this building without someone watching and it's not every day someone tries to top themself in the lift.' She crossed herself again then moved to shut the door.

'Before you go . . .' Andy placed a hand on the door frame so she'd have to snap his fingers inside if she wanted to close it. 'Can you think of any other details about the paramedics? Like I said, it's not on record so—'

'Make-up.'

'Sorry?'

'The young one was wearing far too much make-up for a job like that. Had a tan as well but it might well have been one of those fake ones, you know? A wee bit orange to be real.'

She looked like she was going to say something else but instead she glanced over Andy's shoulder then quickly retreated into her flat, as if she'd seen someone or something in the corridor behind him. Andy followed her gaze but there was nobody there, no trace of any movement at all. The old lady's door clicked shut behind him.

Andy could have kicked himself. There was only one paramedic on their team who wore make-up and it was Vicky Steele. If he'd told Vicky the name of the patient he was looking for on the computer, he could have saved himself precious time and energy. She could have told him right away if Stef had been there too, saving the life of Alex Mitchell.

That would explain how and why and where their lives had connected.

But it still didn't make sense.

The office staff who created the rotas were often arseholes but nobody was stupid or cruel enough to make Stef and Vicky work together on the same ambulance. The two women had barely spoken since Andy and Vicky's notorious kiss last year.

He had no idea why they'd have been working together that night – or why there was no record of what had happened here. Paramedics tried to get a name and address for every patient they attended so that details of the incident could be added to their medical records. From time to time people would refuse to give details or abscond before they were taken. It was annoying but there was nothing they could do. But if the patient fled and paramedics believed they were at risk of harming themselves, or others, the police would be contacted and a search carried out before they left the scene.

Was that what had happened here? Had Alex Mitchell fled without giving his name?

Andy turned to the lift; silver, silent, sterile. For a few seconds he closed his eyes, pictured Stef kneeling over a bleeding man, doing whatever she could to save him. What was it she always said? *Keep the heid, stem the bleed.* This would be one of a dozen cases she'd attended that night and she'd had no reason to tell Andy about this particular patient. This wasn't a job you chatted about while you chopped sweet potatoes for your curry. They'd made an agreement years back that they'd avoid discussing the lives that passed through their hands. But this was different. He hoped Vicky would be willing and able to give him details of what had really happened that night.

Andy returned to his car, was about to call Vicky when his phone lit up and Sandy Hamilton's name appeared on the screen. 'Andy? You busy?'

'Kind of. I'm—'

'*Kind of* can wait,' he said. 'Get yourself to Green Den Studios, now.'

CHAPTER 26

Betty did a few slow laps of the streets closest to Stef and Andy's house then gave up and dumped her car at the soft-play centre. Hunger tugged her into a bakery and she grabbed a sandwich for lunch, ate it straight from the paper bag as she walked. Heavy grey clouds hung over the Portobello rooftops, sucked the light from a sky that rumbled louder than any stomach ever could.

She stood in a bus stop across the street before she approached Stef and Andy's house. One of the upstairs lights was on. Betty's heart lit up as well. Had Stef come home? Maybe. But it could just be that lamp in the upstairs landing that was always kept on a timer. It switched on for two hours at a time throughout the day so burglars might believe there was somebody inside and target their neighbour's house instead.

Betty had been warned from day one not to unplug it, had paid heed. She'd often imagined how good life would feel if a bright light was all that was needed to protect you from harm.

She'd come straight here from that outhouse.

A few flies had followed her to her car, buzzed around her head all the way, a noisier version of what was happening on the other side of her skin. Thoughts and theories flew in all directions, wouldn't settle. She wondered again about calling the police but resisted. She wasn't yet ready for uniforms or questions or the places they might lead.

She'd see if Andy was home, tell him instead.

He didn't like Richard Owens at the best of times, would hopefully share her concern once she told him about his odd behaviour at the outhouse – and the flies.

Betty crossed the road and stepped into the front garden, carefully picked her way past the outstretched branches of the rose bush by the front door. She rang the bell, winced at how loud it sounded. There was certainly no way someone inside could miss it.

But what if Stef *was* there but couldn't answer? Maybe she'd come home from the retreat and gone to bed, exhausted. She could be *feeling a bit delicate*, as Andy often said.

What harm would it do if she sneaked inside for a minute, just to check?

Betty rang the bell again then waited, counted to one minute by soundlessly turning a penny sixty times in her hand. It was also a good way to keep her fingers busy, to pretend they weren't trembling. But the façade fell when she fetched the spare keys from the hiding place then tried to unlock their door. She gripped them as tightly as she could but still kept missing the target, hitting the door instead of the shiny brass lock. Maybe it was fate, warning her to go home, to never again cross the threshold of this house. Usually when she stood on this doorstep Betty's chest felt like it was full of bubbles. But today they were heavy and menacing, as if they could burst any second and spray her insides with something that would sting even more than that stinking alcohol rub her mother used to dap on her cuts.

It'll make you stronger, her mum used to say, and Betty would obediently nod even though, back then, she really didn't understand how pain like that could make anything better.

Key in, door unlocked, handle turned.

She could tell right away there was nobody in the house. She'd worked as a cleaner for long enough to know that every home felt different when people were in it; even if they didn't make a single sound. It was something about the stillness of unbreathed air, the purity of it. But she went upstairs anyway, calling Stef's name as she went.

Nothing. Nobody.

She went back downstairs and washed the dried blood off her hands. The bleeding had mostly stopped but once the wound was clean, she could see the deep gash that broken window had left on her. It'd definitely leave a scar; another one.

She dried her hands on her jeans then switched on the little lamp on the sideboard, under the map, stared for a moment at the stilled faces of Stef and Andy in those holiday photos. They needed a good dusting, some of them, and a frame to stop the corners curling. Betty pulled a paper hankie from the box on the sideboard and gently rubbed the surface of the one photo they'd got framed; the two of them side by side in shorts and hiking boots, sitting on a black rock, sandwiches in their hands and smiles on their faces and woolly hats on their heads. They were outside that little stone-walled bothy Stef depicted so often in her paintings. Behind them was a peak, a ridge, and a woodland – the same scene painted on the card she'd found in Richard's office.

The majority of Stef's creations matched the landscape in that photo but she'd change the weather in each one, use sunlight and shadows to set the mood.

Stef had caught Betty staring at her paintings one day, asked her what she thought of them. Betty had said *unique* and Stef had laughed then explained that she painted the same scene over and over to prove nature is never stilled completely; that even things that appear static at first glance have ways of evolving, reinventing themselves. Life moves, she said, looking a bit wistful. Betty flushed, not really knowing what she meant; then plucked up the courage to ask.

'Basically, that's my favourite place,' Stef said. 'I feel closer to heaven up there.'

Betty then asked her if that meant she wanted to die in a place like that and Stef had flinched then looked at her with an expression she'd never seen before. She'd told Betty she'd never really thought about it and Betty blushed; pretended she hadn't either.

Andy had come in at that point, told Stef the robin was back and she'd leapt up and stared out of the window with a smile that was pure love and Betty wished she had wings too.

As it was, Betty just had hands and fingers, but she could do what she needed with them.

She cleaned the dust off Stef's face first, circling it with the tip of her finger until it shone again. She left Andy's as it was then sat down and waited.

She noticed the funny smell right away. Something rotting. She got up again and checked the bins then the floor, then the soles of her shoes in case she'd stepped on something dead or dying in the woods. All clean, all clear. It was only when she properly inspected the kitchen table that she noticed the festering contents of the fruit bowl; an orange with a green cap of mould on one side and a sticky puncture wound on the other. The plum beside it was now brown and mushy, along with a squashed, spotty banana at the very bottom. She hadn't noticed it when she'd cleaned the house yesterday but rot never took long to spread, did it? She pulled the bowl towards her and carried it to the sink. Food scraps went into the little grey bin beside the draining board. Betty tipped the rotting fruit into the bin then peeled a soggy takeaway menu from the base of the wooden bowl. According to Stef, Andy was forever shoving junk mail in there instead walking three more steps and placing it in the paper recycling bin outside. It's not exactly hard, is it? No, Stef, it is not.

Betty didn't need to be told twice.

She pinched the soggy menu between two fingers and headed for the back door, counting her steps as she went and concluding Stef's strides must be much longer than hers were even though they were more or less the same height. Outside, she lifted the bin lid with her free hand but when she let go of the menu it stayed where it was, glued to her fingers by the sticky juice of rotten fruit. She used her elbow to hold open the lid then peeled it off with both hands and dropped it on top of a greasy pizza box. Andy had clearly forgotten to leave the bin out for collection on Monday night.

She was about to close the lid when she noticed the sketches; a few scrunched-up pages of that thick white paper Stef used when she made rough drafts of her paintings.

Sometimes Stef would sit for hours at the bottom of the garden, partly hidden from view by trees and the shadows they cast. She'd often be surrounded by balls of paper, failed attempts at some new technique she'd learned in her lessons with Richard Owens. But failing didn't seem to bother or discourage her. She stuck at it, wouldn't come inside until she'd mastered it; done what she intended to do. Then the scraps would be scooped up and dumped in the recycling bin before she came into the kitchen, brandishing her latest creation. Betty would often see the rough drafts in there, squashed and soiled, when she was outside dumping old toilet rolls and badly folded newspapers and the cardboard sleeves of hummus. She'd often thought about taking a sly glance but never had, worried it could be perceived a betrayal of some kind, like reading someone's diary.

But sometimes that was the only way to find the truth.

Betty glanced over her shoulder, even though she knew she was alone, then reached into the bin.

The paper was thicker than the kind used for bills and official letters. It would tear less easily and give deeper cuts and when she ran the soft side of her finger along it the sound was louder than the usual whisper. One side was blank except for a smudge, a greasy mark from somebody else's finger or thumb. These were the lines she knew coated coins but couldn't usually be seen, unless the coin was just minted, still had that rare sheen that caught the eye from a distance, drew you in. She passed the soft part of her thumb over the smudge then turned over the crumpled piece of paper to see what lay on the other side.

The page was filled with a series of drawings locked inside boxes. They were drawn in blue pen, one that had spat out clots of ink that now clung like sticky little fruits to some of the lines. Whoever did the drawings would have a trace of blue on the side of their hand, colour dragged off the page and on to their skin before it dried.

But Betty cared less about that than the faces looking back at her from the page.

The artist had drawn nine boxes on the long side of the page and five running down the shorter side, forty-five in total. In each one the background was the same – the mountain landscape Stef had painted so many times before. But the dominant image in each box was Stef; stilled and staring at the viewer.

But Betty had never known her to paint self-portraits.

The artist had managed to capture perfectly the shape of her face; the way she held her head slightly to one side; her off-centre parting and those stray hairs that often fell over her eyes. Even on the page, they held Betty's attention and made the coldest parts of her shake themselves awake and wriggle into life.

It was only when Betty tore her eyes away from Stef's face that she noticed the differences between the first box and the last. Stef's expression didn't change much and neither did the backdrop. But little by little the artist had picked Stef's body apart, removed the tip of a finger from one hand then a nail from a toe in the next one. It went on and on until all that was left in the last drawing was Stef's head – but with no body beneath.

Her mouth was hanging open in the last few boxes, as if she wanted to speak. But even there, there was a growing absence; a gradual disappearing of her tongue until all that was left was a face with a deep, black empty hole in the middle of it. In the very last box the artist had stuffed something into her mouth. It looked like a rag at first, something to silence her. It was only when she held it up to the light that Betty realised the lines filling Stef's gaping mouth were actually letters, bent horribly out of shape. Four letters, one word.

Help.

CHAPTER 27

The windscreen of Andy's car was dotted with yellowing leaves from some unseen tree, held against the wet glass like X-rays stuck on a light box, their tiny skeletons and rotting edges exposed even though the sky was dull. He started the engine and the wipers shuddered into action, swept them out of view as he sped away from Hartfield Court, towards Green Den.

Sandy's call had been innocent enough, on the surface.

He wanted Andy to know there was a heavy police presence at the studio – and that the police press office had issued a statement saying they were trying to contact all artists who regularly worked there. He advised Andy call the police to let them know Stef was at a retreat and that's why she wouldn't be responding to their calls. *So they know she's safe,* said Sandy, and Andy said nothing but ended the call before grief snatched his voice from him.

He called Vicky after that, chest prickling with irritation when she didn't pick up right away. That woman was never more than two inches from her phone and never ever set it to silent. She'd be waging some pathetic digital war to show who was in charge. When she finally answered she used a voice that made her sound surprised, as if the call didn't come in with his name on the screen.

'Andy? Where are you? And what happened with that awful policewoman? I've been worried.'

'I'll explain another time,' he said. 'Right now, I need you to answer a simple question. Did you and Stef work together during her final week? Just before Christmas?'

'Doubt it. I don't think we've worked a shift together since *you know what*. Nobody wants a cat fight on an ambulance. But why can't you ask Stef?'

Vicky was clicking her tongue.

'Apparently Stef went off the head at you while she was treating him?'

'Oh, shit. Yes. *That* night. Someone called in sick and Stef was covering for them so we were forced to work together. How could I forget? Blocked it out, probably. No offence, but she was totally unprofessional, speaking to me like that in front of all a patient.

And his neighbours. But you're right, she got signed off a few days later, didn't she?'

'Aye.'

'I've always felt a bit guilty about that, to be honest. Can't help feeling *we* were partly responsible for her stress. It couldn't have been easy for her, bumping into me every single day at the station after what happened between me and you.'

Andy gritted his teeth. 'You mind if we talk about the patient?'

'What about him?'

'There's no record of it, Vicky. That's what I was looking for at the station.'

'Och, Andy, you numpty. That's because he legged it before we got his name and home address. He'd done a pretty decent job, almost cut deep enough to do the job. Stef took the lead but she seemed distracted, took forever to get him cleaned up. I offered to help and was told where to go. Meanwhile the man was getting more and more agitated, told her to leave him alone, let him die, all the usual stuff they don't really mean. But then he pushed Stef and when we tried to calm him down he fled. We informed the police, as per protocol, but he was long gone. The job was automatically logged – but without his name and address as we couldn't assume those flats were his home. But that explains why your search didn't work. If you'd searched *job location* on its own, you'd have found a file relating to that case and all the other jobs we've done at that skyrise over the years. But if you searched the location *and* that patient's name together the search would come back blank. I wish you'd just asked me. You've gone and got yourself a disciplinary meeting over nothing. Bert thinks you'll be suspended.'

'You're kidding.'

'He hasn't called you?'

'No, he bloody well hasn't. Jesus Christ. And what about you?'

'Scolded but saved, for now.' Vicky sighed. 'What's all of this about anyway? Why the sudden interest in a runaway patient from six months ago?'

'You don't know what happened, do you? You don't know who he is?'

'No. Do you?'

'His name's Alex Mitchell. Ex-con with a long history of assault charges, now linked to the disappearance of a pensioner called Maureen Aitken.'

'So we saved a criminal? Sure, it wouldn't be the first time,' said Vicky. 'And strictly speaking, Stef saved him. Is that why you're worried?'

'Who said I'm worried?'

'Andy, I know you. Something's going on. It's fine if you don't want to tell me but please – ask for help if you need it. As a pal. I promise there's not a single string attached. OK?'

Andy sighed. 'There is something, actually. Would you be able to go to my house, check something? I can tell you where we keep the spare key.'

'Not sure Stef will approve of that.'

'She's . . . not there.'

'In that case, I'm all yours.'

He'd just turned into the driveway of Green Den Studios when they finally hung up. After much humming and hawing and another lecture about Andy being a jealous husband, Vicky had agreed to go to his house later and let herself in using the spare key. She'd then check the *Recent Calls* list on Stef's mobile phone and tell Andy what numbers had been dialled on Monday. She'd not been happy about it, warned him this was the last favour.

It was a risk, sending somebody else. Especially someone with a gob as big as Vicky's – but he needed to know for sure if Farida's claims were true; that Stef had phoned Alex Mitchell's flat hours after his release on Monday afternoon – hours before she'd left their home for the very last time. And only once he'd established that fact beyond all doubt would he start asking why.

Right now, he had enough to think about.

The old Volvo groaned as he belted over potholes but he kept his foot down as he powered between the trees towards the old barn that Richard Owens had converted into a complex of art studios. Ideas above his station, that one.

Richard Owens was absolutely convinced he was a genius, was forever coming up with absurd installations and exhibitions that he'd describe as cutting-edge, though the handful of people who visited were usually family and despite that, rarely agreed.

For his last exhibition he'd dumped an old-fashioned computer printer in an empty room then built a tower of scaffolding around it. Apparently it was social commentary of some sort, but Andy hadn't felt remotely moved by it. Stef had loved it, jumped to Richard's defence the moment Andy dared criticise him. But why did she get art lessons from a man who didn't even paint much these days? More talent, less ego, that's what made a good teacher. Needless to say, Stef had tutted loudly when he said that, then booked her next lesson regardless. Andy hated the thought of Richard leaning over her, placing his fingers on the slender handle of her brush, gently steadying her hand.

He was such a pretentious twat.

But he wasn't any more harmful than that, was he?

Andy saw the pulse of blue lights, got the feeling he was about to find out.

CHAPTER 28

The first thing Betty did after finding the *help* note was fold it up and slip it into her pocket.

She didn't believe in coincidences. She'd found the sketch because it was *meant* for her and Andy had chosen her for the cleaning job because it was what Fate wanted. It was the same power that drove Finders towards her lucky coins, but now it was helping Betty instead.

After that she went to the utility room and took Stef's red running jacket off the hook. It hadn't been moved since yesterday, but Stef's phone had. The pocket were empty and the jacket weighed almost nothing. Betty clutched it close, a child with a blanket.

But it offered no comfort to anyone.

If Stef's phone wasn't here, where was it? And in whose hands?

She pulled out her mobile, scrolled to Stef's number then held her hand over the call button, hesitant.

If Stef answered she'd be relieved and say she was calling about Tuesday's missing payment. But what would she say if somebody else picked up? The best thing was nothing at all. She'd stay completely quiet, as if she'd rolled on to her phone when she was napping. She pressed the call button then closed her eyes and waited, waited, waited.

No answer. And silence in the house.

Yesterday she'd heard the phone vibrating when she called, noticed the glow of the screen through the lightweight material of Stef's running jacket. She redialled, scanning the room for a screen, lit up. Nothing. When the call switched to voicemail she hung up before the beep then tried again, moving from room to room then heading upstairs.

An unused metal coat-hanger rattled against the door of the master bedroom when Betty pushed it open, peered in. Even though it was early afternoon and would be eternally embarrassing, a tiny part of Betty had hoped she'd find Stef and Andy there, wrapped up in each other and their sheets. But the covers were flat, the bed empty.

Her steps softened when she stepped inside, a hangover from the days she'd sneak into her mum's room to swipe the coins left in the pockets of her unwashed clothes.

Stef and Andy's bedroom had white walls and a big window, was bright despite the grey skies outside. One of wardrobe doors was wide open and Betty recognised some of Stef's favourite clothes, knew they'd fit her too if she sucked in her tummy. But some shoes were missing from the rack beneath and the gaps reminded Betty of the painting from the bin; Stef's body stripped of fingers and toes; her head without a neck and her mouth stretched around that word. *Help*.

She shut the wardrobe door and dialled Stef's number, again.

Plastic vibrated on glass and Betty saw right away that Stef's phone was on the dressing table, sitting between her hairbrush and hand cream and that little black-and-white photo of her mother. Her brain jammed, couldn't decide which label to stick on that fact. Was this good news or bad? Did it mean Stef had been home, moved it here herself?

Betty silenced the call; then froze.

Footsteps crunched on the gravel outside.

She inched towards the window then peered around the edge of the thick velvet curtains. A woman wearing heeled leopard-skin boots was standing in the garden, staring at the unvarnished wooden shelves where Stef kept dozens of unused plant pots, stacked by size. She picked one off the top shelf, tipped it upside down then shook it. A few crisp, curled leaves fell out. She put back the pot and checked the next one, and the next.

She'd be looking for the spare keys, the ones in Betty's pocket.

But had Betty locked the back door when she came inside from the paper recycling bin? She couldn't remember, but doubted it. She liked to know she had an easy escape route. As Betty's pulse and mind raced a blackbird perched on the windowsill and started singing cheerfully, as if God had mixed up the soundtrack of that moment with another.

If the woman in the garden was looking for the keys that meant she was hoping to come inside and if she did that meant she'd find Betty here, in Stef and Andy's bedroom. Betty would lose their trust and her job and the chance to right her wrongs.

She had to leave, now.

Betty chose speed over silence, bounded down the stairs then slipped out the front door – it opened and closed with the flick of a Yale lock – and hurried to her car. She was still holding Stef's red running jacket, and another souvenir she'd swiped from their room. A children's rhyme filled her head as she ran and she hoped that this one wasn't true; that the words weren't some kind of bitter premonition.

Finders keepers; losers weepers.

CHAPTER 29

Andy pulled into the car park at Green Den Studios, was waved to a stop by a police officer wearing a uniform two sizes too big. He lowered his window, leaned out. 'What's going on?'

'Police incident.'

'I guessed that much,' said Andy, nodding to the police tape strung between two fence posts, closing off the car park entrance. 'My wife paints here. I really need to get through.'

'What's her name?'

'Stef,' he said. 'Stef Campbell.'

The officer looked at him, chewing her bottom lip. 'Give me a minute,' she said, then turned and walked towards a patrol car. Andy parked up and got out, straining to see what was happening closer to the studio. He could see two police officers standing in front of the main door. One of them was taking notes as he chatted to grey-haired woman Andy recognised from

Stef's exhibition just before Christmas. Ellie, her name was. She'd been friendly to him at the exhibition but had given him daggers every time they'd met since – why, he did not know and Stef said he was imagining it. Maybe she was born sour-faced. But either way, he'd try speaking to her, see if she knew what was happening.

Some bedraggled news reporters were nearby. He couldn't see Sandy Hamilton but he knew a few other journalists who'd tried to get some background on patients for their crime stories, recognised one of the older men. Big Stevie, they called him, a proper wizened hack from one of the nationals.

He only came to good ones; when good meant bad.

Stevie was staring at the sky, smoking, and beside him a girl from the TV was staring at her mobile phone with a deliberately serious face, determined to look like she was working. She was probably checking Facebook. He was scouring the other faces when a police van pulled up behind him and honked its horn. He edged forward and let it through, only noticed the writing once it had passed him. *Forensics*.

He'd waited long enough. Andy ducked under the police tape, was heading for the main door when it was pushed open by two men in police uniform. They turned to their right and it was only then that Andy noticed a few more officers standing in the woods.

What was going on here?

His insides burned as he ran towards the woods, slipping between trees before the officers could see and stop him. He slowed to a walk once he was surrounded by that moist gloom that was so familiar to him, usually such a source of comfort. He could hear the buzz of a radio up ahead so worked his way towards it, gently pushing long spindly branches out of his path. He stopped when he saw the outhouse, squat and stone and guarded by Farida McPherson. She was on her own and for once looked flustered; was waving her arms in the air, batting away shifting clouds of flies that ducked and dived and buzzed around her head. Andy couldn't see anything beyond the open door behind her but even from where he stood, he could smell *that* smell.

Blood. It permeated the air, nippy as chopped onions, rancid as pissed-in pants, unmistakable as garlic. He stepped out of the woods. 'What the hell's happened here?'

Farida flinched when she saw him.

'You shouldn't be here,' she said, at the precise moment a man in uniform burst out of the door, gagging, then vomited at her feet. Farida took a tiny sidestep, handed the officer a paper hankie from a new plastic pack then instructed him to escort Andy to a patrol car.

He was led through the woods and into the car park, past the branches that had scratched his arms on the way past. Now, they parted, let him pass – but the press pack had their claws out instead. Andy spotted Ellie there as well, clutching her mobile phone to her chest like a crucifix. Cameras clicked, the sound of a catwalk in a muddy car park. A few of them shouted questions, called him by name. They knew him, wanted to watch a hero fall. And the fact he was being dragged out of the woods by police meant they'd assume that whatever had happened in that wee stone outhouse was linked to him. And it wasn't, was it?

Right now, he wasn't sure he could answer his own question.

Next thing he knew a damp hand shoved his head downwards and he was being pushed into the back of a patrol car, door slammed behind him before he had time to react. A meathead in uniform sat in the driver's seat, ignoring Andy's protests as thunder rumbled overhead, the starting gun for a proper summer storm. Rain hammered the metal roof, drops so big and fat they sounded like hailstones.

Andy pulled out his phone, was texting Sandy for more information when the press pack shifted suddenly, swarmed the main door of the studio like a crowd at a festival, surging forward when the main act hits the stage. He persuaded the officer to open the window an inch to stop it steaming up. In reality, he wanted to hear better. The lassie from the TV was perfecting her serious face and some guy from the radio was holding a furry microphone in one hand and jabbing a cable into a digital recorder with the other.

And then she came.

There was an immediate hush when Farida walked out of the woods towards the front door of the studio, calm and controlled as ever despite the sudden wild weather. She batted away impatient questions and a few fat bluebottles that had followed her from the woods. Hers was instant, effortless authority.

Reporters dumped umbrellas and flicked to a fresh page in their pads; the TV girl side-stepped so the cameraman could capture Farida, and the radio boy was kneeling on the ground in front of everyone else, angling his oversized microphone towards her.

'You don't waste your time, you lot,' she said. She looked in Andy's direction. It was like that game he used to play with his wee sister, staring at each other until one of them blinked. But Farida McPherson must be the national bloody champion. A few of the press pack turned their heads, anxious to see what or who had caught her attention. That was exactly what he didn't want.

Farida's eyes were like a spotlight, singling him out, stripping him bare. She could probably smell the dread that crept from his belly to his throat when he finally managed to translate the expression on her face. *Pity.* He blinked. Game over.

She gave him the faintest of nods, then turned her attention to the journalists.

'Earlier today we received a call from an artist at Green Den Studios, in relation to a derelict property in the grounds, a short distance from the main building.' When Farida paused for breath Ellie took a tiny step forward, arm held across her body like a shield, mouth flapping open and closed like she was psyching herself up to make a speech. The officer to her right tugged her sleeve then pulled her into the crowd, shaking his head. Nobody spoke over Farida. 'Investigations are ongoing and we'll issue a statement later. In the meantime all enquiries should go via the press office.'

That's it?

That was it.

She batted away a fly that was making loops in the air, swooping at her hair. 'Questions?'

'Aye.' All eyes shifted to Big Stevie. He always had a fag on his lips and a question on his tongue. 'What are the flies like on the inside?'

'I'd prefer *relevant* questions,' she said, scanning the press pack. 'Anyone?'

'It's just . . . I heard there's evidence of human remains. Can you confirm that?'

'What do you think?'

It took Andy a moment to register what they'd said. His blood started churning faster, getting hotter, stinging his veins. Big Stevie stepped forward, fag clamped between his lips. 'I think you're good at not answering questions.'

'I think you're bad at asking them.'

Cue a few whispered howls, some quickly silenced sniggers, and all eyes still on Stevie. He took a few puffs of his fag then tossed it on the ground, stubbed it out with an unpolished shoe. 'Eighty quid fine if you leave the stub there, pal,' said Farida, then turned and went inside. The click of the door was a muted starter's gun.

Shoulders relaxed, phones were pulled out of pockets, cameramen and photographers stooped over their viewfinders to revise what they'd captured. Big Stevie snuck away before anybody could take the piss, headed towards his car with a phone to his ear. A few optimistic reporters lingered, seemingly oblivious to the downpour.

Andy was staring at them out of a rain-streaked window when Farida opened the driver's door, told the meathead he could leave. She buckled her seat-belt before she twisted around in her seat and looked at Andy. 'We need to talk,' she said, then started the engine. 'At the station.'

CHAPTER 30

*S*tef closed the front door behind her and immediately felt the tension loosen. She'd been scheduled to take a few more days off to support Andy during his compassionate leave but she'd called Amechi when Andy was in the shower the previous night, arranged to swap shifts. Officially, all rota changes were meant to be arranged by email via the workforce planning team but in reality paramedics at the same station often organised it themselves using a text message and the promise of a pint. Amechi had transferred from one of the Glasgow stations a few months back, was keen to make friends and prove he was one of the team. That was why Stef knew he'd accept her request at such short notice.

He'd hesitated when Stef asked him the second part of the favour – to tell anyone who asked that he'd been the one who asked for a rota change. Not her. She couldn't have Andy knowing that she wanted to work, to get away from him. He had no idea what her

236

world had really become while his eyes were locked on another woman's arse.

Vicky Steele was the least of her worries.

Stef zipped up her coat, cursing the endless winter chill, then paused for a moment to inspect the rose bushes that lined their garden path, stretching up from a little square of soil that was hemmed in with concrete slabs. She'd often wondered where roses grew naturally, in the wild, but had never remembered to look it up and had only ever known them like these ones, tied to canes with green twine and fed with chemicals and clipped when they grew too tall. A thorn clawed at her jacket just before she reached the gate, forced her to retreat a few steps. On other days she might have read it as a sign that she should stay at home, be with Andy, put him first. But not today.

Instead she tutted, tugged it, then headed for her car.

When she reached the station she saw Bert standing outside fire escape next to a bin stuffed with scrappy pieces of tinsel thrown out when they hung this year's decorations. He was talking on his mobile phone but he waved then signalled for her to go over once she'd parked.

Once she switched off the engine she fumbled around in the glove box as if she were looking for something, hoping an emergency would force Bert inside before they had time to chat. No such luck.

He nodded to her as she approached. 'Didn't expect to see you here today.'

'I swapped.'

'With?'

'Amechi. A favour.' She hoped she could explain the deal without directly lying. It was exhausting, always watching what she said. 'Just today.'

Bert clicked his tongue. 'Not very considerate of him.'

'I'm fine.'

'You know it's Vicky you're working with?'

'I'll cope.'

'And Andy? How he's doing after the funeral?'

'A few more days and he'll be fine too,' she said, then deliberately looked at her watch. 'I should get going. If I don't get a cup of tea before my shift I'll be no good to anybody. God knows why I thought it would be a good idea to drink whisky last night.'

Bert smiled, exposed rot wrapped in pink. 'About that.'

She'd started to move away but then stopped, turned. 'About what?'

'There's been another complaint, Stef.' Bert sighed after he said it, moved his eyes away from hers. 'Or *maybe I should rephrase that. Another colleague has raised concerns about your conduct.'*

Her insides shrank. 'What's been said this time?'

Bert lowered his head and scratched the tiny space between his unclipped eyebrows. 'A staff member contacted me the other day, made some pretty serious claims. They said you seemed drunk on the job.'

'Drunk? Please tell me you're kidding.' She stepped back, stumbled a little as fury filled her veins instead of blood. Or shame. Maybe both. 'And you believed them?'

'I'm obliged to look into it.'

'So you don't trust me now, is that it?'

'This isn't about trust.'

'Then what's it about?'

'Patient safety. And concerns for your . . . mental health.'

'You're kidding.'

'I'm not. You and Andy have had a hard time of it these past few months, what with his mother being so unwell and . . . well . . . what happened at the Halloween party. I feel for you, Stef, coming in to work, knowing Vicky Steele will be here as well. It's not a surprise that you're struggling but you can't look after other folk if you don't look after yourself,

can you? And believe you me, I'm speaking from personal experience. The fact is I need to take all complaints and concerns seriously and I suggest you do too.' He studied the scuffs on his shoes before he spoke again. 'The staff member claimed you were unsteady on your feet and that your speech was slightly slurred. The Stef I employed twenty years ago wouldn't be seen dead in public in that condition – and she certainly wouldn't be driving one of my ambulances.'

'I've never had a drop of alcohol at work. Come on, Bert. You know me.'

'Aye, and I know you like a drink.'

'I do. Same as all of us. But that's not the same as drinking on the job.'

'I'm glad we agree on something.'

'Who made the complaint?

'That's irrelevant.'

'For you, maybe.' Rage made Stef's cheeks flush and she cursed her body for exposing the parts of herself that she'd much rather hide. 'So what happens now?'

'Once I log the complaint online it's out of my hands. The regional managers will get involved and you'll be called to a disciplinary hearing. You might be suspended at that stage, or struck off the register.

Health professionals cannot be drunk at work, full stop. But we've been working together a long time, Stef, and we all know you're under pressure. I'm risking my own job here to save yours. But here's the deal. If you agree to take some time off I won't start formal proceedings. Go to your GP first thing tomorrow and get a sick line. You need time off to sort out your head, and your marriage. It's too late to cover this week's shifts, especially with Andy on compassionate leave – but as of this weekend you've to stay away from the station, and that's an order. We can sort the paperwork later.'

Stef nodded then went inside, ignored Bert's half-hearted attempts to call her back.

When she reached the mess she flipped on the kettle and when steam wafted out of the spout she leaned into the cloud, let the heat of it sting eyes until they watered.

At least she could use that as an excuse.

She was still standing there when Vicky Steele burst into the mess, carrying an illuminated tabletop Christmas tree and a takeaway coffee and filling the room with the reek of that fruity perfume she often wore. Andy used to joke it was like working beside a ripe mango and Stef had found herself searching for that scent on him ever since his grand confession after the Halloween party. Still, he swore he preferred the smell of Stef – mud and turps and dried sweat on second-day running clothes. I'd bottle you if I could, he'd often told her, and they'd laugh at the image of him as a crazy old man in a care home, grasping a corked bottle marked Stef, *holding it to his nose and breathing her in.*

Across the table Vicky Steele blew on her coffee, took a tiny sip, winced as she swallowed. 'Damn stuff always smells better than it really is,' she said, then winked at Stef and tossed her cup into the bin.

CHAPTER 31

Andy pulled his hands out of his pockets and squeezed the polystyrene cup, but felt no comfort from the warmth of it. The surface rippled, coffee lapping higher the longer he held it. He looked up, found Farida's eyes.

'Before I tell you any details about our . . . findings near the studio, I'm going to ask you exactly the same thing I've asked you before. Where is Stef?'

'How many times do I have to tell you? She's at—'

'An art retreat, up north. No signal, no phone, no address. Correct?'

'Aye.' Andy sighed, cupped his nose and mouth inside his hands. They smelled unfamiliar. Police station soap. It smelled like those bars in cheap hotels that disintegrate after five minutes; cheap fat and chemical lemons and soggy cardboard. 'Stef left for a retreat on Monday evening and I've haven't seen or heard from her since. And before you ask me for the tenth time – no, I don't know exactly where the retreat is located. Now, will you just tell me what you found? I've been in my job enough years to recognise the reek of blood wafting out of that place. Please tell me it's got nothing to do with Stef.'

'Funny, I was just going to ask you the same thing,' she said.

Andy felt sick, suddenly missed Stef. He screwed up his eyes, pictured a world without their kitchen table or the place mats they'd got as a wedding gift and never liked but never changed; without Stef's mother's old teapot or the tray bakes they sometimes made on rainy weekends. But that wasn't his future now, was it? If he told Farida the truth, he'd spend years eating meals of someone else's choosing, from a plate he didn't own, with forks and spoons that had been inside a hundred different mouths before his. And it wouldn't just be him who was locked up, would it?

He had to get out of here as quickly as possible – and he had to call Alyson, regardless of what they'd agreed. An officer had taken his mobile phone when he arrived – standard procedure, said Farida. *Standard my arse*. Maybe it was a way to make sure he didn't leg it. But whatever the reason, he hoped they didn't check his messages. Alyson would have sent him the signal by now. *Surely.*

'Investigations are ongoing,' said Farida. 'But I'll share the few facts we've been able to establish so far. A call came in around one o' clock today from one of the artists who works at the studio. She'd gone for a walk in the woods when she became aware of a large number of flies close to one of the outhouses on the Green Den estate. She called the police and officers tried to gain access to the building without success before attempting to contact the owner, a Mr . . .' She glanced at her notes. 'Mr Richard Owens. When we—'

'*Richard* is behind this?'

'You know him?'

'He was Stef's art teacher.'

For a moment Farida was completely still. '*Was*, or *is*?'

'Is.' He stared at her, fury like a stinking smoke bomb spreading into every part of him. Farida turned back to her notes, continued where she'd left off.

'When we failed to make contact with Mr Owens, officers forced entry to the outhouse but were initially hindered due to problems created by the large infestation of insects.'

'The flies?'

'Correct.' Farida tried to contain a shudder but it slipped out, the faintest of tremors in her shoulders. If she'd been in that building for long, they'd have been crawling all over her.

'And what about the human remains that Big Stevie mention at the press conference?'

Farida clasped her hands on the table in front of her, leaned forward.

'Forensic investigations are ongoing but officers attending the scene observed a large number of flies swarming out of the outhouse via a broken window and noted they were drawn to another area of woodland close to the building. When they investigated it quickly became obvious they were dealing with a crime scene. The flies had acted like a beacon, drawing them towards a shallow grave and the remains it held.'

'Human?'

Farida nodded, Andy ached.

'Is it Stef?'

'I'm unable to comment any further,' she said, 'I'm sure you appreciate our investigations are at a very early stage.'

Andy exhaled, hoped tears would soothe the burning in him. 'Please,' he said, desperate for Farida to remove the possibility that Stef's body had been found there, flies sucking on the scraps of her. Instead, she changed the subject.

'Samples of the remains have been taken to the lab for analysis and I'll keep you informed,' she said. 'But in fact we believe the flies originated within the building, drawn primarily to two key . . . *substances*.'

'What kind of substances?'

'Blood,' she said. 'And semen.'

Another bomb exploded in Andy's chest, blew his voice to pieces. His head started shaking of its own accord. His hands followed moments later and when he reached for the flimsy vending machine cup, it spilled, shot pools of burning coffee right across the table. Both of them leapt up and stepped back, watched as steaming brown liquid reached the chipped edges and started dripping down on to the floor. Andy's chair toppled over. He was bending down to pick it up when Farida spoke again, looking down at him from the other side of the room.

'I brought you here because we found something else in the outhouse that is causing me great concern, especially in light of our recent conversations. There are paintings, Andy. Of Stef.'

Andy righted the chair, leaned on it as he slowly pulled himself up. 'What kind of paintings?'

'Portraits.'

'Plural?'

'Dozens of them.'

'And all of Stef?'

Farida nodded. 'Most of them appeared to be unfinished.'

'What do you mean *appeared*?'

'The flies have caused extensive damage to the canvases so it's difficult to make out all the details. But I've crossed paths with Stef often enough to know it's her face in the painting. And given her connection to Green Den Studios it makes—'

'Sense? I don't bloody think so.' Andy's jaw tightened. 'Why would some paint my wife *dozens* of times then dump the canvases in a stinking outhouse? Who would do that?'

Farida's face was still, gave nothing away. 'Officers are working hard to establish the identity of the artist. We're currently interviewing all members of the studio to establish which of them, if any, stores their work in the outhouses. Do you know if Stef does?'

Andy shook his head. 'I sincerely doubt it. She either leaves it inside the studio – they all have their own locker – or she brings it home. No artist in their right mind would leave their work in a damp outhouse if they really cared about it. But my money says this will be something to do with Richard Owens. It *must* be.'

Farida cleared her throat. 'We hope to confirm that as soon as we locate him,' she said. 'In the meantime, are you able to confirm the nature of their relationship?'

Andy dropped his head. He didn't want to admit this to Farida; didn't want to say out loud what he'd heard for so many months, as if that would somehow make it true.

Life hurt more on this side of the game, didn't it?

'There have been rumours,' he said. 'Stef said it was nonsense and I chose to believe her. But there's no doubt in my mind that he'd jump at the chance.'

'To be clear, your wife denies any suggestion of—?'

'An affair? Aye. Categorically denied.'

Farida wrote something in her notepad then turned the page and kept writing. For a few moments the only sound in the room was the scratch of pen on paper and the ticking of the wall clock. Andy watched the little red hand spinning smoothly around the dial as if this were a normal day, same as any other. 'How long will it take to get lab results?'

'It varies. But I'll advise you when we do.'

'So what now?'

'Now I'd suggest you have a long, hard think about how to contact your wife – and call me the moment you get hold of her.'

'You think something bad has happened to her, don't you?'

'What I *think* is irrelevant,' she said. 'I work only with facts.'

'So that means yes.'

'It means speculation has no place in a police investigation.' She pulled her chair away from the puddle of coffee, placed it directly between Andy and the door, then sat down, legs wide, elbows firmly planted on her knees. 'But I'll let you in on a secret, Andy – I trust my feelings. And right now I get the distinct impression you're keeping something from me. I don't know what and I don't know why, but I definitely sense it.'

She sniffed after she said that, as if the sweat seeping out of him held the scent of Stef's body. It was impossible to think of where she was now, of death holding her instead of him. Andy opened his mouth to speak but Farida held up a hand to silence him. 'But you can rest assured that wherever she is, Andy, we *will* find her – whether you want us to or not.'

'And what's that supposed to mean?'

'It means exactly what I said.'

'I want the best for my wife.'

'*Best* is a relative word, don't you think?'

Andy didn't answer, couldn't. She held his gaze for a few moments then stood up, headed for the door.

'Farida?'

She turned, still gripping the door handle.

'There's something else. I found . . . a connection,' he said. 'Between Stef and Alex Mitchell.'

'Go on.'

'Stef saved his life. He'd slit his wrists.'

She let go of the handle, faced him. 'Why didn't you tell me this earlier?'

'I've only just found out,' he said. 'I didn't find any record of it at the station because I'm crap with computers and was searching for the wrong thing. Alex Mitchell fled the scene before they'd taken his name but one of his neighbours told me what happened and the other paramedic working that shift confirmed it. He tried to kill himself just before he attacked that pub landlady but as we know, Maureen Aitken disappeared around the same time. Maybe guilt drove him to it? Maybe he killed her then tried to kill himself.'

'And you're *sure* it was Stef who saved him?'

Andy nodded.

Farida stared at him, unblinking. 'Tell me, have you read the papers this week?'

'I avoid them. Why?'

'Wait here,' she said, then left, shutting the door behind her. Andy heard footsteps in the corridor and words spoken too quietly for him to understand. He heard a door open and a blend of noises seep out; laughter, the beep of a microwave, the clink of mugs in a sink. The soundtrack of a staffroom, same ones he immersed himself in at the ambulance station mess. Or used to. He'd been hoping he could persuade Bert to reconsider his disciplinary hearing but if those photos from Green Den Studios ended up on the front page he'd be done for, good and proper.

Off-Duty Paramedic Dragged From Murder Scene.
Calm down, Andy. Nobody's mentioned murder, yet.

The word was still on his mind when Farida came into the room holding a dog-eared newspaper, rolled up like she was going to swat a fly with it. His remembered those swarming black clouds around the outhouse, the reek of blood in the air; he imagined Stef's portraits in the gloom, every inch of canvas covered in those shifting, shiny bodies.

Farida slowly unrolled the paper and started flicking through it, fingers pinching the tops of each page. It was the same newspaper that Sandy wrote for, he saw. From where he was standing Andy could see the sports pages and a front-page headline about some counsellor caught in a sex scandal. The usual. When Farida handed him the paper their fingers touched, just for a moment. Andy flinched. 'Sorry for this,' she said, then let the paper go. But it was only when he started reading the article that he realised what her apology was really for. It was a court story, telling the tale of Alex Mitchell walking free on Monday. There was nothing new there, nothing that shocked him. But then Farida pointed to the final few paragraphs, a bit of colour from the reporter, depicting the scene outside the courthouse once the trial was over.

Alex Mitchell, walking out of court; a free man. Alex Mitchell, lighting a cigarette in cupped hands then turning to face the small crowd that had gathered on the pavement. Then a screech from a tanned woman who was pushing strangers aside, steaming towards him, insisting he was a useless, murdering bastard who'd killed her poor mother, Maureen Aitken.

And Alex Mitchell, riled, adamant that *he* wasn't to blame for any of this. Alex Mitchell, desperately searching the crowd until he found the face he was looking for, then pointed at it.

Alex Mitchell, saying Maureen Aitken would still be alive if it wasn't for *that bitch*; the one who hadn't listened to him; the one who'd taken away his choice; the one who'd saved his life against his will.

Andy read those last paragraphs numerous times, trying to make sense of them. In trying to defend himself Alex Mitchell had accidentally linked himself to the disappearance and death of Maureen Aitken. Andy already knew Stef had saved his life around the time she went missing – but now he could see that the order of events was the opposite of what he had assumed.

Alex hadn't tried to kill himself because he felt guilty about killing Maureen Aitken. He'd tried to kill himself to stop himself from doing it.

'Stef saved Alex's life *before* Maureen Aitken went missing?'

'It would appear so,' said Farida, and Andy's heart felt ready to explode. If Alex Mitchell had killed an innocent old woman then hidden her body – what would he do to the woman he blamed for his crime?

CHAPTER 32

The police officer didn't look at Andy when she handed over his phone. He wondered if this was the only job they gave her, if she spent her days stripping folk of coins and iPhones and scrunched-up hankies and chewing gum, all the things they carried that linked them to the life they might never live again.

She glanced at Andy then tapped a blank space at the bottom of a form. Her fingernails were painted a shimmering pale pink colour and he pictured her at some posh beauty salon, telling tales of the scum she dealt with at work. Andy leaned in and signed the page, wondered what life she invented for him when she looked at his hands.

He had the urge to set her straight, tell her *some* folk thought he was a hero.

Apparent strangers would tap him on the shoulder in the bagel shop or gently tug his sleeve when he strolling along Portobello Promenade on a day off. They all had different faces but their expression was the same: a mixture of awe and shyness, like they were meeting someone famous. Whatever words they actually said, the meaning was the same.

You saved me.

What would they say if they saw him now? If they knew the truth about him and Alyson?

He signed and pushed the form and pen towards the officer. She filed it then pulled out a packet of disinfectant wipes, wiped her hands clean; as if she couldn't bear to touch what he'd touched.

'Want one?'

Andy spread his fingers into stars, stared at them. Paramedic hands were scrubbed and disinfected and at the end of every job. But the filth on him went deeper than that, didn't it?

He shook his head, picked up his phone, and left.

He'd expected to have messages from Vicky and from Alyson when he checked his phone but there was nothing from either. He checked the time, felt sick. Vicky should have found the spare house key and checked Stef's phone by now. And why the silence from Alyson? If the day was unfolding as planned then she would contact him soon, tell him it was done; over. Mission complete, and just like that his world would change shape; be ripped into a Before and an After. Then Alyson would call the police, officially report what she'd found.

Stef, a what instead of a who.

But what about the where? The discoveries at the Green Den outhouse had thrown his mind off course, created the possibility that Stef, somehow, was not in the place they'd planned.

Andy's hands were trembling as he scrolled through his phone, desperate for distraction.

First of all he needed to collect his car from Green Den. He'd refused the offer of a ride from Farida, didn't want to extend the conversation with her or spend any more time inside a police car.

He hailed a taxi to take him to the studio, called Sandy on the way. He wanted to speak to the reporter who'd covered Alex Mitchell's trial on Monday; needed to know who Alex had seen in the crowd waiting outside court; the person he blamed for his crime.

If Stef had gone to Alex's trial she'd not mentioned it to Andy.

She'd gone out for a few hours on Monday morning, dressed in her running gear; told him she'd gone to the beach for a jog. But could she have used her clothes as a decoy and gone to court instead? It was possible. And that meant it was possible Alex Mitchell *was* looking at Stef when he batted back the murder accusations from Maureen's family and blamed *that bitch* for his crimes.

'That's why I need to speak to the court reporter at your paper,' he said, and Sandy repeated his line about liking long shots, said this one would break all records. But aye, he'd help. For Stef.

The taxi dropped Andy at the Green Den car park. Police officers chatted and checked their phones behind strips of flapping plastic tape but Andy kept his eyes down, climbed into Stef's old Volvo and left before anyone recognised him or started asking questions.

When he reached the newspaper office he parked at the main entrance then walked around the building until he reached the makeshift smoking shelter at the back. Sandy was waiting for him there. He flipped a half-smoked cigarette into a puddle then kicked away the stone holding open the fire door.

'Follow me,' he said, then disappeared inside.

Andy was shocked for a moment by the roar and rattle of the printing press; the whirr of the conveyer belts and the thud when a bound stack of newly printed papers landed in the back of an awaiting van. Thousands of words and hundreds of lives, bound together for one day only. The cement walls were bare except for filth and even though there were wide windows high above them the whole place was dark, as if sprays of ink had mottled the light. It smelled of paper and the sweat of the staff working the machines.

A few of them glanced up when Andy walked in. He followed Sandy down a corridor that led to a set of double doors. The moment they opened he heard the buzz of a newsroom – a dozen TVs blaring out the same news from different points of view, phones ringing, laughter, the metallic clatter of stationary cupboard doors, the hum and clicks of a photocopier. Sandy was a few steps ahead of him, shouting something about Desmond Tutu to a skinny lad at the other side of the room before he called to a girl who looked like she'd been raised on a strict diet of lentils and world music. Half her head was shaved and the other sprouted long purple hair. Jesus. He wouldn't be surprised if she shook his hand with a Taser. The girl pushed back her roller chair then stood up, smiled at him then continued typing, hunched over her keyboard.

She said something to the boy beside her before she left, made him laugh. Then she headed for Andy, held out her hand. 'I'm Hazel Auchenstell,' she said. 'Crime reporter. Sandy said you're interested in the

Alex Mitchell case? That you need to know what happened after court on Monday?'

'Kind of, aye.' Andy looked for Sandy but he'd vanished. 'Did he explain . . . ?'

'More or less,' she said, then pulled a face that was halfway between a smile and a grimace; the expression nurses have before they take blood. 'Should we go somewhere quieter?'

She pushed through a door into a pale blue corridor that made their steps echo and led him up a flight of stairs lit by a flickering tube light. She held open another set of double doors at the top. 'Welcome to the archives,' she said. 'Otherwise known as the cuttings room. Sorry about the dust but at least nobody will disturb us up here.'

The cuttings room looked like a library; high ceilings and labelled folders stored on row after row of tall wooden shelves that would move if you turned a handle on the end. Hazel headed for a big table up the back, switched on an old-fashioned brass lamp with a dusty green shade and motioned for Andy to sit down on a plastic chair that creaked when he did.

'Sandy said you covered the whole case?'

Hazel nodded. 'I wasn't hugely surprised when I saw his name on the court list again. Another woman, another assault. Seems to be his forte. But the attack on Melanie Best – the pub landlady – just before Christmas was mild by comparison to his previous convictions. To be fair to him, he *had* managed to stay out of trouble for years. But given his long history, he was still considered a danger to the public which is why he was jailed, awaiting the trial for that assault.'

Andy nodded. 'Sandy explained this to me already. He spent six months in jail waiting for the trial and when he was found guilty he was then *sentenced* to six months – which he'd already served. Right? Which is why he walked free on Monday despite the fact he was convicted of the crime.'

Hazel nodded. 'Exactly. It doesn't make sense to a lot of people, but that's the law for you.'

'And what about the disappearance of Maureen Aitken and her dog? I've heard Farida McPherson has her suspicions but do *you* think he's involved?'

'It's definitely a possibility,' said Hazel. 'I covered that story from day one as well. To begin with it seemed like a typical *old-person-goes-AWOL* story but then somebody mentioned this reformed ex-con she'd had working for her. Nobody remembered his name but from the description it sounded like Alex.

I've seen him in court *a lot* over the years. So I dug a little deeper and tried speaking to people who knew Alex instead. Unfortunately people connected to violent criminals aren't keen to speak to the press on the record, for obvious reasons. I've got dozens of notepads filled with notes that I'll probably never be able to use. But that doesn't mean I don't have a theory.'

'Which is?'

'Complicated, but bear with me.' Hazel shifted in her chair, pulled her feet under her legs like a yogi. 'Various people told me Alex had been doing odd jobs for Maureen Aitken for almost a year – but apparently they'd had a "disagreement" about money a few weeks before Christmas – a good few weeks before she disappeared. She'd accused him of stealing, apparently, and he was furious.'

'You got a date for that?'

Hazel shook her head. 'I'll double-check my notepads with the interviews but I'm quite sure no specific date was given. Why – do you know something I don't?'

'Doubt it,' said Andy but his mind jumped to the case file on Bert's computer, the details of the injuries Maureen had sustained when she'd supposedly fallen over at home just before Christmas. 'So what happened after that disagreement? Did she fire him?'

Hazel shrugged. 'I asked her neighbours the same question but nobody was sure. From what I was told he didn't have a regular schedule, just did odd jobs as and when Maureen needed. What we do know is that a few weeks later he was locked up for the pub landlady assault and shortly after that Maureen's daughter registered her mother as missing. I'm not a great believer in coincidences but . . . who knows. There's no blood, no body, no sign of forced entry at her house. But in my view the police need to get their arse in gear and find Maureen's body – and her poor dog. The search effort was massively hampered by the awful snow we had over New Year but there doesn't appear to have been much happening since then. I'm hoping Alex's accidental confession outside court will rekindle interest in the case – despite the fact he clearly holds someone else responsible for Maureen's death.'

Andy sighed. 'That's actually what I wanted to talk to you about,' he said. 'Turns out my wife saved Alex Mitchell's life around the same time Maureen Aitken went missing – and apparently he'd begged her *not* to help him. When she did he got abusive then fled the scene. I heard what Alex said after court and it made me wonder if he blames Stef for his crimes. As in, if she hadn't saved his life against his will, he wouldn't have murdered Maureen Aitken. If Stef went to court that day, I knew nothing about it. But maybe you'd have seen her?' Andy pulled out his phone, opened a photo of Stef and slid it across the table towards Hazel. 'Recognise her?'

Hazel picked up his phone and studied the photo, the screen lighting up her face in the gloom of the cuttings room. 'I honestly can't be sure,' she said. 'Court's always packed out on a Monday, inside and out. All the driftwood from the weekend, washed up in one day. When Alex walked out after the trial it was obvious he was looking for someone specific but I really couldn't be sure who – or if your wife was there.'

'Would anyone else know?'

She bunched up her lips. 'You could try asking the security guards at court? They man the doors all day, see everyone who's coming and going. Can't guarantee they'd remember an individual face but it might be worth a shot. Tell them I sent you and they'll be friendly.'

Andy smiled, stood up. 'I'll head there right now. Thanks.'

He left Hazel in the cuttings room, was halfway along that dull grey corridor when his phone started ringing. Vicky, at last. He took a deep breath before he answered, tried to sound calm.

'Andy? So sorry I took so long for me to get back in touch. Believe it or not I've just made it to your house now – got caught up in flash flooding. Anyway I've got good news and bad news. I'll start with the bad – your spare key isn't where you said it was. I've been searching the back garden for ages and there's no sign of it.'

Andy sighed. He should have gone home himself. 'And the good news?'

'Your back door was unlocked so I'm inside anyway.'

'How is that good news? Jesus. Has anything been taken?'

'Everything looked in order at first, but . . . I can't find the mobile phone, Andy. I dialled Stef's number a few times, hoping to hear it ring. But it's not here. I've searched everywhere, twice. I felt bad, poking around your house, worrying Stef would turn up at any second. But I swear on my mother's life that it's not in the house.'

'That's impossible.'

'It's a fact.'

'But I *definitely* took it upstairs,' said Andy. 'And the spare keys are *always* in that plant pot. Are you totally sure you checked everywhere?'

'Positive.'

Andy's brain was ready to burst. If Stef's phone wasn't there, where was it? Who would dare slip into their house on a Wednesday morning – and why would a thief only take Stef's phone? The only other explanation was that the keys were in their usual place but that Vicky hadn't found them – but that meant he'd left home without locking the doors. He'd never done it before but he'd barely slept and his head was a mess so it was possible.

His own speculations made his skin crawl. He needed Stef's phone so he could check Farida's claims – see for himself if Stef had called Alex Mitchell's landline on Monday night or not. But without the phone, he'd have to take her word for it.

'Earth to Andy? I said the answerphone in the hall is flashing red so that probably means you've got a new message. You know how to check it remotely?'

'Not a clue.'

'Want me to listen and tell you who it is?'

Of course he wanted to know. He *needed* to know. Chances were it would be a salesman or a dentist, some kind of courtesy call. But what if it was something else? What if it was the one call he'd been hoping for and dreading all at once? He had no idea why Alyson would call his landline instead of his mobile but maybe there was no signal in the cuttings room or maybe he'd been on another call when she tried to get through.

'Andy? You still there?'

Andy's pictured Vicky in his hall, pressing play on that old machine and listening to a muffled message that she probably wouldn't understand at first; or wouldn't believe, even if she did. She only knew the part of Andy that he'd chosen to show her; knew nothing of his dark edges. But the shadows were here, now, and they'd swallow everything if she pressed that button and heard that voice and knew what was really happening; that a lifesaver was capable of the opposite. Could he really trust Vicky Steele with a secret as big as this one?

Probably not, but he needed to take the chance.

'Aye, go for it,' said Andy.

'One second and I'll put you on hands-free.'

He heard a clunk, pictured Vicky sitting her phone on that table in the hall; her painted nails pushing down on the play button of their answerphone. It was uncomfortable to think of Vicky standing in their home, eyes scanning the framed photos of him and Stef on their campervan adventures. He had no idea how that would make her feel, if she'd be smug or sad at the sight of them. A computer-generated voice disturbed his thoughts, told him there was one new message, received today at 2:30 p.m.

'You hear that OK, Andy?'

'More or less,' he said, then his hall at home and the phone line was filled with a voice he didn't recognise. A woman cleared her throat, then introduced herself as Morven Owens – Richard's wife. She was struggling to get hold of him and wondered if Stef knew where he was? She'd had the police at her door, looking for her husband after the discoveries at Green Den. The woman started to speak again then hesitated, as if she wanted to say something else but didn't dare to. 'I know he . . . confides in you,' she said, then hung up.

For a moment there was silence then Vicky picked up her phone. 'Mean anything to you?'

'Aye,' said Andy, then ended the call before Vicky asked any questions.

His mind was clogged with anxious thoughts, a motorway at home time. The fact that Richard Owens had gone missing on the same day that human remains were discovered at Green Den could mean a hundred different things – but two theories lingered. Maybe Richard Owens was the one who'd been killed.

Or maybe, just maybe, it was him who'd done the killing.

CHAPTER 33

The road was quiet. Betty pulled over at a rural petrol station, parked far enough away from the service window that the skinny boy working there wouldn't see her or what she was looking at. She switched off the engine, glanced at the red running jacket on the passenger seat. When she picked it up she heard a sound that was more familiar to her than any other; the gentle tap of one coin rattling against another. She zipped open the pocket, then pushed her fingers into the corner of the stitched seam. She pulled out a few coins and among them, there it was. The shiny penny from 1988; the one Stef had bent down and picked up from that crack on Portobello Promenade; the one that, in some ways, had led her here. But where had it led Stef?

She slipped it into her own pocket then turned her attention to the other thing she'd grabbed from Stef and Andy's house. Stef's mobile phone, now in Betty's hands.

It was lighter and newer and probably more expensive than hers. She knew it had fingerprint recognition to unlock the home screen. But she also knew that Stef had disabled it, said that did her no good when she was out on a job with someone else's piss or shit or vomit or blood on the hand that gave her access. A PIN code was better, could be entered with a knuckle if and when necessary. And since they always used the same one, it wouldn't be forgotten. Betty brought the screen to life then typed in the date of Stef and Andy's wedding anniversary, the one they used for the burglar alarm on the rare occasion they remembered to switch it on. And just like that, the phone opened.

The photo on Stef's home screen was that same mountain view she always tried to capture in her paintings. It was the same scene recreated in the sketch she'd found in the paper bin – and the same one shown on the card she'd stolen from Richard's office. Betty pulled it out of the door cavity, read again the words Stef had written for Richard.

All Yours x

But now she saw something else.

Stef had written on the right-hand side but on the left there was a trace of something sticky. Betty looked closer, made out the straight lines left by a strip of

Sellotape, now torn off. And cutting through those straight lines was an indentation pressed into the cardboard; round at one end, flat along the top and a row of uneven teeth along the bottom. A key.

She closed the card again, stared at the bothy in the picture and its little wooden door. Maybe the key fitted that lock and the card was a map to let Richard know Stef was there.

But why? Simple: to paint.

Betty tried hard to convince herself that it sounded like a sensible and logical explanation; even conjured up a lovely bucolic scene in her mind featuring Stef and Richard, smiling serenely as they painted the landscape from a different angle then made cups of tea on a tiny gas stove on the ground. But then came the memory of that sketch from the bin; Stef's body, picked apart piece by piece. Then her brain would take the image of the bothy and turn it into the Green Den outhouse instead; a place that was dark and swarmed with flies; where bulging bin liners were dragged from the boot of Richard's car and dumped inside; and where her own skin had been split by a jagged glass edge.

The only way to find out if Stef had gone to the bothy – without or without Richard – was to hike that hill, see for herself what and who lay behind that little wooden door. She had the chance to become the hero she'd so often imagined herself to be, saving dogs from frozen lakes and children from crumbling cliffs and old ladies from housebreakers and heartbroken husbands from the edge of bridges and Stef from the person who'd splattered her blood on the bathroom wall. She imagined neighbours hailing her homecoming, the whispers that would pass between them.

We always knew that Betty Stevenson was something special.

But part of her dismissed the idea as silly, even before it had fully formed.

She was Betty Stevenson, a cleaner and a seeker of lucky pennies and a giver of good luck. She hiked Arthur's Seat at least once a week to drop a penny at the summit but she was not Indiana Jones and was probably letting her imagination run away with itself. Yes, she knew this was Stef's favourite mountain; but she had no idea where it was.

Andy could name every peak in the country by its silhouette, but Betty would have to work harder than that.

She opened the photo album on Stef's phone, eyes pricking as she scrolled through images of the life she lived when Betty wasn't there. Stef had thousands of images. Chances were she'd taken multiple pictures of that mountain scene – and her phone tagged the location of all photos – but it would take Betty all day to find the right ones.

There had to be an easier way to work out where the bothy was.

She returned to the main screen, decided to check calls, messages and emails.

There was nothing from Andy or Richard but other than her, one caller had phoned Stef's mobile several times since Monday. They'd left voicemails but when Betty tried to access the messages she was asked for a password. Betty typed in the code Stef used for everything else but this time it didn't match. She tried three times, then gave up.

There were no text messages but Stef had a few dozen unread emails, marked in bold. She scanned through the previews without opening them. One from a running app, saying someone had stolen her record. One from her bank. One from a friend with a Spanish name. The other ones seemed to be marketing campaigns from a clothes store and an airline and a hotel chain. The usual. She scrolled through the earlier emails, trying to find one from Andy or Richard or Alyson; the few folk who might know the location of the bothy.

But there were none.

She returned to the main inbox, was about to close the email app when she noticed a name on the very top message. It was a survey sent by trainline, was generic and impersonal and would no doubt have been deleted by Stef if she'd seen it. But instead Betty opened it, found exactly what she was looking for. The email asked Stef to fill out the form, based on her most recent travel experience; a train she'd booked to Lewistown on Monday night. Betty had never heard of the place. But was Stef there, safe?

She typed the village name into her maps application and when the red marker zoomed in on the location a few photos appeared on her screen beside it. Betty stared, stunned. The photos on the screen looked exactly like Stef's paintings. That scene, again.

She was on the right track.

Outside the car, a single ray of light split the grey and in Betty's head, a single memory did the same.

Betty shut the maps application and opened Stef's *Health* folder – the one she and Andy used to record their hikes – and the one she'd been so busy studying on her phone last Friday when Betty had gone round to clean. Alyson had popped round later that morning and the pair of them had sat on the back doorstep as

Stef talked her sister through some route and showed her images of key waypoints along the way. They often did that before big hikes, eyes gleaming with anticipation as they gazed at photos of the high-up places they were heading to. Sometimes, if Betty made the right noises, Stef would call her over to see and Betty would act surprised and say it looked lovely and wish she was invited. But Alyson's response that day had been muted.

She'd waited until Betty was out of sight then spoke to Stef in whispers that she'd only just managed to hear from the hall. It's too risky, Alyson had said.

Stef protested but Alyson smothered her sister's words with her own.

Too risky, she said, louder this time.

It was one thing having a GPS recording of the route, Alyson said, but the key question was this – would Stef have mobile phone signal to call for help if required?

When Stef said no, Alyson had stood up and gone outside.

Betty had taken her chance and slipped into the kitchen, hoped Stef would show her the route instead, knowing she was guaranteed a positive reaction. But Stef hadn't noticed Betty at all, just sat on the back step staring at Alyson as she paced their the little lawn, flick flick flicking her lighter.

It made Betty wonder if it was the duty of all big sisters to worry about their younger siblings the same way a dead mother would've done. Or rather, should have done.

Betty still preferred maps to apps but this one was easy to navigate. She knew how to search for routes and follow the paths of those who'd walked there before you. When she typed Lewistown into the search box a few dozen hiker icons appeared on the map, each one representing a route previously recorded by someone else who had passed close to the spot. Most people gave their hikes dull but practical names like *Myrton Woods to Almont Estate* but Betty knew Stef and Andy chose names that meant something to them. She scrolled through the list, quickly found theirs; a hike from Lewistown that Stef and Andy had done together but recorded on his account. They'd posted that photo of themselves at the summit and they'd given it a name that made Betty's skin crawl. *Closer to Heaven.*

When Betty opened the hike and pressed a button marked *GO*, a message popped up on the screen telling her she was too far away from the starting point – and asking if she'd like directions on how to get there? Betty clicked YES then and pulled out that scrap of paper from the bin, tears pricking her eyes as she stared at the sketched portraits of Stef in front of that same mountain scene. Stef, mutilated and asking for help.

Closer to heaven, they'd said.

Betty started the car and headed north, hoped it wasn't hell she'd find instead.

CHAPTER 34

Stef had just caught sight of the man slumped in the open lift when Vicky reached the top of the stairs, paramedic kitbag in tow, breaths like a comma between every word.

'Thought you said you had a sore foot? Bloody hell. Six flights, that was. That's the last time I'm attending a skyrise with a broken lift.' Vicky stuck out her bottom lip and blew her fringe off her forehead but a few hairs stuck to her sweat-smudged make-up, bright orange foundation now slick and greasy as butter spread on hot toast. If only that'd teach her.

Stef forced a smile then let it fall, signalled towards the lift. 'Over here.'

Someone had rammed a wooden kitchen chair between the automatic doors so they wouldn't close but they were still switched on and shuddering. The injured man was sprawled awkwardly on the lift floor; lips pulled tightly against clenched teeth. His eyes were closed but he was breathing heavily, like he'd just finished a sprint. Both arms were bleeding, skin neatly sliced from the wrist upwards.

Crouched beside him was a woman with leggings and a fleece and skin that looked sticky to the touch. Her eyes were on his face and her hands were on his shoulder and her pale grey slippers were soaking up blood from the puddles forming beneath them. First things first, they'd need to remove the woman from the scene.

'Can you step back please?'

The woman didn't budge.

Stef leaned in and pushed the emergency stop button. An alarm started ringing, feebly, and the metal doors came to a standstill. Stef unzipped her jacket and tossed it on the floor outside the lift then opened her kit bag, adrenalin surging as she struggled with the latex gloves, fingers finding all the wrong places. Vicky was watching her and her lips were moving, as if she was silently counting the seconds Stef was wasting as she fumbled with basic kit and simple procedures. She needed to calm down, check the man's vital signs and assess his injuries before they decided the best way to treat him.

She talked to the woman as she worked. 'Was it you who found him?'

The woman nodded.

'He said not to phone the ambulance.'

'You did the right thing. But I really need you to move out of the way' Stef was firm, but kind. The woman lifted herself off the floor, legs visibly trembling as she stepped over the bleeding man. She wasn't Stef's priority but she clearly needed help.

'That's it. I'm here for you, love.'

The woman reminded Stef of those dogs at the rescue centre that cowered when you reached out to give them a biscuit, that knew hands only as weapons.

'Do you know his name?'

The woman had just opened her mouth to speak when the man roared and lashed out. He tried hauling himself to his feet but his bloody hands slipped on the metal sides, left smudges of red on the shiny surface. He spat out blood and bits of words, teeth bared.

Stef tugged the woman out of the way then quickly stepped back, put herself out of danger as well. Vicky appeared beside them then directed the woman towards the neighbours who'd gathered by the stairs. She told them in no uncertain terms to bugger off then strode back to the lift and crouched down in front of the bleeding man. 'If you die because touching you puts us at harm, that's your problem. OK?'

The man roared again then flopped on to the floor; a firework, spent.

Stef hunched beside him. Some of her colleagues treated self-harming patients like they were deaf and dumb and selfish as well as depressed; talked over them and down to them and inferred a blame that had no place.

Even the phrase some of them still used – attempted suicide – held the suggestion that the patient had failed; that they couldn't even do that properly. But scratch below the surface of these lives and you'll soon stop whinging about your own. In theory, anyway.

She examined his arms, decided to deal with the right one first.

'This might sting a bit,' she said, expecting him to flinch when she pressed a thick antiseptic wipe on to the gorge he'd carved into his underarm, from elbow to wrist. But the flinch turned into a shove that didn't knock her over but would leave a bruise. 'One more move like that and we'll get the police in, OK? You need to let me do my job.'

'Don't.'

He spat out the word with such force that she felt it on her cheeks, wished she was wearing a face mask.

The next words were blood-coated. 'Please,' he said, louder now. 'Don't'.

'It'll only hurt for a second.'

The man started shaking his head when Stef said that and making a noise that was more animal than human.

'Please, don't,' he said.

He struggled, tried to wriggle away from her while she treated his wounds; reminded Stef of that deer she and Andy had knocked down last summer on the back road to Stonehaven. Flash, thud, and it had bounced off the bonnet. They found it lying in a ditch a few metres further on, eyes wide, snorting saliva, scrambling on soggy ground as it tried and failed to stand. It was only when Stef went to help it that she realised its hind leg was missing, was somewhere on the road behind them. She'd stayed with the deer while Andy called a vet but when he came off the phone he crouched beside her, shaking his head as he gently placed his hands on its sticky, quivering belly. 'Vet says there's nothing he can do.'

'And us?'

He'd looked at her then, given a shake of the head so slight that most people wouldn't have noticed it. But she knew by the way he'd bitten down on his bottom lip that his mind was elsewhere; that the vet must have used the one phrase he couldn't bear the sound of. Put it out of its misery, *she'd have said and Andy's eyes would have filled up at the mere thought of it; of the day that same decision had been made for his wee sister, because of him.*

That wee face, unchanged for ever. His mum and dad, flattened by the horror of a decision like that. Flick the switch, turn off a life. Their choice. But Andy still believed it was him who'd forced them into that corner, so deep and dark it'd sucked all the light from his family.

She'd put her hands on top of his and they'd stayed with the deer until its heart had stopped beating. Then Andy had stood up, spat repeatedly in his hands then rubbed them together to wash off the blood. He'd gone to the car without a word and Stef had fought a surge of nausea when she picked up the stray leg and moved it off the road. No amount of stitches could have held that life in place. But she'd done a pretty good job of the man in the lift. They'd got here on time, done their job, saved a life.

He'd be sore and scarred but would survive. She pulled some more wipes from the kit bag, was struggling to find the opening when Vicky leaned into the lift. 'Need a hand? They're a bugger to open, those ones.'

'I'm fine,' said Stef, wondering if it was Vicky who'd claimed she was drunk on the job; if she'd taken Bert aside and warned him to keep an eye on her, just in case. Vicky would be on red alert, searching for further evidence: slurring, stumbling, shaking hands.

'You sure, Stef? I really don't mind taking over.'

Stef glared into Vicky's fake-tan face. 'I said I'm fine, OK?'

And that was when the man pushed her again. She fell backwards, arse landing in a pool of blood as the man leaned over her. For a moment there was only the reek of his laboured breath and a few centimetres between them. For a millisecond, their noses touched. Then came the words, wrapped in bloody spit.

'You had no right,' he said, then pushed past Vicky and stumbled towards the stairs, leaving a line of bloody footprints on the pale green floor as he pushed passed neighbours who'd been enjoying the show. When Stef tried to get up her hands slipped on the sheer metal sides of the lift and by the time Vicky leaned in and helped her up he was long gone.

They called the police, let them know they'd had a runner – and a bloody one, at that. Officers came but the man was nowhere to be found and there was no sign of the woman from the lift either, the one who'd *made the call. Later, Stef and Vicky peeled off their uniforms in the station's laundry room and stuffed them into the machines with too much powder and a hot wash, hoping to remove all stains. That was when Stef realised she'd left her jacket at the flats, tossed on the floor beside the lift. Any other day she'd have gone back for it on the way home but she didn't fancy running into that bleeding man by accident when she was on her own. Bert had grumbled when she'd asked him to issue new kit and ID card for her last few days, acted as if she'd done it on purpose.*

She hadn't, but something about that job had unsettled her.

'Please, don't,' he'd said.

She and Andy had an agreement that they didn't discuss patients outside of work. But days later, with her last shift completed and Andy by her side and wine in her veins and bad news on the TV she saw that same man's face on her screen alongside the blackening eyes and burst lips of the pub landlady he'd recently attacked.

The words tumbled out of her, then, disguised as a hypothetical question.

'You ever had a patient flee the scene?'

Andy screwed up his face. 'Couple of times.'

'*And you didn't chase them?*'

'*Not our job. We just let the police know, left them to track them down.*'

'*Makes me uncomfortable.* '

'*It's their choice to run.*'

'*True,*' said Stef. '*But what if we'd already taken choice from him?*'

Andy sat down his glass, turned to face her. '*Meaning?*'

'*What if someone doesn't want to be saved?*'

'*It's irrelevant. We do our job. Save lives; save families from grieving.*'

He looked away from her, glanced at the order of service from his mum's funeral, sitting on the table alongside dozens of sympathy cards that all said the same thing.

I'm sorry for your loss.

Stef downed the remainder of her drink, hoping to drown out the part of her brain that pushed a bitter truth to the very end of her tongue where it festered, unspoken. She wondered if any other paramedic or doctor or nurse had ever looked at a life they'd saved and regretted it as deeply as she did; if they'd thought the four awful words that she did now.

I'm sorry you survived.

CHAPTER 35

Andy dumped his car at Charlotte Square, decided to walk from there to the courthouse. In Edinburgh city centre you had to take what parking you could get and two feet often proved faster than four wheels. Saying that, the weather was often cruel to walkers.

The storm had driven the lunchtime crowd indoors, off the cobbles and into the warm, lit-up places that lined the streets. Scottish pubs were made for days like these, and there were plenty of them. What he wouldn't give for an ordinary afternoon on the beers with Stef, putting the world to rights and truly believing it mattered.

He checked his phone, again.

Why hadn't Alyson called him back? He'd given up waiting and called her, was politely informed her phone was out of signal or switched off. And what about Stef's phone?

He'd made Vicky do a final check of the house before she left but she insisted there was no sign of it. So unless she was lying, that meant somebody had been in their house and taken Stef's phone. But who? Dozens of people knew where they hid the spare keys. He'd been saying for ages that they should change the hiding place, just in case. *Just in case of what?* Stef had said.

He'd had no answer, then; could think of a few now.

Vicky had also asked if he'd wanted to her to replay Morven Owens's message on their old answerphone but there was no need. At least the facts on that were clear.

Richard Owens had disappeared on the same day human remains and defaced portraits of Stef were found close to Green Den Studios. Farida McPherson was looking for him, as was his wife. Could he be the one who took Stef's phone? He definitely knew where they lived.

But why take her mobile?

Andy couldn't bear to think about it.

He knew he should call Farida, tell her about the answerphone message for Stef and the sad way Richard's wife had said the word 'confide'; a word that carried with it the suggestion of secrets shared between those two; a bond between a husband and wife who were already bound to others. But Farida already sensed Andy was keeping something from her and he couldn't face any more of her clever questions. Every single one was like a shoulder charge, knocking him off course, weakening his resolve, tempting him to fall to his knees and repent.

He couldn't allow it, shoved his phone in his pocket and tried distracting himself with the views that usually inspired him; the castle on the rock, the jagged silhouette of spires and domes and peaked roofs of the Royal Mile, the green glory of Princes Street gardens, dividing the Old Town and the New Town. His calves complained when he turned on to the Mound, made the steep climb up to the Royal Mile then turned left and headed downhill.

The symmetrical High Court building stood opposite St Giles's Cathedral and in front of that was the spittle-splattered Heart of Midlothian mosaic on the pavement. Stand there long enough and you'd see it, locals and tourists stopping to spit on the spot where, long ago, prisoners were kept before a trial. A few more steps on was the Mercat Cross and the gruesome tales of wrongdoers who were nailed to it by their ears.

This part of the Royal Mile was human morals built in stone; a reminder of what people should and should not do; of sinners and their sins.

A few folk lingered outside the main doors of the courthouse, backs hard against the wall to avoid the worst of the rain. Inside a curly-haired woman wearing too much perfume and a baton on her belt pointed him in the direction of the scanner. A security card hung around her neck on a tatty lanyard, said her name was Maria Elena Biznaga. The name looked Spanish. Her face did not. He dropped his phone and wallet into a plastic tray, got a nod of approval when he walked under the archway. Then he stopped in front of her chair, forced a smile.

'I'm a friend of Hazel Auchenstell,' he said. 'A reporter, from *The Journal*?'

'Good for you, pal.'

He held his smile in place. 'She said you might be able to help me?'

'With?'

'I'm trying to find out if my wife was here on Monday.'

'If she's an offender you'll need to check the court lists for that.' She turned away from him, stared at the blank screen of the scanning machine. There was nobody waiting in line, nothing on the belt. She glanced at him, irritated, when he didn't leave. 'Ask at the office, eh?'

'What if she was in the public gallery? Or waiting outside?'

The woman spun her seat round a little. 'I scan their bags, son. I don't take their picture.'

'You don't need to. I've got one here.' Andy held out his phone, open at a photo of Stef. 'Long story, but I need to know if she was here on the day of the Alex Mitchell trial.'

'Is that the wife beater who went off his head when they let him out?'

'Aye,' said Andy. 'My wife's a paramedic. She saved his life, a while back.'

The woman pulled a face like he'd spat on her. 'And why in God's name did she do that?'

'It's not really a matter of choice.'

'I suppose not.' She shrugged. 'But I'm confused – why do you need to know if she was here? Can you not just ask her?'

'It's complicated.'

'Always is, pal.' She straightened up, pulled a pair of glasses out of the chest pocket of her short-sleeved white shirt. 'Go on then, let me have a look at her,' she said, peering at his phone. She pursed her chapped lips then shook her head. 'Not ringing any bells.'

'Would anyone else know?'

'Doubt it. It's chaos in here on a Monday and it was even worse than usual after that arsewipe kicked off. Kirstie usually watches the front door but she ended up in the office on Monday morning playing agony aunt to some woman who'd keeled over in court. Anyway, I radioed Angus and he covered for Kirstie until the scanner broke and he had to come in here and fix it. Typical. And God knows where Magnus was. Skiving, probably. But whatever the reason, I was left watching the doors on my own. Just me and the savages. To be honest, it was so busy I doubt I'd have noticed my own mother sitting there, never mind your wife.'

She looked past Andy towards the main door. One of the smokers had come in from the rain, was wringing out the soggy corners of his jacket on to the marble floor. She tutted loudly. 'Speaking of savages . . .' She winked at him then turned back to the scanner, waved the lad through. 'I'm sorry I couldn't help you, pal. Tell Hazel I was asking for her, will you?'

'Will do,' said Andy, tugging up his collar as he walked out on to the Royal Mile.

He headed for the nearest coffee shop, became the last soggy customer in a long soggy queue. Almost everyone stood with their heads bowed, eyes on their phones. Andy did the same. Hazel had left a long message, asking how he got on at court. She was still trawling through old articles in the cuttings room and scouring her shorthand notepads to see if she could find any clues in her old interviews; anything that would link Stef's life to either Alex Mitchell or to Maureen Aitken. Vicky had sent a text message as well, telling him she'd left the house and asking if she could do anything else to help. He was typing a reply to Vicky when his phone made a noise he didn't recognise and a notification popped up. He'd removed that option from his text messages and emails years back. He'd chose to read messages in his own time, didn't need his phone to prod him in the ribs every time somebody else wanted to contact him.

So what was this?

He slid his thumb upwards to get rid of it but in the second before it disappeared he saw two words on his screen that made no sense; that both terrified him and gave him hope. He slid back to the menu screen and opened the notifications tab. And there it was. His hiking app had sent him a message telling him someone had just pressed GO on one of his recorded hiking trails. It asked if he wanted to send them a thumbs up or a message to thank them for choosing his route over all the others on the app. There was a photo of the other user, the person supposedly walking in his footsteps this very second.

Andy had taken that photo, remembered why she was laughing when he took it.

The other user was Stef Campbell.

This would lead him to whoever had her phone.

He was still staring at the screen, mind whirring, when the barista leaned over the counter and gently tapped his arm, asked if he was OK. 'Look like you've seen a ghost.'

In some ways, he had.

And now, he knew where it was walking.

CHAPTER 36

The first Monday of sick leave was a day Stef would never forget, however much she'd have liked to. It started as soon as Andy left for work. She could still feel the spot of warmth on her lips where he'd kissed her on his way out, wished her a good day; told her to rest. She'd managed a smile and to hold the tears in until his back was turned.

But already, home felt different.

The threat was everywhere, turned her body to ice when it materialised.

She was in the shower, trying to lose herself in the simple pleasures of hot water and soap and steam and a song from the radio trapped by her head then released by her voice. And it was there, in a room full of mint-scented steam, that the first blow came.

She'd imagined a thousand endings, but not that one.

Stef, there, eye to eye with the blood that was leaking out of her head and on to the white tiles. And that voice, taunting her as she lay weeping in warm puddles of herself.

Don't say you weren't warned.

She called out and when no help came she dragged herself up and off the floor, pressed a cold cloth to her head and tossed old beach towels over the blood. She scrubbed clean the walls and floor, tried to do the same to the one thought that played on loop in her head; the one truth she did not want to acknowledge. Even though she'd scooped herself up and plastered herself back together it did not mean she was safe, or saved from anything. It just meant there would be more of her to unpick before the job was done.

This was the just beginning.

CHAPTER 37

When Betty reached Lewistown the hiking app told her to drive right through, towards the mountain and the start of the walk. Instead she pulled over then hurried downhill towards the scattering of solid stone buildings, mist lingering so close to the roofs it was as if the slates were steaming. She'd have a quick look for Stef in the village before she set off and if she saw anyone she'd show them a photo of her, ask if and when they'd seen her.

She'd never been before but had walked every single street and mapped them in her mind within ten minutes. The streets were empty – not surprising, given the weather and the warnings on the radio of much worse to come. She'd try businesses instead. Betty went into the wee shop and the tea room but both were empty except for the staff. She smiled and showed the photo; got shrugs and shaking heads in return.

The hotel was her last chance. It was one of those Victorian hunting lodges that had been converted in the seventies and not upgraded since. The kind of place that, if it were a person, would have dandruff.

Reception was dark and empty but she saw light and heard voices through a swing door adorned with an oversized, unpolished brass sign screwed into the plywood. *Public Bar.*

The bar consisted of a cushioned bench that ran the length of two walls and was covered in once-plush red velvet. The *public* consisted of a very tall man wearing a short-sleeved rugby shirt and three squat pensioners wearing almost identical beige anoraks with damp patches on their backs. All of them were drinking pints and looked like they had been all afternoon. They nodded to Betty then returned to their conversation, which also involved the barman, a skinny man who'd have slipped neatly into the tall man's pocket. Stef definitely wasn't there but she'd ask anyway.

She'd just pulled out Stef's phone, open at the photo of her face, when the barman hushed the public mid-conversation and nodded to the huge TV mounted on the wall. 'I've got a bet on Elgin to win against Stranraer,' he said, a comment which prompted hoots of laughter from the other men.

The more the barman hushed them the louder they talked.

Betty was psyching herself up to interrupt them when the image on the screen changed from a TV studio to a live report – but it wasn't the sports news. It started with an aerial shot of trees then zoomed in to a converted farm building she knew only too well: Green Den Studios. The footage changed again and she saw that derelict outhouse, now swarmed by police instead of flies.

Betty could see the window where she'd cut her hand, found herself touching the wound while she watched. Meanwhile the barman was under the TV, reaching above his head and fiddling with the controls. Suddenly the channel flipped to a weather report showing the map of Scotland covered in grey clouds and lightning rays and a weatherwoman who was doing her best to pull a grave expression. Cue more abuse from the customers. Then the tall man stepped forward, flipped to the news and turned up the volume, full blast. He slapped the barman on the back then returned to his pals. The report was finishing but Betty heard all she needed to hear.

Unconfirmed reports of human remains.

At the very end of the report the screen flashed to a computer-generated image showing two different cars and giving details of their number plates. The reporter said police were keen to trace the owners of both vehicles in connection to the discoveries at Green Den and urged members of the public to contact police immediately if they saw them. But she also warned people to stay alert and keep their distance, especially women.

Betty stared, stunned. She knew both of those cars.

One of them belonged to Richard Owens. She'd driven behind it for long enough to memorise the number plate; but now that human remains had been found at Green Den it was the police tracking him instead of her.

And the other car?

It was hers.

The news ended and the football results came and went and still Betty stood, eyes fixed on the screen, fingernails picking the crust off the cut from that broken window at the outhouse. Blood dribbled out, left a dark stain on Stef's bright red running jacket.

When the barman called out to her, offering a plaster, she didn't respond; and when he when came close and tapped her arm she flinched then lashed out to defend herself before muttering an apology and fleeing the bar. She stumbled down an echoing corridor, towards the ladies' toilet. She'd compose herself there, stem the bleed with loo roll.

Inside a surprisingly plush carpet lined the floor, leading to a long line of cubicles. Betty chose the one at the end, slipped inside without locking the door behind her. She just needed a minute to calm down, to work out what all of this meant and what she needed to do.

But she'd only been in there a few seconds when the main door opened.

For a moment she heard laughter from the bar but then a woman's voice filled the bathroom, even though she was speaking in whispers. 'Stef's not where she should be,' she said.

The woman's voice trembled when she said it and afterwards Betty could sense the same shake catching her breath, pushing it through a grater before it left her mouth and hit the phone. 'Yes – *of course*, I waited. And *of course* I'm sure it was the right place – in that clearing, close to the . . . the burial place.'

For a few moments all Betty could hear was the rustle of waterproof clothes as the woman paced the floor. When she stopped a new sound came, the scraping metallic flick of a lighter. There was no smell of tobacco and Betty was sure alarms would have sounded if she'd lit up a cigarette – but the woman kept on flick flick flicking. 'I couldn't have stayed any longer without putting myself *at risk*.' She said those last two words slowly, like Betty's mum used to do when she spoke to anybody foreign. 'I was drenched and freezing and those damn clouds just wouldn't lift. If I'd stayed on the hill you might have had two bodies to deal with. And surely one body is more than enough.'

The tremble in the woman's voice fattened and turned to tears that almost drowned out the next thing she said but Betty heard, felt her heart shrink and shrivel in her chest when she heard the woman's question. The words were pushed out between sobs, bent out of shape by grief. 'What have we done, Andy?'

A tiny gasp slipped out of Betty's mouth and then she froze, eyes closed.

'Shit, there's someone in here,' the woman said, barely whispering now. 'I don't know. Andy, will you listen to me? Let me check. I'll call you back.'

Betty held her breath.

'Hello? Is someone in here?'

The voice was inches from her. If she'd reached out she could probably have touched the woman, held her hand over that mouth to keep it silent. As it was, Betty pressed herself against the walls of the cubicle, wished she could slip into the tiny pores of the mouldy grout that held the pale blue wall tiles in place. Then the footsteps stopped and familiar hiking shoes appeared on the other side of the door. Betty felt helpless, then realised that she had a choice: wait to be found or, for once, make herself seen.

She pulled open the door and stepped out.

Their eyes met, lingered for a few seconds more than was comfortable. Did Alyson recognise her? It was unlikely. Betty was just the cleaner, after all. She'd notice if Stef's floors needed a scrub, no doubt, but would rarely spare a thought for the one who kept them clean.

But then Alyson's eyes fell on the blood staining Betty's sleeve and her face stretched into an expression that held something else; a look Betty knew from her mother.

Blame.

'That's Stef's jacket,' said Alyson. 'And the blood? Jesus Christ, is that my sister's blood?'

Alyson stepped back, head shaking, fingers already fumbling for the call button on her phone. 'I'm calling the police.'

When she glanced at the screen Betty took her chance; ran.

She burst out of hotel and ducked down a side street she knew led to her car, was tugging her keys out of her pocket when she remembered the news report, the search that was already underway. If police were looking for this car, she couldn't be seen anywhere near it. From now on, she'd walk; reach the start of the hike by foot.

Her lungs and legs protested but she continued out of the village, following a narrow path that snaked upwards, towards sodden woodland and the cloud-topped ridge that lay beyond it. She only stopped when the app pinged, told her she'd finally reached the starting point. Betty bent over, shuddering, until she got her breath back. And when she straightened up and looked to the stretch of path ahead she realised she knew exactly where she was, despite the fact she'd never been there before.

She was standing inside Stef's favourite mountain scene.

She glanced back at the village then started walking uphill, following the GPS route through woodland and on to the bothy, towards the summit. Betty knew now that she wasn't the only person looking for Stef.

Alyson was here, Andy was on his way – and if her suspicions were correct Richard Owens might be here as well, clutching a key in his hand. But Betty was the only one with a pocket full of lucky pennies.

She set off, clutching copper, hoping that today the Finder would be her.

CHAPTER 38

For months she blamed open doors and slippery floors for the bruises left on her.

But when the questions finally came they brought with them her decision; to leave.

Her last morning at home started with a run along Portobello Promenade, ended when she found a lucky penny. A sign, she hoped; but then skin was split and blood stained tiles, again. Hours later, Stef stood alone on her own front step, staring at glossy yellow paint on wood and the polished brass and the creep of rust around the screws. She pictured Andy inches away from her on the other side of the door.

The first time they met he'd called her Stephanie, read straight off her ID card at work with a sly glimpse and that smile she'd grown to love so much and to inspire in him so often, from that day until this. She'd been standing by the kettle at the station, watching steam rise, fingertips spotted with grease leached from the half-eaten croissant sitting next to her mug. When the water boiled Stef had made her tea then stepped back, stamped down hard on Andy's bare feet. He'd just dumped his uniform in the laundry room, was walking to his locker to get his shoes when it happened. Stef had lamented her spilled tea, then apologised.

'I'll live . . . Stephanie,' he'd said – and at their wedding two years later he had shushed the drunk cousins who whooped and whistled when he stood up and said he'd loved her from that very first moment; that he'd known the rest of the living he'd do would be by her side.

That was the start of it. And the end?

Stef leaned against the front door, shut her eyes. This close, the yellow paint still smelled new despite the fact they'd painted it years back, not long after they'd bought the house.

They'd moved to Portobello at her suggestion. It was all big skies and endless sand, one of those beaches that tripled in size at low tide. She loved the fact you could stand waist-high in the water ten metres from the shore then turn around and see the green lumps of Arthur's Seat and the Salisbury Crags. Edinburgh was sandwiched in between; sea and hills framing the city. At that time prices were cheaper there so they'd bought a house with their own front and back door and a garden that wasn't littered with other people's blackened disposable barbecues.

It was the perfect size for two. They'd both flushed when the estate agent had said that, beaming in his too-shiny suit, as if that was all any couple would ever want or conceive of. 'And wait until you see this!' he'd said, bounding into the garden and signalling for them to follow. Andy had hung back, said he wanted to check the number of sockets in the living room. And there it was, that distance; a silent confirmation of the truth he'd never dared to say out loud.

Her body had failed them both.

Stef curled her hands into pathetic fists, remembering those losses; the children who'd spent every day of their short lives inside of her. If they'd lived they'd have been teenagers by now but it was impossible to imagine their faces when all they'd ever seen of them were photos after scans, a nose and ear and eye built of black-and-white pixels.

Now, fifteen years later, she was snuffing out Andy's dreams all over again.

For a few moments she stayed on the doorstep, staring at her hands. She wanted to bang white-tight *knuckles against the door and to hear footsteps in the hall and feel that familiar rush in her chest when Andy opened up; forgave her and welcomed her home.*

Instead she stuffed her hands into her pockets and pictured him inside, alone; perched on the big radiator, listening for the gurgle and whispers of pipes. If he felt lonely he'd close his eyes and listen for sirens and tyres ripping over those uneven cobbles near the bus stop and that blackbird that always sang on their outhouse roof in the evenings. She knew him, knew it was the silence in the house that would bother him more than anything else.

Her doing.

When she and Alyson were wee her mum liked using the word 'undoing' whenever she and Alyson were playing up, demanding more than they deserved. 'You two will be my undoing,' she'd say, but the words would come with a light shake of the head and a gentle laughter that spelled out the opposite. They made her, and each other. And when she had become undone they'd made every possible effort to keep her together until there was nothing left to hold except paper hankies to her dripping mouth.

Stef moved away from their door and the memories, then turned her back on them. As she walked away she thought the hardest part was over; let herself believe that she held her future in her own hands. Then behind her, a door opened and closed.

She spun round and scanned the rows of houses. It would just be a neighbour, taking out their bins. A breeze caught her hair, brought a chill to the evening air and the scent of salt from the beach she loved, but was leaving. She shivered then kept on walking.

But it wasn't just fear that followed her.

CHAPTER 39

Betty could see for miles, wondered if she could be seen.

The bothy was just ahead of her now. If there was anybody inside they'd see her coming. Likewise nobody could leave without being spotted by Betty.

She'd followed the path for almost an hour but now she stepped on to the grass in front of it, remembered photos of Stef and Andy, here; cold hands wrapped round hot metal mugs, faces obscured by the rising steam.

Now, a curtain of condensation blocked the window.

But the door was ajar.

Betty peered inside, could see right angles and smooth, straight edges; a table, a chair, a bench. A bottle corked with a candle.

But there was something else; someone else.

The woman inside was sitting on the floor with her knees pulled up to her chin and her face turned towards the cold fireplace. From where Betty was standing, she saw Stef's face in perfect profile. It made her think of pennies and the magic they held and of the Queen's eyes, always staring directly ahead. Until now she'd never wondered what the Queen might be looking at; what had caught and held her attention, on the other edge of the coin.

Betty kept one hand in her pocket, squeezing a penny against her palm as she reached out with the other hand to push open the door.

Even from the door Betty could tell Stef's clothes were drenched and once she stepped inside she realised her whole body was trembling, reminding Betty of how her mum would look when she didn't have enough money to go boozing. She stopped within touching distance, spoke in a voice that was far too loud for the distance between them.

'Stef?'

Stef glanced at her, wide eyes looking over Betty's shoulder and out of the door, as if she expected to see someone else. 'Why are you here?'

That stung, wasn't the reaction Betty had imagined. 'I was worried. I saw blood in your bathroom, then I found your phone and then . . . *this*.' She reached into her pocket and pulled out the scrap of paper with the forty-five portraits of Stef and that word at the end. *Help*.

Stef stared at it, shaking her head. A single tear rolled down her cheek.

'I thought . . .' Words left Betty, were replaced by shame. The whole thing seemed so ridiculous now. Stef would think she was being hysterical, should be locked up.

'What time is it?'

Betty glanced at Stef's phone, still in her hand, still open at the recording of that route. The word *autopause* flashed on the screen. 'It's just gone four o' clock.'

'No, no, no.' Stef reached for the chair, hauled herself on to her feet. She winced when she put weight on her right ankle. That was when Betty noticed the cuts on her hands, still raw, and mud caked to her trousers. 'Are you hurt?'

Stef nodded. 'But I can't be *here*. They're coming for me, Betty.' She inched towards the door, sucking in breath with every step. 'I need to get to the woodland.'

'You can barely walk.'

'Will you help me?' Stef leaned on Betty.

She'd dreamed of moments like this one. She nodded then pulled off the red running jacket, wrapped it around Stef's shoulders.

'I'll get help,' she said then. 'I'm going to call an ambulance.'

It was a shock to hear herself speak those words again, dragged her back to the last time she'd said it; that night just before Christmas when she'd found her wee brother Alex, bleeding on their kitchen floor.

He'd slit his arms open with the knife she sharpened weekly and she'd called an ambulance even when he'd pleaded her not to. He was *choosing* to die, he said, to stop himself from killing someone else.

He'd confessed to pushing Maureen a few weeks earlier when she'd accused him of stealing. She'd fallen over and bled a little, he said. But now he wanted to hurt her more.

He'd told Betty where his mind was going, how black and how bleak his thoughts had become. He *wanted* to kill Maureen, could no longer fight the urge.

But Betty had been unable to believe that of her one and only brother; unwilling to stand and do nothing while he bled to death. He'd fled when she phoned the ambulance; only making it as far as the lift. Then help came. She'd felt proud at first, for saving him. But if she hadn't? That was the crushing weight Betty had carried with her ever since; the shame she tried to miti-gate by dropping lucky pennies in the hope she'd bring moments of goodness to strangers, instead of death. If she'd done what Alex said and let him die, Maureen Aitken would still be alive.

He'd murdered her two days later; his own wounds still weeping and the old lady's blood fresh on his hands when he got home to their flat at Hartfield Court. He'd dragged Betty out of her single bed and pinned her down on their kitchen floor, in the same place he'd tried to take his own life the day before.

This is your fault, he'd said. *You shouldn't have saved me.*

He said he didn't care about the paramedics who'd tried stitching his wounds. It was their job. They had no choice. But Betty did. She was his big sister – his only remaining family – and she should have listened to him.

But she'd called the ambulance instead.

She remembered closing her eyes when she heard the sirens that night, the control it wielded over the lives of others; the instant, unequivocal respect it demanded and received. All over the city people were stepping back from crossings and pulling cars to the side of the road, momentarily putting another's life before their own. And that night, for once, it was Betty's family that had mattered the most.

She'd pictured the ambulance zooming through red lights and swinging around corners, doing all that it could to reach their Hartfield Court flat Before It Was Too Late. Little by little it got louder and closer and Betty had imagined the faces of people who'd see it and wonder why it was there, concern etched into their faces and relief in their hearts that, this time, they were not the ones needing help. Next came the click of doors opening and the thud as they were slammed shut. Footsteps on the stairs, the beep of radios. Then Stef had crouched down beside her and Alex in the lift, brought with her the scent of disinfectant; of an angel. And those words that she'd clung to ever since.

You did the right thing.

After that Stef and the other paramedic had thrown complicated words between themselves, names of drugs and equipment and techniques that brought them to the moment of crescendo when Stef said the words that nobody else ever had, before or since; the words that made her want to be part of Stef's world in any way she could.

I'm here for you, love.

And now, at last, Betty was there for Stef.

She pulled out both mobile phones, was checking them for signal when Stef reached for Betty with bloody fingers. For a moment the two women stared into each other's eyes, their shifting pupils writing out a sad, silent contract between them.

Then came the same two words that Betty had heard from her brother.

'Please,' said Stef. 'Don't.'

CHAPTER 40

The hiking app led Andy north, a drive with few cars and far too many memories.

He drove fast, sadness squeezing his throat as he crossed the Forth Bridge, wheels bumping noisily over the joins. To his right a train sped over the red lattice of the rail bridge and ahead of him the land started creeping higher; rounded green knolls replaced by bare grey rock; the neat order of cities and motorways exchanged for big skies and the ragged outlines of trees.

Up ahead the clouds were lifting and the cheerful man on the radio said the storm had changed direction, would shed its load over the sea instead. The phone conversation with Alyson lingered, however, cast shadows on all the parts of him that still believed their story could have ended differently. Stef wasn't where she should be, despite all those months of planning; him and Alyson doing everything they could to make sure it ended there and then. Alyson had tried calling him back a few minutes after the first call but he'd let it ring out, couldn't bear any more words. He wasn't strong enough to carry her guilt and her fears along with his own. Why had he ever agreed to this in the first place?

Maybe witnessing death from a distance had seemed like the easier choice and he'd been stupid enough to believe it would mean he could stand at the edge of his wife's grave with a clear conscience. A hole, and her in it; and a world, now, without her.

He couldn't believe it; wouldn't, until he saw it for himself.

The satnav told him he was five minutes from Lewistown, where the walk began. Alyson had told him she'd put on dry clothes and wait for him at the hotel so they could follow together the route she'd walked alone that afternoon. But Andy had already decided he wouldn't stop, would head to the mountain without her. He hadn't told her about the notification on his phone; the confirmation that someone else was following Stef's favourite hiking route – and that they were holding Stef's phone in their hand as they walked.

Would he find Alex Mitchell roaming the mountain? Or Richard Owens? He pictured Stef's slender, soft hands and wondered who would be the last person she touched.

He dumped the car in a lay-by and started walking that familiar path. The world became green, the sky silver as sunlight tried to burst through grey storm clouds.

But the shadows came soon enough when the path turned into the woods. These were the landscapes Stef loved to paint, the places light rarely reached. He walked until he reached a fence with a tall stile, winced as he stretched his leg over the top and wished Stef was waiting on the other side, hand outstretched, assuring him they didn't have far to go. He stuck his head inside the bothy on the way past. There was nobody in there; the sunlight was pushing through the window, painting rainbows on a few shards of broken glass scattered around the legs of an old wooden table. The colours drew his gaze to the floor and to a few drops of blood that had long since dried into the stone. He slammed shut the door and kept going.

His legs and lungs felt heavy, like his body was filled with sand. But it was nothing compared to that ache of the grief that was lodged in his throat. He'd got used to it over time, taught himself an endless variety of ways to act like it wasn't there at all. But in moments like this it was there when he swallowed, as hard and sharp and real as a razor blade snagged in the flesh. Stef would say he was wrong about that, of course; told him that the grief stayed there because he held on to it. Grief didn't grip him but the other way around.

Let it go, she said. Made it sound easy.

As he entered the next area of woodland he paused to catch his breath and it was there that he heard it. Somebody else was in the trees. Or something.

'Stef?'

Nothing.

He turned, eyes narrowed. The trees here had been planted in neat rows with little man-made valleys in between, their steep sides thick with last year's browning pine needles. Usually the forestry workers would chop off the lowest, narrowest branches; the ones that would act like kindling on the rare occasion a fire took hold. That hadn't happened here. Even when he hunched down he could barely see past the second row of trees, their trunks and the space between them obscured by twiggy fingers so thickly intertwined that even dogs would struggle to push through. It was a different story when he looked up. The treetops moved gently from side to side, offering him glimpses of sky and throwing out the creaks and squeaks and groans that were impossible to place, or ignore.

Andy held his breath and tried to listen for the sound he'd heard before; the one thing that lay beyond the thump, thump, thump that shook his body from the inside and the scrape of one bending tree bumping against another. He closed his eyes. Focus, Andy. Listen for it.

And there it was.

In. Out. In. Out. It was here, now, and not too far away.

Somewhere close, he could hear someone else's breath.

Andy pushed though branches that seemed to push back, jagged edges stabbing at his hands and face and legs as he hunched down and forced himself forward through the thick lattice of branches.

And suddenly there she was, just out of touching distance.

Stef didn't respond when he called her name but he could see a faint movement as her lungs did their duty, made her back rise and fall with each breath. There was no sign of anybody else in the clearing; not Richard Owens or Alex Mitchell or anyone else he'd feared might want to harm her. It was just the two of them; Stef and Andy, back together.

'I'm here, love, I'm here.'

She was lying among hardened roots and softening pine needles. It was a world of ragged edges and uneven lines, of endless rot and strong shoots pushing through; life and death, inseparable.

Andy reached for her stilled fingers.

Her hands were passive, now; were held but could not hold.

It was then that the glint of a sharp edge caught his eye on the far side of her; a metal tip; man-made and guaranteed to break a heart.

It had really happened, and it had happened here.

He noticed a one-pence piece as well, solid and shiny on dull, soggy ground. He'd always insisted he didn't believe in luck; said life was all about making choices and learning from them. But he reached for the coin all the same, had just picked it up when a twig snapped nearby.

He scoured the gloom. 'Is somebody there?'

No answer came but again he heard a breath, sensed movement in the trees.

Then Stef groaned. He inched forward until his face was above hers, inches apart.

Her eyes were closed and the cheek that was facing skywards was spotted with tiny specs of dirt that had fallen from the canopy and floated earthwards. He reached out, held his hand in front of her mouth and waited, waited, waited until he felt the fleeting warmth of a shallow breath. Then reached for her free hand, took her wrist between his fingers and tried to find a pulse. He closed his eyes, tried to separate the thud of his own heartbeat from hers. In bed he'd often hold her for a long time after she'd fallen asleep, soothed by the sensation of their two pulses blended together. He loved the fact he couldn't tell the difference between them, that hers was as familiar to him as his own. But now he listened only for hers, was forced for the first time to see her life and his life as two completely separate entities. But then it came; weak and slow and tired, but it was there.

He pulled out his mobile, checked for a signal he already knew he wouldn't find. Stef was still alive, could still be saved. That's what he was made for, wasn't it? It was an instinct he couldn't fight and didn't want to. But it wasn't what he'd promised and it wasn't what they'd planned. He dialled the number anyway. Silence. But then Stef spoke.

'Please don't let me go,' she said, words slurred, sleepy. His heart thundered when her eyes locked on his and she said the same words again. But this time, he heard what she really wanted to say – and not what he'd wanted to hear.

'Please, *don't*,' she said. Then a final, deliberate pause. 'Let me go.'

Andy breathed in the scent of crisp mountain air and pine needles in that light-dappled forest, all the parts of the world that Stef loved most; then he lay down beside his wife and held her for the last time. When her heart stopped, his broke.

And all around them, quietly, life continued.

CHAPTER 41

Andy was still there when light and dark had changed places and the wail of a siren smothered all other sounds. When he heard movement in the woods he knew it was over. Footsteps crunching, branches cracking. But still he held on.

He had little concept of what would happen next. There would be grief. There would be police and there would be questions and there would be judgement. He would no longer have a wife.

There were voices now, one of them on a walkie-talkie. He tried not to listen, but he heard boots snapping twigs and scattering rocks, the scratch of branches on waterproof jackets.

He felt the vibrations of footsteps on the forest floor, walking towards him. He heard the click of the radio button, the crackle of static, a call for assistance and when the answer came it brought with it the background sounds of a life elsewhere.

The mountain was noisy now, no longer theirs. But still Andy stayed where he was.

He held Stef a little tighter, a little closer, a little longer.

Then finally, a voice came. 'Andy Campbell?'

Good question.

'Are you hurt, pal?'

Andy thought about all the times he'd asked that same question, leaning over someone who'd been literally ripped to pieces by something sharp, something hard. Andy kept his eyes shut, wondered how he'd have reacted if he came upon this scene the police were seeing now.

Warm fingertips touched his hand and the soft skin of an open palm rested on his knuckles. A thumb touched his and squeezed. *Stef. Please be Stef.*

'Move him.'

The hand on his was gentle but insistent as it eased open his fingers one by one. *This is it, Andy. The last time you'll touch her. How could that even be possible?*

This is *Stef.*

He tensed, tried to shake off the hand that was not hers. *I'm still here, sweetheart.* Someone touched his back, his waist, his feet, tugged him away from her. He opened his eyes for what might have been the first time in hours or days or weeks. It made no difference, now.

Andy knew the science of it, but was still amazed how quickly she'd turned grey.

He stretched out, managed to grasp a few strands of her hair between his fingers.

'Let go, Andy.'

It was the right thing to do. He knew that, he knew that, he knew that. But all they'd really bring was blue lights and plastic tape and all they'd really do was zip her up in a bag then slide her into a freezer until she was ready to be burned.

Andy's legs wobbled when the paramedics helped him to his feet. As they walked away he caught glimpses of Stef's body and of the strangers now crowded around her; people in uniforms anxiously batting away flies as they talked quickly and quietly into radios and to each other. The paramedics led Andy in the other direction and he looked at her for the last time. Stef, stilled, yet free; from suffering and from the dread of it.

This wasn't the ending he'd ever have wanted but he knew this loss was different to the others. His wee sister's death brought with it blame and the torment of all the tiny decisions that could have changed things. When he and Stef had come here all those years ago to make a grave for their lost children they did so in the knowledge life had made that decision for them. But here, there was something else, held firmly in Stef's limp hands.

Choice.

CHAPTER 42

Present Day

A chorus of creaks cracked the heavy silence in the courtroom, dozens of people standing up in unison when an officer opened the door behind the bench. *All rise.* The judge sat down and adjusted his glasses then glanced towards the public gallery and nodded, signalling for them to sit as well. Cue more creaks, zips opening and closing, hands rummaging the contents of bags, failed attempts to catch sneezes.

The judge started to speak, but Andy waited only for the words that mattered.

Would it be one word or two? Guilty, or not guilty?

He wondered what Stef would have said if she'd been sitting there beside him during the trial, if she'd ever imagined her final moments would be picked apart in public like old bones. That was the one part they'd never really talked about; the part they knew couldn't be planned for. Even with the best of intentions, the final verdict was beyond their control.

But they'd done what she wanted; what they'd promised.

She'd only been off work for a few days when she told him about the diagnosis, even though she'd known about it for months. She'd been sneaking out for hospital appointments while he was at work; keeping it to herself until her mind was made up about the part that came next. 'Before my hands go, I go,' she'd said.

She'd sat him down at the kitchen table, handed him one of the many letters she'd scooped off the front-door mat before he'd woken up; an envelope with the hospital logo, sent from Dr Lachlan, the doctor she'd bumped into that day on the summit of Arthur's Seat. He was the gentle specialist who'd given her the diagnosis; a polite death threat.

Stef admitted that he had urged her time and again to tell her family about her illness, long before she did. When she made excuses he'd warned her that the disease would speak for itself soon enough anyway, turn words to slurs and walks to stumbles.

The complaints at work were testament to that.

Andy had stared at the letter for a long time after he'd read it. He could tell Stef wanted him to raise his head and let his eyes meet hers, but he could not. He knew what this meant. Their time was up. This disease did not allow for happy endings.

'Andy?'

Her voice would go before she did. He wondered how many more times he'd hear her say his name before it went; a burst bubble that could not be remade.

'When did all of this start?'

'Around the same time your mother got ill,' she said. 'Tiny changes I tried to ignore – and even once I got the diagnosis I didn't believe it, convinced myself it was all a mistake; that I'd be the exception. But it came to a head the night I was treating Alex Mitchell. Or trying to. My hands got so weak I could barely get my gloves on. Vicky noticed and, of course, I took it out on her. I was actually relieved when Bert forced me to take time off. I knew I couldn't keep working on the ambulance when my own body was so obviously failing me.'

'You said the doctor signed you off for stress.'

'I was trying to protect you. And myself.'

'And that's why you fell in the bathroom? The day you split your head?'

She nodded. 'There's a weakness in me now. In my feet. In my hands. It comes and goes but it'll just keep taking more.'

She leaned forward and took the letter from his hands. He let it go, watched her fold it and slip it into the envelope; his wife's name trapped behind the little plastic window, their world flattened by three words printed on that page. That diagnosis. That bloody illness.

Motor neurone disease.

The slow-motion killer, paralyses you completely from the vocal cords down; locks you inside your own body but keeps your brain intact so you don't miss a single moment of your own demise. Stef's mother had suffered it and she and her sister had grown up in fear of history repeating itself.

'So what happens now?'

'We've talked about this before.' She didn't look at him. 'We agreed.'

'You can't just . . . end it. Not *now*. Not *yet*, Stef.'

'I can.'

He bit down on his bottom lip, hoped the sting of it would dull the ache that held the rest of him. All that was left were the different ways to die. Sooner or later. Here or there. Alone or with him beside her. By her own hand or somebody else's.

If Stef's mind was made up then he had only one question left. One word. He must have said it a million times in his life and he'd say it a million times more but never again would it burn like it did now. One word, one question and an answer that would destroy a life; would bring with it the dawn of a world that looked totally different to the one he and Stef had built for themselves.

'When?' he said, thinking again of his wee sister and The Decision being made. Life support being removed. And aye, he'd asked the same question back then. His parents hadn't asked for his opinion and he'd never dared ask if they'd had doubts and how long they'd lingered. But his doubts had stayed, hardened into a certainty that life was *always* worth fighting for; a commitment that he'd do all he could to preserve it.

'When, Stef?'

'Soon. Before my hands go, I go,' she said, then slowly clenched the fingers of her free hand, made a pathetic fist. 'I could barely burst a bubble with this one.'

'Then let me burst your bubbles for you,' he said. 'It's just about learning a different way of living. I mean, you can walk. And you can talk, no bother. You can probably still paint as well. You might have years left, for all we know.'

'That's just it. Nobody knows.'

'Lots of folk live good lives without their hands, Stef. And their legs. You'll manage.'

She'd shaken her head then, no doubt knew he was avoiding the obvious. 'It's not the living part I'm worried about,' she said, then reached into her pocket again and pulled out a stiff plastic packet that held a syringe. 'I need to be capable of taking my own life, *on my own*. No assistance of any kind, at any stage. I'll need a strong grip to pull drugs into the syringe. If there's any suspicion that you helped me with this, they could prosecute. Worst-case scenario, you'd be put away for fourteen years.'

'Och, that'll never happen. They'd need proof.'

'It'd still ruin your reputation,' she said.

Andy scoffed. 'Jesus Christ, Stef. You're more important than that.'

'And what about your career? You're only forty-five, Andy. You've got twenty more years to work. Twenty more years to keep saving lives. You have to think of yourself. We both do.'

He'd hesitated for a second, maybe two. But that was enough. 'They can't fire me without good reason,' he said.

'They'd find a way. Especially if it got into the press.'

'Why would it?'

'These things do.' He'd winced when she said that. *These things*, as if she was talking about something that was inconvenient; something that would pass.

'It's just doesn't feel like the right way.'

'It's the only way.'

'Where will you get the drugs?'

'Never you mind.'

Andy looked at her, knew that this time these choices weren't his. They'd both been there, leaning over the bed of the dying, listening to someone gagged by pain but somehow finding the strength to beg; the person pleading for someone to knock them out so that their suffering would end. A victim's pain would go when death eventually took them but the trauma of watching that suffering stalked those left behind.

'I don't want you to die alone.'

'And I don't want your last moment with me to be . . . *that*. I won't have it. You were there when your sister died and I know that's the only thing you see when you think of her.'

'Och, I was just a wee boy.'

'It's my decision, Andy.'

'Can it not be mine as well?'

For a long time neither of them spoke.

'Will you do it here?'

She shook her head. 'You'll be haunted by it, spend the rest of your life avoiding whatever room I chose. I won't have it. I'll go to the hills. Somewhere help can't reach.'

'And wait for a stranger to find you? No way, Stef. I should—'

'I've told my sister. Alyson knows where I'm going and she'll come and find me, first. She'll tell you once . . .' She shrugged. 'Once it's over.'

'I want to be there.'

'No, Andy. I know you too well. You couldn't *not* save me.'

'I could try.'

'I don't want you to,' she said, voice cracking. 'And I need to make sure nobody else saves me either; I'll go somewhere I won't be found by chance. People assume they're doing the right thing by saving a life. And mostly, they are. But once my hands are paralysed, that's it: I won't be able to work a syringe on my own. If I'm saved this time I might not be able to make another attempt, even if I found the courage to try.'

'But it's far too soon, Stef. You're too . . . alive. Too well. You're still totally yourself.'

'That's the whole point,' she said. 'I want to be myself, always. Unlike my mum. Unlike so many of the folk we've treated over the years. I'm doing this for my sake, and yours.'

'Surely you can wait, a bit.' He nodded to the syringe in her hand. 'Use a different method.'

She shook her head. 'Fifteen minutes and the job's done. There's no chance of it going wrong. No mess. No suffering.'

And what about his own suffering? He'd wanted to ask her that but didn't dare.

He had no idea how long they sat at the kitchen table that day. Time slowed down the way it always did when death was close, when he was leaning over someone he knew he couldn't save. He'd be praying for it all to end but at the same time he'd be desperate to give them a few more minutes, to do his best to make them feel safe and secure as life slipped away from them and everything they were became a past tense. People often asked him about souls and whether he'd seen them or felt them and he never knew what to say. There was definitely a change in the air when somebody died, that moment when he'd be waiting, waiting, waiting for an inbreath to come.

But here, now, the verdict came instead.

CHAPTER 43

Two words. *Not guilty.*

Andy's body was a tightrope, cut. Whispers came, were hushed. He felt a hand on his arm, could tell by the light grip and the whiff of white musk that it was his lawyer.

'Come with me, Andy.'

He allowed himself to be led, left the courtroom through a side door then followed her up a set of stairs and into a room that looked like it could be used for interrogation. She pulled out a padded chair for Andy then took a yellow plastic one for herself, tutting when she caught her tights on a chipped edge. When she spoke Andy heard a voice but no words. He wondered if this was what dying felt like, a numb awareness of presence and sound but little more. The window was open and his hearing tuned into the faraway sounds. He heard the hiss of a bus pulling away from traffic lights and when it was gone he heard a blackbird exchanging a song with another one even further away, the pair of them giving it their everything, as if nothing in the world had altered or ever would. He could hear the automatic door of the courthouse clunking open and closed. He could hear voices too, pictured folk smoking in the sunshine outside the pub across the road, staring at a clear blue sky as they clouded their lungs with tobacco. He thought he heard Sandy and Hazel then Amechi and Vicky – but it was Alyson's voice he wanted to hear more than any other. She still blamed herself for the trial.

It was her who'd called the police to the mountain that night when Andy didn't arrive at the hotel. She'd told them of a bloodstained stranger in Stef's red jacket, fleeing the hotel toilets – then, collapsing under the pressure of so many police questions, she'd sent them to the place she knew Stef should be. It was the place she and Stef had agreed on; the place Andy was never supposed to go. But that was where officers had found him, lying alone with Stef's still-warm body in his arms and her bloodstained running jacket on the ground beside him; next to the syringe and the glass vials stolen from the station and her missing mobile phone.

The stranger who fled the hotel toilets had never been traced.

Andy didn't blame Alyson for any of this but still guilt stained her – and Andy's wouldn't disappear with the verdict. But tonight, they'd talk, try to remember that the choice was never in their hands.

There was a knock at the door. The sight of Farida McPherson brought him back to that room. She was speaking to his lawyer, asking her to leave.

'May I?' She'd already pulled out the chair, sat down when he nodded. 'So, case closed.'

'Not guilty,' said Andy, then let out a sound that was caught somewhere between a laugh and a cry. 'Doesn't help, does it?'

'You've been through a lot.'

'No thanks to you.'

'It's standard procedure.'

Andy sighed. 'Standard my arse. We did our homework and there's less than 2 per cent chance of prosecution in "assisted dying" cases, or whatever you want to call them. And as the trial has shown, Stef was meticulous with her planning, wanted to eliminate any danger of . . . *this* happening.'

'You're a free man now.'

'In some ways.'

Farida gave one of her sniffs. 'I noticed Betty Stevenson in court today.'

'Who?'

Farida's tongue pushed against her teeth like she was trying to dislodge something caught between them. An accusation, maybe. 'Alex Mitchell's big sister.'

Farida paused, eyes scanning Andy's face for a reaction. 'I can only tell you this because the case is closed but it was Betty who called an ambulance when he tried to kill himself, the day before he murdered Maureen Aitken. So even though it was Stef who actually saved him, Alex blamed his big sister for calling the ambulance.

'Betty was also the reason officers found Stef's ID card in Alex Mitchell's home the same night Stef went missing. Betty claims Stef had left behind her jacket the night she saved Alex's life – and the ID card was in the pocket. She said she'd been meaning to hand it into the station for months, had left it on the mantelpiece of her flat as a reminder.'

'But in your mind only Alex Mitchell lived there?'

Farida nodded. 'Hence my concern for Stef's safety. It was made worse by the fact neither Alex nor Betty were there to set me straight. Alex had already fled to a hideout flat in Lesmahagow. And Betty was impossible to get hold of – until the day she walked into a police station holding the dog lead her brother had used to strangle Maureen Aitken.

'We *now* know that Alex went on a bender after the pub landlady trial ended that Monday afternoon. He then turned up blind drunk at Hartfield Court, hammering the door and demanding his sister let him move back in with her. When a neighbour told him she wasn't home he kicked in the front door then fled before the police arrived. When we turned up he was gone but we found Stef's ID on the mantelpiece, and then was when I got involved. Neighbours informed us Alex lived there with his sister, Betty Stevenson, but the woman has a miraculous capacity for remaining uncontactable, and unseen.'

For a moment Farida glanced at her own hands, clasped in front of her so they gave nothing away. 'So that explains the presence of Stef's ID card at Alex Mitchell's flat – but there's one thing I still don't understand about this case – why Stef called the landline at his flat that day. There's no logical explanation for it.'

'Who knows,' said Andy, knowing *he* did.

Stef had phoned Betty's mobile and landline to cancel her cleaning shifts that week, not knowing that the number she dialled had any connection to a killer. Chances were she didn't even know Alex Mitchell's name, never mind the fact he was Betty's brother and that he'd taken a life after she saved his. All Stef had wanted to do was make sure Betty didn't come to their house that Tuesday morning, knowing Andy would be stressed and sad and waiting for a sign that said everything was over; that their plan for her ending had become a reality.

Stef would travel to that mountain then take her own life, while she was able.

Alyson would wait, wait, wait, then travel alone to the place Stef had chosen to die. Alyson's job was to find her first, before a stranger stumbled over her body in the woods. Despite their protests Stef had chosen to leave her mobile phone at home, knowing there was no signal where she was going. She didn't want a safety net, the temptation of escape.

Their goodbyes would be in person, in words, at home.

And Andy? His role was simple but devastating: let her go.

Betty hadn't been part of the plan until she rang their doorbell that Tuesday morning as if it were an ordinary day. Then somehow, silently, she'd changed everything.

Farida looked like she was about to say something else when there was a knock at the door and Andy's lawyer popped her head round. 'You ready, Andy?'

'Give me two minutes,' he said, then waited until she was gone until he spoke again. 'I imagine you spotted Richard Owens in court as well?'

Farida rolled her eyes at the mention of that name. They were allies in that, at least.

'Think he was quite pleased with all the free publicity in the end,' said Andy. 'And believe it or not the *Still Life* exhibition's been a huge success. He's taking it to London. Why anyone would pay good money to look at a canvas spotted with fly vomit is beyond me.'

'Unbelievable,' said Farida. 'But hopefully he'll think twice before he tries anything like that again. Complete waste of police time, not to mention the stress it caused to you, and some of the officers who attended the scene. He's lucky he didn't get jailed for it.'

'Or sectioned, more like,' said Andy. 'Didn't have the balls to apologise face to face but wrote me a letter to explain what the whole thing was about. Apparently he got the idea from a *National Geographic* article exploring the way house flies react at crime scenes. Investigators mixed blood, semen and saliva with different colours of paint then placed it all in a room with white walls – and fifty thousand live maggots. The coloured paint allowed them to work out which substance the flies were most attracted to. That was all done for science but Richard thought he'd turn it into art. Got animal blood and semen from a local farmer then set up that outhouse as a lab, of sorts.

As for the portraits of Stef – she usually recycled her practice paintings – but Richard specifically asked her if he could keep the half-finished self-portraits she'd created during their art classes. That's why you saw her face in there – though he confessed to me that Stef didn't know what they'd be used for. She left them all in her locker, gave him the key and he helped himself.'

'And what exactly was he trying to express?'

'The circle of life, apparently. The flies used parts of dead animals to create something new. And he wanted Stef in there because she'd *willingly* chosen to still herself in those self-portraits, but would then be *unwillingly* stilled by the disease. That's how he came up with the name. *Still Life*. He's playing with words, and the whole concept.'

'Interesting,' said Farida.

'That's one word for it,' said Andy. 'To be fair to the man, he *did* ask me before he included Stef's final painting in his exhibition – and that one escaped the fly treatment, thank God. It's far too good a work for any of that nonsense.'

'Is that the painting divided into boxes? I saw it in the paper.'

Andy nodded. 'Forty-five self-portraits, one canvas. Each box represented one year of her life – and one part of her body that the disease stole from her.' He sighed, a fist tightening in his throat. 'I think Richard knew that Stef's painting would be the best work of the whole exhibition – that what the critics are saying, anyway. She'd be chuffed.'

He looked at her when he said that and for a moment they shared the slightest of smiles.

'I suppose we should be thanking Richard as well,' said Farida. 'It was the flies from his experiment that led us to Maureen Aitken's body in the Green Den woods. Did you hear we traced her dog alive and well? Sophie, a poodle, now safely rehomed with a family in Harrogate. But without the flies we might not have found her body, and without it Alex Mitchell would still be a free man. Those flies are the reason he's behind bars.'

'Rather him than me.'

Farida stood up, held out her hand. 'You're a good man, Andy. Don't forget it.'

He hesitated then shook her hand, and left.

The press was waiting for them on the pavement out-side court when Andy's lawyer led him outside, holding a single printed page which she'd offered to read out on his behalf. There were flashes and faces held in deliber-ate sympathy. Big Stevie stepped forward, tossed out the first press question. 'Will you be able to grieve in peace now, Mr Campbell?'

Andy didn't answer, barely noticed any of it. He looked over their heads and expectant faces and microphones and saw Betty Stevenson walking away from the courthouse, heading in the direction of the bridges. Home, maybe, to the address on Stef's *Frequent Destinations* list. Stef used to drive Betty home, every Tuesday and Friday after her shift, dropping her off en route to her art lesson at Green Den.

But he was sure Stef hadn't made the connection to Alex Mitchell. Stef must have attended dozens of paramedic jobs at Hartfield Court during her career, could never have guessed Betty was the sister of that bleeding, blaming man who she'd saved that night in the lift.

It was Hazel who'd told Andy the connection between Betty and Alex.

She'd been searching her notepads for useful information on Alex Mitchell and had found an old interview where one of the neighbours had talked about his big sister, Betty Stevenson. *She's something special*, they'd said, then explained that even though they had different dads and different surnames, Betty and Alex had lived together for most of their lives.

She'd helped raise him then watched him fall; still loved a hated man.

Betty hadn't turned up for a cleaning shift since Stef died and Andy hadn't called, knew it was better for both of them if all contact ended. If Farida found out how closely their lives were connected she'd investigate, maybe re-open the case they'd just closed.

It was better to deny their shared history.

But not quite yet.

Betty paused and looked back; her eyes touching the place Andy stood and then rising, rising, rising to meet his, just for a second. They'd not spoken since that night on the mountain. He'd noticed Betty hiding in the woodland but she'd left him alone with Stef, until he'd felt life leave her. Her body was still warm when Betty came to him with a confession, expecting to be blamed. But Andy had thanked her instead.

And now, here they were, the only two people who knew the whole truth.

The conclusion of the court case wouldn't end anything; his mind would not be suddenly stilled. Grief and guilt held him in their grip but there was gratitude too, for the person who'd been brave enough to make it happen; to give Stef the ending she wanted.

He held up a hand and got a nod in return, Betty's unashamed acknowledgement of the act.

CHAPTER 44

It wasn't love that had led her there, but the lack of it.

Betty stopped a few metres from the table where her brother sat rigid in a wooden chair, arms crossed, eyes locked on the chipped Formica tabletop. Behind him, a door was unlocked then opened, brought cool air and relatives who'd thought twice about what to wear.

Some clutched photos, paper memories of a life that was long since lost for all the people already sitting down. Betty brought fingers that fidgeted inside the pockets of her coat, that mutinied against her command to be still and stay still.

Her brother looked up, did not smile.

She rested a hand on the empty chair before she pulled it out, same way she'd seen other people do in pubs, as if there existed the possibility that her brother would shake his head and say the seat was taken; that he was waiting for someone else.

The chair legs scraped on the concrete floor when she pulled it out, sat down. She doubted she'd ever felt so entirely out of place, so intensely, overwhelmingly distant from a human being that she knew so much about. She knew everything about her brother, could recite facts and dates and addresses; could probably guess his passwords if she had to.

But she'd spent her whole life watching him grow and turn into a person far different from the one he could have been.

He was pressing the palms of his hands together, as if he was praying, although Betty was quite sure that God and Jesus and the Bible hadn't entered her brother's head in years. Decades. Maybe never. The tips of his middle fingers were resting against his chin and as she stared at them she realised she didn't know her brother's hands any more, wouldn't recognise them if they weren't conveniently attached to his body.

When they were little he'd measure the size of his hands against hers, palm to palm, wriggling the tips of his fingers upwards then pausing, silently mouthing numbers as if calculating with scientific precision how many days or weeks or months it would be until his hands were longer and stronger and better than hers.

Even then he was tired of being branded as the useless wee brother; the irresponsible one, incapable of being good or fully loved. But what they told him he was, he became.

He'd used those hands to steal Maureen Aitken's front-door key from the row of little brass hooks on Betty's bedroom wall. Back then she happily took keys from every client she cleaned for, gave each one a specific place on the wall then labelled it with their name, written in block capitals using her favourite blue pen. She knew not to put their address on the key but Alex didn't need one. He'd done numerous odd jobs for Maureen – putting up shelves and mowing her lawns and walking her dog when she felt too tired to do it herself.

Maureen had trusted him, at first; a novelty.

But when he failed her she snatched that trust away and he found he had further than ever to fall.

First he tried using those hands to end his own life.

But, saved, he took Maureen's instead.

Anyone who read the papers now knew Alex had followed Maureen Aitken and her poodle Sophie into the woods near Green Den Studios then strangled her with the dog's lead. The grave that he dug was hidden for months by drifting winter snows, the brown earth above

Maureen's wiry body hard as the ice that covered it. But the guilt stayed fresh, haunted him and Betty both.

When Alex came home the night of the murder he'd used those same hands to hold Betty down on the kitchen floor, beat all the parts of her body that he knew nobody would ever see; stopped only when she bled and agreed the blame was hers. She *shouldn't* have saved him.

Maureen's murder was her fault.

He left Betty there, battered and blamed; but not before he'd hung that bloodstained dog lead on the little brass hook where Maureen's house key should have been; a reminder of what he was capable of and a warning of what would happen if she ever called the police.

When Alex was arrested later that same night for assaulting a pub landlady he held out his hands to be cuffed. He was jailed, awaiting trial. But the dog lead stayed where he'd left it.

That was the reason Betty never took a house key from Stef and Andy, or anyone else she now cleaned for. Never again would she risk her brother getting hold of her clients' keys; accessing their lives, then ending them. When Alex was in jail for the pub attack he'd often called the flat landline, not to chat to his big sister but to taunt her, saying the worst was yet to come. When she stopped answering the landline he'd filled her mobile's voicemail with abuse instead. The off button was her only escape and the reason why her phone wasn't switched on the day Stef had called to cancel her Tuesday cleaning shift.

That missed message had started all of this. Betty searching, finding, helping.

For that, she thanked her brother.

But when police confirmed it was Maureen Aitken's body in that shallow grave, Betty took that dog lead from the hook in her bedroom to the nearest police station. For a long time she stood outside the automatics doors, watching them open and close. When a young officer came out and asked if she'd lost her dog she said no, she'd lost her brother.

In court she'd held the Bible in one hand and a lucky penny in the other when she'd testified against him. But he'd written her a letter last week, asking for a visit – and forgiveness.

Now, a buzzer sounded.

They had five more minutes. Visiting time was like a tatty comfort blanket that was whipped away when the clock changed, ordered home out of the room. It was the point when chairs would scrape on the concrete floor and couples would lean across tables, kiss even if they didn't feel like it. It was when mothers cried and fathers tried not to; the only time of day people talked about things that really mattered.

Betty knew what she had to do; why she'd come. For months she'd imagined this conversation; her words and the ones given in return. It was incomprehensible that the conversation was finally going to happen here. She wanted the sound of a kettle boiling to fill silences, a lucky penny to keep her hands busy and a toilet she could escape to if the weight of it got too much. But here there was a locked door and a prison officer and another inmate less than two metres away, listening to stories of the things he was missing from home.

Betty wondered if her brother missed anything apart from having someone to blame.

'It wasn't my fault. What you did. You know that now, don't you?'

Her brother stared at her then nodded. Betty had never imagined truth could be released with so simple a gesture. A slight drop of the head and her world changed.

Betty reached across the table, held her brother's hands between her own.

She couldn't remember the last time they'd deliberately touched. In fact, she hadn't deliberately touched anybody for months, apart from the little parts of themselves that people left on coins but she wasn't sure that fingerprints counted as human contact.

She'd touched Stef, of course, in the woods.

The moments before death had been less dramatic that she'd envisaged. She'd made sure she didn't look directly into Stef's dying eyes because that would be bad luck but when she saw Andy coming she'd leaned over and kissed Stef on the forehead, felt like a priest or someone who gives blessings to those who need them most. If Stef had opened her eyes and said thank you in that moment Betty would have smiled and told her it was the least she could do.

But really, it was much more than that.

It was Betty Stevenson, being enough.

She'd driven home from Lewistown to Hartfield Court that night but had never touched that car again. It belonged to Alex. That was why she'd seen it on the news. Police had been searching for it – and him – after the Green Den discoveries, rightly suspecting he was linked to the case.

Betty was halfway home from visiting her brother when she realised she'd left her coat at the prison, and with it, a purse full of pennies and all the good luck that they held.

For a moment she hesitated, looked back.

But then she walked, and kept on walking.

CHAPTER 45

It was Betty who'd led Stef, limping, from the bothy to that clearing in the woodland – hours after she should have arrived there on her own with a needle full of poison and her final goodbyes already spoken.

She had no doubt Alyson would have made it to the clearing at the agreed time but she'd have found silence instead of her sister, stilled. Her failing hands had blown their plan to pieces, forced their paths apart. After she'd tried and failed to open the delicate vials and fill the empty syringe, Stef's mind coaxed her to drink the drugs that remained, but she knew her body was wise, would summon vomit to clean her system. It was too risky, too uncertain.

Desperation led her mind and eyes to the ridge and the peak she'd painted so often; some place that was high enough to fall from. She'd pictured herself stepping into sky, watching the top sides of trees as she hurtled towards earth and a messy death. She couldn't risk delay or bear to say goodbye twice. But nature decided for her, sent rain and wind and clouds so thick they nipped her ankles, hid the path that led to the ridge, and her release. She slipped on muddy ground close to the bothy door then dragged herself back inside with a twisted ankle and bleeding hands and a mind that wouldn't rest until she found a way out of the skin that, soon, she'd be trapped inside.

Then Fate brought her Betty.

When they reached the clearing Betty lowered her on to thick, knobbly tree roots that had pushed up through the moist earth; her back against a trunk that moved slightly when she leaned against it. If she'd still had the strength Stef could have dug her nails into the bark and broken it off like flaky skin, exposed a world of tiny creatures that would simply remake their home elsewhere without complaint.

Instead she reached into her pocket and pulled out two of the three cardboard boxes she'd stolen from the ambulance safe on Monday night. Each one contained ten tiny vials of morphine, not much bigger than those miniature perfume bottles her mum used to keep in the bathroom cabinet at home; freebies from department store events or beauty magazines. Each one was smaller than a child's pencil and its smooth glass sides were even harder to grip. It had taken her a while to get the hang of it when she first started working as a paramedic – holding the vial still between two fingers and pushing the pressure point on its delicate neck with the thumb of the other hand. Get it right and the top clicks and snaps off, leaves a smooth edge. Get it wrong and it'll shatter and you'll bleed. She must've done it a thousand times, been so sure she'd manage on her own out here, on this day; her last.

She'd stopped at the bothy on the way up so she'd have shelter for the technical part: opening the delicate glass vial with weakening fingers, filling the syringe, preparing the poison that would silence her suffering. But instead she got broken glass and bloody fingers. Her grip was already too weak to pull the drugs into the syringe.

Her mind coaxed her to drink the drugs that remained but she knew her body was wise, would summon vomit to clean her system. It was too risky, too uncertain.

A death like this one had to be by her own hand, but her own hands had failed her.

The suicide law in Scotland was clear – no help, no assistance – so if death was what she wanted, she had to be the one who made it happen, from the moment she left the house to the moment she'd leave this life. She'd shared her plan with both Andy and Alyson but only her sister knew the precise time and place it would happen; and had agreed to find her, first.

But the train had to be booked and paid for and taken by Stef, alone. No help, no assistance. She'd stolen the drugs from the ambulance station without Andy's knowledge. No help, no assistance. She'd spent her last night of life alone in that hotel, waiting for her final sunrise and a slow, stumbling solo hike to the place she loved more than any other; the one she'd tried to capture on canvas so many times.

Closer to Heaven, they'd called it.

This was the walk she and Andy had done the day they said goodbye to their unborn children; hiked from the bothy to the woodland and buried that little box between trees, in the hope their grief would leave them, or lessen. Now she'd chosen that same place for herself so she could lie beside them at last, end her days in the same spot they had.

Without choosing her own ending, she'd become only breath; only heartbeats. She'd be floppy limbs and a wordless mouth. She'd be eyes that saw only ceiling and sheets.

Stef wanted to wake up, always, and wonder how the weather would affect her day. She wanted to be the announcer of the obvious when curtains were thrown open, to have wind and rain and sun and snow dictate her mood and her clothes. She wanted to sit on the back doorstep after a storm and let the dampness seep through the pockets of her jeans. She wanted a howling gale to blow dust into her eye and crisping leaves into her hair. She wanted to leap over a dead tree and into a puddle that was deeper than it looked, tut when the cold water sucked at her socks. She wanted to poke her head out of a campervan at dawn then screw up her eyes at the brightness of the new day. She wanted sunburn. She wanted to make the most of wet weekends. She wanted to feel the crunch of icy grass under her feet, to sniff the winter air and know that snow was coming, wish she'd brought gloves.

Human life is one long, elaborate escape from bad weather, but today Stef needed to escape from something else: the storm under her own skin, a disease that would not let her be.

She'd come here today to catch her death.

Here, now, while she still had the choice.

When she gave the first vial to Betty she held it in her palm the way a jeweller holds a precious stone, waved away all talk of police and prisons. Stef explained what needed to be done; talked her through the plan that had been thwarted by her own weakening hands.

'Then I'll lend you mine,' said Betty, and did.

Between trees, light flickered. And in Stef, the darkness that had stripped her world of beauty started to fade. The forest floor was spotted with puddles of sun and grey trunks burned yellow. They were at once made of light and of the shadows that lay behind them.

Stef heard Andy's voice, felt love and at home.

Then up high, clouds shifted. And she was gone.

Acknowledgements

I know my name is on the cover of this book but if you were able to sneak backstage you'd see dozens of other people there, cheering me on and offering their expertise. I'm going to name a few, in no particular order.

I'll begin where all of this started; with my agent, Caroline Hardman. Thank you for your endless support and honesty and for so calmly reassuring me it was OK to put that first draft in the bin. To Jon Elek, Rosa Schierenberg, and all the team at my publisher, Welbeck – the most massive of thanks for your patience and belief and unwavering encouragement. High five to Joe Mills at Blacksheep for that brilliant cover. Thanks also to Annabelle and Emma at EDPR for doing what you do.

To my editor, Sophie Wilson. I know writing is my job but it feels almost impossible to capture in words how much I enjoy working with you. A big vermouth-infused thank you for always asking exactly the right question at the exactly the right time. Huge thanks also to crime writer Sophie Hannah, for creating the Dream Author programme and being so incredibly generous with your time and advice.

To the D20 Authors – where do I start? You're every best friend rolled into one. Special thanks to Nikki Smith and Philippa East for patiently guiding me towards the right path when I was so totally lost with this book. Hats off to Gillian Harvey, for the title! And a heartfelt thanks to Trevor Wood, for quietly inspiring.

To the Caledonia Crime Collective – thanks for the enthusiasm and for making me laugh, a lot. Special shout out to Jonathon Whitelaw for cheerfully answering my questions about news reporters and court. Any nonsense that's in there is my fault.

To my paramedic pal, Mel McDevitt – your input has been vital and won't be forgotten. A thousand thanks for answering my thousand questions. You've been astoundingly generous with your time and knowledge. Any errors or inaccuracies are entirely down to me.

Gigantic thanks to Elin, Iain, Ella and Eve Waterston for the writing retreat at Chateau Awesomeville during quarantine. And *mil gracias* to Elena, Maria and Mayo in Mallorca – your beautiful flat was the perfect place for final edits.

Enormous thanks to my early readers: Ruth Forsyth, Andrew Hamilton and Claire Lindsay. Your feedback helped me transform the book, and to believe it was worth the effort. Thanks also to the Porty People Facebook group for unfailing local support.

To mum and dad – all it took was *an idea!* Thank you for helping me find it and for always finding something positive to say. To the sibs, thanks for so widely spreading the word about your wee sister's stories. And to Mari – I love sharing my world with you, and my imaginary ones. Thank you for believing in Betty. And me. And us. And love and stuff. Lunch is on me.

WELBECK

PUBLISHING GROUP

Love books? Join the club.

Sign up and choose your preferred genres to receive
tailored news, deals, extracts, author interviews and
more about your next favourite read.

From heart-racing thrillers to award-winning historical
fiction, through to must-read music tomes, beautiful
picture books and delightful gift ideas, Welbeck is
proud to publish titles that suit every taste.

bit.ly/welbeckpublishing